# RESOLUTION

Adrian O'Donnell

Cover design by: thegreyghost

*For Jo and all our family and friends.*

# PROLOGUE

The sports bar on the outskirts of Orpington in leafy Kent buzzed. It was eight thirty and West Ham were playing Chelsea on the large screen showing Sky Sports.

It was a typically modern set up inside, multi screens, a few pool tables and a large bar area served by young women who made themselves very busy offering easy banter with the punters. A number of gambling machines added to the lively atmosphere and general noise.

Tonight, there were maybe two hundred people inside, the beer was flowing and the lads watching the match shouted encouragement every time West Ham United had the ball. Every single one of them looked like trouble, short hair, muscles and plenty of menace. Not a pub that a stranger would be welcomed into, but never the cause of a lot of hassle. There was a very good reason for this - the owners didn't like the police becoming involved in petty trouble. They preferred to maintain the law and order themselves.

A further door led to a larger back room where two or three burly men acted as gate keepers. It would appear that your face had to very much fit before entry was allowed. Illegal gambling locations were not on the business plan submitted to the council before permission was granted for this club, nor was cocaine dealing or prostitution. But with the right credentials this is what you got; after all, with the Brood Family no expense was spared.

The main bar door opened from the street and a large black man entered looking around. This was his first day out of prison. In HMP Marwood he had been nicknamed Green Mile and he was a man with a gold Willy Wonka ticket to the back room. The gate keepers spotted him and beckoned him over where one took the heavy leather jacket from him and handed it to the bar staff.

"If you would like to get a complementary drink from the bar, we will tell Mr Brood that you are here." They waved to another bar girl and a cold bottle of beer was passed to Green Mile. He drained it in two enormous gulps, the cold beer tasting like nectar after a year inside. He was also excited about a job offer on the table from David Brood, the second in command of the business.

The door opened and David strode over holding out a well-manicured hand.

"I have heard a lot about you Green Mile. Do hope that you don't disappoint."

They strode through the protected doors, David leading the way. Before Green Mile could register his surroundings, the crack of a Taser knocked him off his feet and he collapsed semi-conscious. By the time he recovered his senses he was fully restrained, hands secured in plastic cuffs behind his back, and he was sitting on a dirty wooden high-backed chair.

Through his dazed state, he looked around, registering that the roulette and card tables were moved to one side and twenty or more men stood to his front, all wearing white forensic suits and all armed with saws and meat cleavers. The room was covered in plastic and Green Mile knew that this was not a decorative feature.

"Ok you grassing little cunt, you may wonder why you are sat on a fucking chair two sizes too small for you and in the presence of heavily armed men in paper suits avoiding any evidence trail?" David paused while looking for Green Mile's reaction.

"You, my old son have grassed the family up. I have been given it on good authority that you have told a certain Mr Stephen Byfield that my family wishes to cause him harm. I will give you a chance to answer."

"Not true, I have said fuck all." Green Mile looked him defiantly in the eye.

"Is that the case?" David looked up and nodded. A door to the

left opened up and a hooded figure was dragged in, the cloth hood hiding what must have been a
horrific mess, the blood on his dirty shirt telling the story. Another chair was pulled up in front of Green Mile and the bloodied figure pushed down into it.

"Well old son I half anticipated that answer so let me introduce you to my little singing bird. Excuse his somewhat rearranged features but he needed some encouragement to sing." The hood was pulled off revealing Paul Parker, former Deputy Governor at HMP Marwood who stared blankly at him. Parker had been unceremoniously sacked from the prison service having tried to undermine Stephen Byfield's attempts to bring Marwood up to standard.

"Okay Governor, is this my 'not so little' grass?"
Parker nodded, he couldn't speak, and a frightful gash from his mouth to his ear prevented any sound except a whimper as the hood was replaced. David Brood looked up.

"Kill this grassing screw, but I will allow a quick death, he has served his punishment." Parker was grabbed and dragged back through the door.

"As for you my big friend, I have grand designs, and I'm not talking about the TV show." He laughed at his own joke and the others joined in. Green Mile just stared back before saying "Fill your boots you fat faggot, slow or quick I couldn't give a fuck, do your worst." With a flash of anger in his eyes, unintentionally showing Green Mile that his words had hit home, Brood replied "Slow sounds very good," before turning to his men to give them orders.

"Now gag this ugly cunt and tie him to the chair; I am going to deal with this personally."

West Ham scored a goal and the main bar erupted just as the cut throat razor much favoured by David Brood sliced through the dark flesh removing the left ear in a single swipe. The pain must have been horrific as the blood erupted in the same enthusiastic manner as the crowd. Green Mile passed out without much sound but was quickly revived.

"Bring in the dogs." Brood ordered. The same door that Parker had been dispatched through re-opened and two massive Rottweilers were led in heavily chained but still managing to look ferocious.

"Now my friends here are hungry for meat and very angry as we have unwittingly not fed them for a day or two." The dogs, with the smell of blood in their nostrils, strained at the chains. Brood took his cut throat again and cut off the T Shirt worn by the doomed man. His muscular body looked impressive and David commented, "May take a while to eat this little piggy, boys." Again, there was laughter. In a final parting gesture David stood in front of the blood-soaked chair.

"Now, these boys are going to eat you in record time, and you my friend are going to watch. Good luck." He took the blade and opened the man's stomach leaving innards exposed. Green Mile screamed a long lonely scream as the dogs were released and heads buried into the exposed stomach tearing and snarling.

They were allowed to feast until it was clear that the man was dead. Brood stood watching without a flicker of emotion on his face.

"Ok boys, get these two dirty bastards away and back into the cage. Cut this fucker up and get rid of him. I don't want to see his ugly face again, understand?" The group nodded and got to work with the tools.

# CHAPTER ONE

Stephen awoke with a jolt and tried to gain his bearings. A thin trickle of cold sweat ran from his forehead and dripped on to the pillow beneath his head. The nightmares would not go away, the same dream night after night. Always standing in a long tunnel, the silhouettes of Tanya with a child on either side were in the entrance, the children waving at him.

Behind them Stephen could see the headlights of a truck hurtling towards them from the back, dust kicking off the wheels as the vehicle raced towards the unsuspecting trio.

He tried to shout, but feeling gagged no words would leave his mouth and trying to move his feet was pointless as they felt as if they were made of clay and melded with the ground. He simply stood in the darkness watching the terror play out before his eyes, helpless towards saving those who meant most to him in life. And then, just before impact, he would jolt bolt upright, gasping for breath and sweating horrendously.

Tanya, woken by his sudden movement, stroked his head and spoke softly to him. She was used to this routine and whispered reassurance, "You're dreaming again, it's just a dream." Stephen leaned towards her and kissed her forehead, "Sorry, that dream came back again I wish I knew how to stop it, it feels like I'm out of control, even though I always wake up before disaster."

She smiled, "It's a dream, they are not real, just your brain working things out. Relax, it can't hurt you." Looking at her in the half gloom his heart rate slowly returned to normal. He lay still, controlling his breathing until the feeling had gone.

She was a stunningly beautiful woman, only just thirty years old with a Spanish complexion and brown eyes that when he first met her begged him to look into them for a few seconds more than you should. It was a standing joke amongst all his friends that he was punching above his weight. In truth he agreed, but as he pointed out at the time, men age better. Even the arrival of baby Hector in the last year had not damaged her stunning figure, and the other mothers at the pre-school which Ellie and Harry attended often claimed to be insanely jealous in regards to her ability to lose weight and tone up. She would tell them it was genetics but of course it wasn't, it was hard work alongside caring for three children under the age of five.

As a Governor of a prison in the high security estate, Stephen had seen his fair share of horror but nothing, however, could have ever prepared him for the terrors that hit him last year. No-one in their right mind would ever consider what life felt like being chased by a serial killer, and then sitting trussed up like a chicken while the same man slaughtered your mother and destroyed your belief in God. Martin Heard, serial killer, had been placed on the earth to create misery, death and destruction, and only with the help of a small army, were they able to stop him. But stop him they did, stopped dead and he was now hopefully frying in hell.

But they could not stop what they could not yet see – the merciless eyes of the Brood family. A family so entwined within the gangster culture of London's East End that when they drew blood, the Thames wept red and when they sneezed everyone caught a killer cold. Stephen had already shut down their prison drug racket costing them a small fortune but now with revenge on their minds, that killer cold had Stephen's name all over it. He would need more than a hot honey and lemon to stay healthy with this one.

The Brood brothers headed up the family in unity, but in life they were very different types of men, both enjoyed violence and control but practiced it in their own unique forms. David Brood was approaching his mid-forties, it was difficult to guess how close as he dressed immaculately all the time and styled himself on the old-fashioned mafia father figures which gave him a timeless appearance. He loved art and all things cultural and took pride from learning how to play the piano to a reasonable standard. He disliked his slightly receding brown hair but kept its style short to counteract the look.

In another lifetime he may have made a good friend or someone that you would have a drink with in the golf club after a Saturday morning round. In this existence he was to be avoided at all costs. He would have your life taken in a heartbeat.

Kevin on the other hand was a couple of years older and craved none of the material things enjoyed by his brother. He needed little and was very at home in prison, which was just as well as he had spent a great deal of time getting used to these establishments. His tastes included violence, extreme violence and absolute control. He was married to a lady of sorts who waited for him as he moved from prison to prison. She enjoyed living on his reputation but wished that he had invested more money into a bigger home with an indoor pool, as his brother David had done. Whenever he was out of prison, she played the gangster moll part, acting like Barbara Windsor, all blonde hair and cockney accent while occasionally getting offended by someone in the club in order to see them beaten senseless. Gangster colleagues of the Broods gave her an extra wide berth, just in case a misplaced look upset her.

Kevin always had an air of menace about him, toned body – almost the look of a middleweight boxer, thick, black hair kept relatively short, brown eyes that foretold your death and a slightly dented nose that nobody mentioned. During his periods out of Her Majesty's Prisons, his main vice was a nice car, which changed regularly as did girlfriends. He didn't care who knew and his wife couldn't care less, she didn't want to lose her status, and if he wanted to play with tramps on his nights off, it was his business, she didn't give a damn. She was far too busy mixing with the Essex jet set to let trivialities get in the way of a spa session or spray tan. Anyway, she was no one to preach celibacy. She had a steady flow of young men who liked her way of life while the husband was detained elsewhere.

One rule everyone around him quickly learned, was that if he wound down the car window when he saw you on the street, you ran to see what he wanted, whoever you were. Failing to respect this man meant you were gone. People who knew him said that he carried a weapon in his car at all times and if you saw it you were finished. If the tool didn't get you then the muscle in the car following him would.

# CHAPTER TWO

Stephen dialed Terry's extension. "Come down to my office, I have a couple of things I need to get straight with you before I go on leave. I'll get the kettle on."

Knocking and entering, Terry took the waiting mug of tea before taking a seat at the table. He couldn't help but notice the pile of photographs scattered on Stephen's side.

"What are you up to with all of those dodgy looking people? It looks like a real rogue's gallery."

"I need to have a chat about that in a bit, firstly let's just get the prison business straightened up." Passing over two files Stephen took a sip from his mug.

"I'll be at home for the next two weeks, we are just sorting some domestics out, and I want to spend a few days with my dad. He has really come on over the past month and I want us to build on that foundation, strike while the iron is hot."

"Good idea" Terry agreed, "I'm glad to hear things are looking up for him."

"These two bits of work are key jobs," Stephen continued, "the first one is a security issue, we need to split up some of the gangs forming on the wings, this isn't just our prison, it is area wide. The influx of African drug gangs flooding the towns around the county is having an impact on law and order both inside and out and we need it dealt with. I want you to get the ball rolling with some security intelligence work, nothing too heavy at first and we will pick it up in a couple of weeks when I get back. Any questions on that?" Terry shook his head.

"The second project that has fallen on our laps is related to these people," he pushed the photo's towards Terry, "the Broods. We all know about their influence in and out of prisons, and the sway they hold especially in places such as ours. We need to be alert to staff corruption as they are attempting to undermine our security strategy. It goes without saying that this work is of the highest level of secrecy. Prison Service directors believe that they may have up to a dozen staff on their payroll in every high security prison in England and Wales, it is astonishing."

"Okay, so why am I looking at their faces?" Terry asked.

"Because they are targeting me directly. I took them down a while ago and it seems that they now want revenge for the lost revenue.

These two are the leaders, very well-organized people and top of the police serious crime teams list. The others are their management teams, they operate like a big organization and are good at what they do. Ruthless bastards! It's not the first time I have had direct threats, and it will not be the last. In fact, they are in a large queue of people that want us hurt Terry, it goes with the territory."

"Okay, so what are you doing about this threat, I take it that the police are aware?"

"Yep afraid so, we have some protection around the house, visiting patrols and a direct line to the police, but we want it all stopped, we need normality for once."

"Okay, that's no problem, I will get those things rolling straight away. I will only ring you if the wheels fall off the place, other than that I will see you in a couple of weeks. Have a good break, and don't worry about things here, I've got it."

"Certainly try, we have a lot going on. Don't destroy the place!"

Stephen gathered up the photos and locked them in the safe. "And don't think twice about phoning me Terry, I trust you but we need to get the big decisions right. Okay?"

"Yep, no issues." Terry returned to his own office while Stephen finished some last-minute details before heading through the gate.

Annual Leave was always a great feeling, it didn't matter if you were an officer or the governor, the moment you stepped out of the gate and got into the car, a weight shifted from your shoulders. Smiling as he climbed into the car, he pushed play on the CD player. Let's get out of here he instructed himself.

ACDC thundered on the radio as Stephen drove along the quiet lane on which his cottage was nestled. He turned it off around half a mile from home preparing himself to acknowledge the security patrol around the house. Sometimes the police were sat on the driveway, other times the family were just part of a passing patrol - a cup of tea, a chat and a security brief. He guessed that the patrols would stop soon, they normally did. They would dwindle down to the promise of a rapid response to the security alarms set in most rooms which was normally the way it went.

He pulled into the driveway; and there it was, a police car sat close to the garage giving him enough space to pull alongside it. Opening the kitchen door, he could smell the coffee. Two officers sat at the table chatting to Tanya. "Hi Stephen," she greeted him. "The officers arrived just after you phoned; I thought it best that they wait for you."

The two young men sat at the table looking awkward and introduced themselves whilst one of them took some documents from a black folder. It was the normal dialogue and he had heard it a number of times before. The danger from the Brood family had diminished, Kevin Brood's phone calls had been listened to inside the prison and nothing had been mentioned. For the past two weeks the police had received permission to plant listening devices in Broods cell. Every conversation had been monitored. Not one mention of the Byfield family. In the opinion of the Chief Constable the threat level had been lowered. No more need for the regular patrols or occasional evening visits. The panic buttons could stay for a further month. This would be reviewed in March. This was not unexpected or indeed, unwelcome news. In fact, some return to normality was very welcome. He shook the policemen's hands and thanked them both for their help whilst they gathered their belongings, made their excuses and left. The squad car pulled out of the drive and headed off back into town. Stephen returned to the kitchen,

"I'm just going to see how Dad is doing, have you seen him today?" Tanya looked up from stacking the used mugs in the dishwasher, "Yes he is in good form, stopping me working with his constant chat, but he seems fine."

Stephen walked into the annex and knocked on the door. "Dad, can I come in?" The door opened and there stood Chris. He looked okay but his eyes were empty, a little red as if he had cried within the last few minutes.

"Come in." They sat talking in the small lounge area; they had entered into this ritual on a daily basis and whilst it seemed sometimes that they irritated each other, they both needed the support in their mourning of a much-loved wife and mother.

"Come into the house Dad, let's have an evening together, you need the strength that only a family can give." Stephen tried a smile, 'It's been a hard year." His voice emphasised that it was tough for everyone.

Chris nodded, "A year ago I had everything torn away from me and I couldn't do a damn thing to stop it. She suffered Stephen and it was my fault." He lowered his head and sobbed, "I just wish that I had never set eyes on bloody Martin Heard. Of all the Social Workers in Britain it was me that bumped into him. If only I had left him to his pathetic life this would never have occurred."

"He is dead and he got what he deserved. You couldn't have stopped anything Dad, he was just pure evil. Nothing that we say or do can ever bring Mum back, we just need to try and rebuild our lives without her."

"Yes, you are right, every day gets a little better, but you must still allow me the odd bad day, I am getting there, it just takes time." Stephen nodded, "I miss Mum too, don't forget that."

"I know I am not the only one involved," Chris acknowledged as he pulled out a tissue and wiped his eyes. Anyway, I must pick the twins up from pre-school. The grandchildren are my world you know, without them my life would be very hollow. The innocence of a child is very healing and I will focus on them for Lucy's sake, knowing she would have loved to see them grow up."

He walked to the door and glanced back at Stephen. "I will come over tonight, I need to eat." His eyes lit up briefly. "What's for supper?"

"Whatever you want dad." Stephen gave him a smile before walking back through the connecting door into the main house.

"Tanya, I'm getting a takeaway tonight, Dad's joining us all."

# CHAPTER THREE

## *North Africa.*

Bob Brooker and Ernie Stocken studied the map with the small red light from the torch. The chill from the night air bit into their bones as they considered their next move. The rugged desert landscape had taken its toll on their kit and bodies; they had tabbed for more than thirty kilometers and hadn't slept for more than twenty-four hours. Dropped into this war zone deep in enemy held territory, they were on a mission to find the location of two kidnapped British oil workers, make scaled diagrams of the area, and assess enemy strength, morale, discipline and weapons on show before being extracted back out to sea by a fast-flying helicopter. Simple mission, what could go wrong?

Bob was a thirty-four-year-old SAS Sergeant; he had planned this to be his last period of active service and in truth he had a gutful of war and had been mulling over a number of options before this job arose. Seven years in the frontline had taken its toll and he now felt that he was losing his edge, too quick to think negatives where he once would have worked out solutions. He had been chosen to lead this mission because those in charge couldn't read his mind.

Ernie was at the other end of the scale, razor sharp and keen. He respected Bob and trusted him fully. Bob had taught him a lot and had saved his arse on one splendid occasion when the patrol had been overrun by Taliban. Bob had taken the wheel of the vehicle they were patrolling in, pushing aside the dead Afghan driver. Steering with one hand and letting loose with a 50 Cal with his blood soaked other, he had smashed his way through the ambush and off into the night. One Afghan driver dead and three troopers with minor injuries, not a bad result all things considering. Later estimates suggested that they were outnumbered by a large crew of thirty-five well trained insurgents, Bob had five men with him. He was never slow to remind Ernie that it was him that had grabbed Ernie by the bra straps and thrown him into the back of the wagon.

Ernie was twenty-eight, and originally from the Princess of Wales Royal Regiment and was a bloody good soldier, and those in the know were grooming him for greater things. It had taken him two attempts to get through selection due to an infected insect bite that nearly cost him his hand but the second time he stood out head and shoulders above everyone else. He was going to need every ounce of that grit tonight as things were going very wrong.

Poor navigation by the chopper pilot had led to the problem, six very pissed off men dropped off on a freezing cold but clear night twenty kilometers from the correct drop off position. The rest of the patrol thought the American pilot had lost his bottle and didn't want a hot drop off before bedtime. Bob knew that he had just fucked up, anyway a hot drop off and every enemy soldier in the country would know that they were there. That wasn't in the script.

The communications had caused another massive headache as despite repeated checks, all communications were lost within the first hour. The guys were going to have to operate under their own initiative and trust that nothing went too badly wrong. Help was a long way away and probably trying to work out how to re-establish comms themselves.

Two of the lads wanted to bin the operation but Bob saw no reason that they couldn't salvage something from the nightmare. Chances of a contact were substantial but Bob trusted the team and the bug out plan was still safe. Worse case they would set up a safe RV area and wait for the chopper to come in as planned.

The red light died as the torch was turned off. Bob spoke silently to the patrol. They were two kilometers away from the compound where the Brits were held. They would patrol up until they reached the final RV area, Ernie and one other team member would move forward, circumnavigate the compound, gain any information and return. They had five hours to get this done before they needed to head back for extraction. Ernie crept forward, the two-man patrol keeping a distance of two or three metres between them. It was dark enough for Ernie to feel that they could work unseen, and there was sufficient cover to hide behind. He scanned the compound fence with his night vision equipment. Just as he expected, no great security around the wire perimeter, but a thick copse of trees a few hundred metres to the left was interesting. If this held more soldiers, then any attacking force could find themselves under fire from the flank.

They edged over towards it, slowly crawling through the first trees, stomachs and chest hugging the ground. They stopped and listened, five minutes of controlled breathing, ears straining for whispered voices or the sound of men sleeping. Apart from a distant hum from the camp, there were no sounds.

Up onto their feet they patrolled further in. It was clear that this wooded area was only a hundred metres deep until a solid brick wall appeared in front of them, seeming very out of place. They moved along it, observing it from all angles. No signs of life but a set of brick steps led down into a cellar area, the door long since gone. Ernie's team mate, Jonny Mulk scanned the area. A long serving SAS trooper, he had seen every IED going and he strained his eyes for anything that could trigger an explosion. Creeping slowly forward, feeling every inch before he moved, he gave the sign to Ernie that it was clear.

"Jon, stay here while I have a quick look, give me two minutes," Ernie ordered. Jonny nodded and Ernie slowly descended into the stinking basement. Again, he stopped at the door and listened. All clear. He could make out a mountain of wooden crates stacked to one side and creeping forward he prised the lid off the first one with his combat knife. Weapons. The crate was filled with brand new automatic weapons and explosives. He opened the next crate to be met with bundles of hundred-dollar bills, thousands of them, just sitting there, waiting to be taken by God knows who. He prised open a few more before concluding that he had crate after crate of money and weapons sitting unguarded in front of him. Ernie silently took photos and moved back out into the fresh air. He silently signaled to Jon that there was nothing there and the two moved on with the patrol.

It was a faultless patrol, just as Bob hoped. Despite the biting chill they stayed upbeat and hyper alert, no signs of danger, no livestock to spook, no dogs to alert the bad guys. It was routine work. Three hours passed and Ernie returned to give his report.

"All good Bob, we have everything we need, small compound, no guards, everyone is asleep. It looks as though our two guys are in a wire cage in the centre of the camp, we counted five prisoners in total. There are only two vehicles of note, neither armoured. I have pictures of everything for clarity."

"Good work mate," Bob replied giving him a slap on the back "I think it's time to get going out of here and then have a brew before pickup." Silently they slipped back into the night and to the pickup point.

On the chopper going back Ernie looked in deep thought.

"You okay Ernie, you look a bit lost in your thoughts," Bob observed.

"Yeah I'm fine mate but I need to have a chat with you, you know, just us." Bob nodded and dozed off wondering what was getting to Ernie.

The midday sun was burning down onto the ship's deck. The debrief had gone splendidly, Ernie had done an excellent job and a major force was in place to create havoc in that little compound. Ernie and Bob found themselves alone under the shade of one of the gun mounts and Ernie looked at Bob, the same way that you look at your best friend when you have something to say but don't know where to start.

"What's up then mate?" Bob could see Ernie was troubled.

"Off the record, Bob?"

"Course" Bob agreed. Their mutual respect made that easy.

"I know that you want out Bob and I have a solution, one where we could make a lot of money and both get out."

"What are you chattering about you fucking idiot, you are mad for it." Bob knew that the army was Ernie's life and couldn't imagine why he would want out too.

"I was Bob, I just have other options outside that are interesting me, and I think that I need to spread my wings a bit," Ernie explained.

"What sort of things Ernie, security type work?"

"Kind of, just a bit different. I'm keeping it low key at the moment but I have had an offer." Ernie glanced down at the deck.

"Go on then mate," Bob encouraged, "how are we going to make enough money to live the dream?"

"Dirty money."

Bob looked up and snapped, "Are you crazy, what do you mean dirty money?"

"Last night, I found a weapons dump, fucking millions of dollars worth of hardware, sat in a bunker doing fuck all. There was also a stash of money you wouldn't believe. I was the only one to see it, it's less than two hundred meters from the compound and hidden. When the bad guys are dead, I'm the only one to know it's there, apart from you. I have had contact with some old friends from the UK, a mob called the Broods who are interested."

"Fuck me Ernie, they are the biggest firm in the UK,.What are you doing knowing and chatting to organised crime gangs like that?"

Ernie knew he only had a short time to convince Bob that this was a viable idea.

"I grew up with them Bob and if I hadn't joined up, I would have been working for them. They can have buyers for everything that we can lift, they will sell every weapon and we can make millions mate. What do you say?"

"What do you mean what do I say, I haven't got a clue about what to say." Ernie had blindsided him with this proposition.

"Let me sleep on it and say nothing else about it. We don't want anyone getting suspicious or we could be in deep shit. Is this where your job offer has come from?"

"Easy money Bob. Let's face it, I've got fuck all, I've been shot at in five different countries and all for fucking what? You do the maths." Ever since he had discovered the stash, Ernie had been doing a lot of thinking, and the more he thought about it, the more it was appealing to him.

It was a statement that Bob couldn't argue with. He had served with a lot of brave men, some now dead, some sat in rented housing and one poor bastard was homeless sleeping on the streets of Eastbourne somewhere. One poor git had flung himself from the top of a town centre car park. One thing they all had in common, none of them had two pennies to rub together.

"You have a point there mate, I saw that one of the lads who went into the Iranian Embassy siege is homeless. The perpetrator is out of jail sat in a nice place paid for by the tax payer. You couldn't make that shit up. Anyway, I'm going to try get some sleep, we'll talk more tomorrow."

Bob hardly slept, it was too hot and his brain was on fire but he thought he had the answer. Ernie was awoken by a bang on his door. It was Bob who wasted no time in firing out the questions.

"Firstly, how do we get the cash and weapons out? You were talking about millions, how does that work out?" Ernie, who had also had little sleep, had anticipated these questions and had the answers ready.

"We deliver the firearms to a tribe just across the border; they pay us a down payment which will be in diamonds. The Broods have contacts in their Government, they will negotiate the safe keeping of these in Africa, their onward journey and payments to us. We will get a good cut of the profits. However, we need to get the stuff across the border first though. It's a hell of a lot of stuff and that's where you come in Mr Logistics." Bob thought for a few minutes. "I know a guy who is based nearby at the moment, he is a Chinook pilot and he owes me a big favour. Let me speak to him, he's someone we can trust with this."

The briefing for the mission to recover the hostages went smoothly. Bob gave thorough instructions, showing the detailed photos Ernie had taken to the Nigerian Officers and explaining the mission in the smallest details, leaving no room for any errors.

The assault force had been practicing for days on a remote camp somewhere in the southern desert. A mockup of the enemy camp had been put together based on the reconnaissance made by Ernie and Jonny and every man knew the part they were responsible for. Bob and Ernie were impressed by the professionalism of this team, they just prayed that they would get the job done and not ask questions about where the advisors were during the fire fight.

The following morning two Special Forces advisors flew into battle with an African force with the strength of two companies, in total a hundred and twenty heavily armed well-trained soldiers. The hostages were released, the compound destroyed and a laden helicopter had briefly entered a neighbouring country with an important cargo. Ernie and Bob had completed both missions, official and unofficial without hitches. The money and weapons were safe and they were back on the boat heading home before anyone noticed that they were gone.

# CHAPTER FOUR

Chris Byfield stood in the annex of the house, the rest of the family having disappeared on a shopping trip into Birmingham. He hated shopping so had decided to stay at home and catch up on some domestics. He had a pile of washing to do and he had also wanted to paint his hallway since the day he had moved in. He hadn't wanted to seem ungrateful so just bided his time until he felt strong enough to say that he didn't like mint green.

The dust sheets covered the hard wood floor and radio two accompanied him, Ken Bruce was rattling through the pop master challenge coaching and cajoling some poor van driver into remembering hit songs from the 1980's. Out of nowhere the black cloud arrived and at first Chris tried to push the thoughts back. He had been here before when thoughts of Lucy and the horrific way she died overwhelmed him but he had always managed to fight through. He began painting but nothing seemed to be going right. Paint splashed on the floor through a small unprotected part in the dust sheets, he tried to clean it up, but it just got bigger, he stopped trying. This seemed to be the pattern of the past few months, try to clean up a mess yourself and it seems to grow and become a greater problem.

The solution lay in his own hands and he was never going to find the answer by sitting in the annex. Showering and changing into fresh clothes, he climbed into the car and headed off to the golf club. He guessed that he had a couple of hours until the family returned and parking up, he entered the bar. Looking towards the far end he saw them, all the golf buddies who he had ignored for so long, rejecting their calls and voice mails as he drowned in his misery. They called him over and once more he was swept into the heart of friendship, as though he had only just gone out to put his clubs in the boot after the last round. The warmth and conversation invigorated him, no conversation was off the table as they chatted about times, good and bad and checking the time, he thanked them before putting another twenty pounds behind the bar for the guys.

"Chris, before you go, we are one short for a four-ball next week, how do you feel about it?"

"I will be rusty, but count me in," he replied with a smile.

The family car swept back into the driveway bursting at the seams with shopping. Chris met them outside of the house and he was smiling, so happy to be here and loved by such a wonderful family. Stephen noticing the change in his face asked "Everything okay Dad?"

"Yes, I think it will be," Chris smiled. "at last I feel as though I can move on. Don't ask me why, I don't think I even know myself." Tanya gave him a hug, "Okay, let's take it a day at a time, no pressure. You will have good and bad days ahead, but I think we will have more good days. Let's get in with the children and have a drink, I think we've all earned it."

# CHAPTER FIVE

Terry knew when a wing was bubbling, all the tell-tale signs were there. Assaults were up and prisoners desperate to avoid the coming storm were trying to move to other wings. They didn't care where they went, they just wanted to avoid the coming trouble. Information reports from all staff were raining down into the security system inbox. Drugs on B Wing were out of control and gang related violence was all over the wing. Groups were openly congregating in strategic corners of the open areas of the wing and weapons had been found hidden in the shower area, clearly left there for a sinister reason at a chosen moment. Some staff had been warned by prisoners to stay away from B Wing on Saturday. It was as clear as clear could be. This Saturday was going to be epic. Prisoners knew it, staff knew it and the Brood family sitting a hundred or so miles away from the prison knew it. They had planned it, they had a score to settle with a little gang from North London who were getting a bit too heavily involved in the importation of legal highs into the prison.

In the Brood world too many bent officers led to chaos. They controlled who, how and when in all aspects of the import and export trade into Marwood Prison and two-bit operators would be shut down and put out of business. In this world it was vital that calling cards must be left to dissuade others from spreading their ambitions too wide.

Terry looked at the Duty Governor sheet for the coming weekend. It was Andy Liphook a newly promoted guy who had replaced Martha, one of the governors who had come to a particularly sticky end at the hands of the serial killer Martin Heard. Martha had fallen for his charms while Heard was in prison, he had butchered her the first opportunity he had, a brutal ending for a kind woman.

Andy seemed good value but a bit untested. This weekend could be a blooding in more senses than one. Terry called him into the office as even he felt a little tense with what was happening and wasted no time in getting down to business.

"Andy, we think that it could all kick off this weekend. We still have a couple of days to go so we have teams coming in from Area to conduct a full lock down search on B wing. What we are going to do is have a wing meeting with all the known faces. We will explain the situation to them and that we don't expect any trouble to continue otherwise there will be consequences for everyone. Hopefully when they all know that the game is up it may calm down. I have also arranged for a few key players to be lifted and transferred. The North London lot will be gone ASAP but that knowledge is to stay in this office." Andy nodded. "And a couple more will follow in the coming weeks," Terry continued. "Hopefully this search will find more weapons and shut this thing down for good." With work to do, Andy left the office to get things moving, the last thing that he wanted on his first weekend as Duty Governor was trouble.

Staff congregated in the prison chapel. Terry had called an emergency full staff meeting. One hundred and twenty officers sat in silence as Terry began to speak.

"Okay, you will all be aware of the unrest on B Wing of late. I am not prepared to allow any of our staff to be put at risk therefore I am shutting the prison down for the rest of the day. All staff will search B Wing for weapons. In a moment you will be put into teams, we will all move down together and hit the wing before the prisoners realise what is going on. The main players who have been named as instigators of this trouble will be searched first. Every prisoner will be stripped searched and anyone offering resistance will be placed into the Segregation Unit. Any questions before we tell you what teams you will be on?"

There were none. Teams were divided and the staff hit the

wing as one. Five cell doors were opened simultaneously and the search began. Terry stood in the Central area of the prison, he could see the whole of B Wing from there and a hive of activity stretched out before him. He noticed that the prisoners were taking this well. In his experience the majority of the prisoners wanted the weapons gone and the leading players would have ensured that there was not a scrap of evidence in their cells.

Four hours later the Security manager, Charlie Peters knocked on Terry's door.

"Hi Terry, not a lot found. Couple of phones, small amount of cannabis and a couple of razor blades found in the shower, apart from that nothing."

"Well done Charlie, if you can brief the staff for me once the evening meal is served, I will be grateful. I will phone Area office and Stephen and let them know the situation." Terry still had an uneasy feeling in his stomach. He phoned the Duty Governor and arranged that the ten key prisoners from B Wing should be taken to the chapel. He wanted to speak with them.

Ten minutes later he walked up the stairs and into the chapel. In front of him sat the ten prisoners who knew the answers to the question. He sat facing them at first saying nothing, just allowing them to contemplate what the Governor wanted with them. Terry had done this a number of times with mixed results. He then asked them outright,

"Okay fellas, I will get the point of why we are here. You know and I know that there has been a lot of tension on the wing lately. I don't want you or my staff hurt. What is going on?"

A young prisoner, early twenties, looked up. He was wearing a blue prison T Shirt, gray tracksuit bottoms and bright white trainers.

"Too much bang up and your staff are a joke. Do you really think that you are going to come onto the wing and find stuff? Fucking joke man," he sneered at Terry

Another older prisoner then spoke up, "Look, we have had a few little disagreements on the wing but it's all sweet now. If you leave it alone it will be sorted." The group then fell silent, meeting over. Staff took them back to the wing as Terry walked back to his office. What more could he do, even as his instincts were screaming at him that this was far from over.

## Saturday

Everything had gone well during the morning time, the R.C service and the Muslim prayer group had passed by without incident, staff started to relax a little and the tension seemed to ease. Music was playing from the cells and there seemed to be a lack of any disagreements. The visit lists were distributed, Andy had a look at B Wing but nothing leapt out at him. Visit runners came and collected the prisoners. For the first session thirty-eight tables were booked and each table could take four visitors which all in all was a busy first session.

Sarah Cross was in charge of the visits room, she had a lot of experience and Andy was pleased that she was around. She was a Supervising Officer which was the first jump on the promotion ladder but raising a family and other commitments had taken more importance in her early career. She should have progressed a great deal more and probably would, now her children were older and she had the time to commit to the job.

It was indeed a bustling visits session when Sarah became aware of an argument breaking out between a group of visitors queuing at the coffee bar. One of the prisoners had recognised a female visitor who was part of the North London gang. He pointed her out and accused her of being a whore. Shouting back at him inflamed the argument. The three large men she had arrived with stood up and recognised the prisoner, a rival gang member. Diving across the tables they attacked him with a flurry of blows knocking him unconscious to the floor. Cups of coffee and tea sprayed across the room covering dozens of people. Several other visitors then became involved which was not in Sarah's script for a good afternoon. She hit the alarm bell and called an urgent message on the radio as things were getting very out of control. By now at least five people were fighting, children were crying and visitors were flooding towards the locked door to try to escape the violence. These same doors then burst open as a dozen or so staff poured in. They grabbed hold of anyone offering violence and threw them out of the prison. As quickly as it had started it had been stopped.

The visitors had been ushered out but thirty-eight very unhappy prisoners were left staring at Sarah. Some of these men had only received fifteen minutes on the visit before the session was ended and although she tried to explain, the feeling in the room was that these North London boys had overstepped the mark. There would be consequences and soon.

All prisoners were returned to the wings where B Wing prisoners were out, playing pool and making phone calls. The noise of the disruptive prisoners coming back onto the wing drowned out all other common sense. In that moment, in that very fragile moment the truce was smashed and it broke with the ferocity of a volcanic eruption. A primeval scream turned into a roar which then melted into thunder. Groups of armed men cascaded out onto the landings spilling down the staircases like a waterfall of terror. Staff who saw it coming ran for the gates, the lucky three made it before a tidal wave of hate hit the gate. One poor officer didn't make it, she had been talking to a suicidal prisoner on the top landing and she had no hope of escape. To her surprise and relief the prisoner pulled her into the cell and locked them both in.

"Hide yourself Miss, if they see you, you'll be dead," he urgently whispered to her.

She quickly pulled a blanket over herself and hid under the bed as chaos sounded out everywhere. It was incessant, fed by hate and growing stronger by the minute. The fury swept up and down the landings. The North London gang stood no chance, battered and broken they were thrown over the railings by people who cared not if they were alive or dead. One of the gang fled and racing down his landing, he rushed into his cell and slammed his door shut. This was his only chance to avoid a beating but he was seen and tracked down by the mob. Lighted paper and cloths were pushed through his broken observation panel as he begged for his life, the cell filling with choking smoke. But there were no staff to save him and he died a choking smoky death in that dingy little cell. Once the mob had hunted down this final member of the North London gang, they focused on other targets, old scores were settled, wing offices ransacked and documentation read and re read.

Then, on the top landing the cell flap opened.

"Oy! Who have you got in there?" The prisoner in the cell said nothing as the young officer hiding under the bed tried to make herself smaller.

"You've got a fucking screw in your cell, I can see the key chain. Oy oy everyone, we've got ourselves a screw!" he shouted gleefully as he smashed his homemade weapon against the viewing panel.

Meanwhile, the command suit at Marwood had burst into life as the ferocity of the riot had become apparent. Andy had taken the role of Silver Command until Terry arrived, he had been phoned five minutes ago and would be at least an hour until he could get into the prison. This meant that Andy would be the lead in a crisis situation, and the phones were a hive of activity. Everyone who was anyone was kept in the loop. The police, Fire and Rescue and Ambulance were on route as were National Tactical Resources. Control and restraint teams from the entire area were also notified and on the way.

"Okay listen in," Andy instructed, "I want the entire area sealed, all external gates must be secured with chains and padlocks, and this must be contained. I also want negotiators up here, let's prepare for the worst. I also want a full staff check, let's make sure all of our boys and girls are safe."

There were only twenty-five staff on duty that day and twenty-four could be accounted for. One officer was missing, twenty-three-year-old Jenny Saunders, last seen on B Wing.

Andy ran back the CCTV to the time of the incident, there she was chatting to a prisoner on the top landing, and then dragged into a cell, B423. The prisoner had physically dragged her in and they had to assume she was a hostage. There were no more feeds on CCTV as the cameras had been smashed and she was on her own.

With this information, the tempo kicked up. Andy took the phone and dialed Gold Command in London. He gave the update slowly and carefully, he didn't want to miss a single detail. Gold Command's voice was very calm, it sounded like a youngish man and someone very precise. It would have been one of the Deputy Directors of Custody, Andy just wasn't sure which one just yet. Everything that Andy could do was being done, the level of violence throughout the wing had subsided slightly, something else was keeping the prisoners busy and Andy knew exactly what the distraction was.

The radio in front of Andy burst into life, it was the Custodial Manager controlling the scene down on the wing.

"Okay boss, we need to talk on the phone, this is not good." One minute later his phone rang, it was Neil Thatcher and he was flapping big time.

"Neil, get a grip, calm down and talk to me," Andy instructed him.

"Okay boss, they have stopped smashing things up and trying to kill each other and we are in contact with one of the gang who is at the gate. He tells me that one man is dead, burnt out in his cell. And they have an Officer locked in a cell on the top landing."

"Right, firstly, can we confirm the identity of the Officer, the dead prisoner, and finally what they want from us?"

"Not sure who the Officer is other than female, the dead guy is Jamie Saunders, one of the London gang. They want full immunity from everything that has happened, they want all CCTV destroyed and will send out someone to see it deleted. If we don't agree they are going to smash through the cell wall and rape and kill the officer."

"Stall, tell them that we have no access at the moment to any CCTV and it is just too dangerous to allow people on or off the wing. Stall them Neil, we don't need long."

Andy got his Control and Restraint advisors together. "I want a down and dirty plan, if we have to get her out, I want to be able to do it. What do I need?"

"I have looked at it boss," one of them replied. "It's a risk and we need everything we can get. However, we can get to within twenty feet of the cell door, the Control and Restraint stairway is located near that end of the landing so we can get there without being spotted."

"How many staff will I need?"

"You will never have enough boss, you just need some people with big bollocks and a lot of speed and aggression. We can do it if we need to, but we may well take casualties."

"Draw me up a plan." Andy instructed.

The phone rang again, it was Neil. "Boss, she is in big trouble, they are hammering beds into the walls from the cells on either side, trying to smash their way in."

"Okay, keep me informed." Andy was thinking on his feet. This was a life or death decision so he phoned Gold Command.

"I am sorry for what I am about to do, but one of my officers is about to be killed. I need to intervene."

Silence, and then "Send me your plan."

Andy emailed it straight through, he had managed to get thirty staff together and still more were reporting for duty.

Again, the phone rang. "Can you pull this off?"

"Yes."

"Is this officer's life in danger?"

"Imminent."

"Your shout Governor, good luck to you all." Andy had the go ahead he needed but he was now on his own.

Jenny Saunders had climbed out from under the bed, she knew that she was in a massive amount of trouble so this was a time for a clear head. She had a prize asset still on her person as the keys were still attached to her key chain. She moved to the window and looked down. A dog handler was standing around one hundred yards away looking up at her cell window so she threw the keys down towards him and heard them clattering onto the ground before he dashed over and retrieved them.

She then sat on the bed while she considered her options. At least the prisoner sharing this cell was friendly, and in fact he was as scared as she was. Prisoners outside were banging on the door, screams of 'rape that bitch' rang out and it was clear what the intentions were. The wall in the next cell reverberated to the hammering of something solid against it. Jenny calculated that it wouldn't take much more effort before they got to her and carried out their threats. She let out a small sob but realised that crying was futile. She would fight once the wall came through as she would rather die fighting than give in.

She stood up and took her baton from her belt extending it as she did so. Here goes fuck all she thought as the wall in front of her started to buckle. Prisoners banged at the cell door as they howled like a baying mob. As far as they were concerned, she was dead. A small hole appeared in the wall and a hand came through and pulled away some more bricks, Jenny could see him smiling as he tore it away with his hands.

"You are going die a long and painful death bitch, but I'm going to fuck you first." he leered at her as he pulled the bricks away with his bare hands.

Jenny stood facing him, bracing herself for what was on its way. Suddenly the faces from the cell window disappeared as if smashed aside by an unseen force.

BOOM! BOOM! Two massive blasts sounded outside of the cell as the door burst open and there stood her heroes all dressed in black and covered in brick dust.

"Quick, come with us, we need to move fast." They dragged her out of the door as the wall crashed through and she was saved with literally seconds to spare. The shields offered some protection as the staff fought their way back to the secure stairway as bricks and metal poles smashed among the brave group. The officer holding Jenny had his right arm broken with a brick, he howled in pain but carried on dragging Jenny along with his other arm. A large metal pipe smashed into the helmet of the officer at the front of the group but she carried on regardless. They reached the stairs, shoved their way through and locked the door off behind them. All were safe.

Laughter filled the stairwell, the sort of laughter that only people who have faced death and survived can give. The leader got onto the radio.

"Silver, we have the Officer; we are all safe and reporting to the holding area. Two officers down, both walking wounded."

Andy punched the air and grabbed the phone and phoned Gold command.

"She is safe, now can we win our prison back?"

"Yes we can, just in our own time now, well done Andy."

By the time Terry had arrived into the command suit most of the area control and restraint teams were in position. The visits room was a staging post, around two hundred staff sat around propped against walls or laying on kit bags. The National lead was standing by the reception desk. He received an email, quickly read it and spoke with his second in command before turning to address the room

"Okay, listen in, we will be ready to go in twenty minutes, everyone know what to do?" The staff nodded.

"Good. All commanders over here, one last briefing and then its game on, let's get our prison back."

The final briefing over, staff checked equipment for the last time before a "Let's go" was called. The staff formed up and made their way to the start point. B Wing gate was heavily barricaded but would pose no significant problems, it wasn't well protected, and most prisoners were off their faces after emptying the pharmacy.

The main metal gate swung open and a number of staff covered by shields ferreted their way in. Lumps of barricade were thrown back until an entrance way was formed. One prisoner attacked the staff but lost his balance and fell forward, his right arm within the grasp of the staff. This was duly grabbed and a shield smashed into the struggling prisoner's face. His forehead split open in good style as a cheer went up through the staff. He was dragged back into the middle of the team and dispatched to the segregation unit.

The teams poured into the main area of the Wing as prisoners surrendered everywhere. Again, they were taken to segregation where a fleet of escort vehicles were waiting. No sooner were they taken to segregation than they were dispatched onto the vans. Like clockwork they were driven off to various prisons around the country where they would be unable to communicate with each other thereby preventing further trouble.

A small group of prisoners stood their ground, they were up for the fight but unluckily for them so were the staff. It was a rout, teams tore into the prisoners, dragging them from the wing and down onto the vans, any resistance dealt with quickly and mercilessly with no time for sob stories. If you stood in front of a team you were taken down.

One last prisoner stood on the netting between the landings, he was armed with a table leg and dustbin lid like a pound shop version of Spartacus. Fair play to him he was going to have a go. One of the staff recognised him. "That is Doug Franks, around two hours ago he was the one who wanted to rape Jenny. You dirty nonce!" he shouted up at the prisoner.

Franks had a reputation on the wing, he didn't take any nonsense and this would be his moment of fame. He jumped from the netting back onto the hard surface of the landing, a group of around thirty staff were on the landing below him and a further sixty staff were behind him.

He rushed for the stairs and managed to get half way down before the staff had seen him and a roar went up. Franks did not disappoint. He dived the final ten feet of the stairs and launched himself into the middle of the waiting staff. His body swallowed up by the mob, he received a fearful beating until the crowd parted. Franks was pinned to the floor, laying face up and legs spread. He was still shouting and swearing at everyone in earshot when suddenly he spotted someone that he had a deep hatred for. He sent a thick lump of spit straight at the officer. Wiping the green mess from his shoulder the Officer ran forward and ploughed his boot directly into Frank's unprotected testicles. Game set and match to the staff. The riot was over.

Forensic units swarmed over the wing. Cell B 3.13 was a murder scene. Burnt paper and clothing littered the floor of the cell, all pushed under the door and through the broken observation panel. It must have been a terrifying way to die and Saunders was found pressed against the window, obviously trying to get a last breath. It would appear that the Brood family had had their way. The North London gang was smashed, one dead, five in hospital with multiple injuries and their business well and truly shut down. There was also a crystal-clear message to all the wannabe gangsters. Play with fire and we will burn you to the ground.

The following days were a blizzard of debriefs. It would appear that Andy had performed outstandingly. His handling of the incident was faultless and his quick thinking had probably saved the life of the Officer. No blame could be attributed to any of the actions taken by the prison and two culprits were identified and charged by the police for the murder of the prisoner Jamie Saunders. A further fifteen prisoners were charged with rioting and could expect serious prison sentences. The prisoner who rescued the Officer by pulling her into his cell was recommended for release. He was eligible for parole and achieved this first time around. There were a number of accusations from prisoners regarding the treatment they received at the hands of the staff. Mr Franks claimed that he had been badly assaulted. Unfortunately, the CCTV had been broken by the rioters so no evidence could be found. It was, as some would say, CASE CLOSED.

# CHAPTER SIX

Kevin Brood lay on his prison bed at HMP Blandford House, an old manor house converted into an open prison. The thought of someone such as him ever being transferred to this prison was unbelievable, but he had managed to avoid many of the risk assessments which should have stopped the move before it was even mentioned. Only a short time ago he was sitting in a severe personality disorder unit but he had contacts and these people could get things moving for the right price. Sometimes the fear of a murky past uncovered was just enough motivation to cooperate.

The illegal phone hidden under his pillow vibrated, he pushed his room door shut and took the call. It was his smart younger brother David explaining that the recent troubles at Marwood were over and had been a total success. Kevin slapped his hand down onto his thigh,

"Brilliant mate, has the message been passed that we will not be fucked with?"

"One hundred percent, all of the London boys are in a terrible condition, one dead and the rest smashed to bits. We nearly ended up with a screw." David roared with laughter as he recalled the story. "She shit herself but got lucky, the teams came in and rescued her."

"Lucky bitch." Keven chuckled, "What about Byfield, how are we doing dealing with him?"

"It's all good, leave that to me."

"Will do mate but keep me up to date." Kevin hung up and hid the phone. The sound of a broom sweeping the corridor outside caught his attention; he hopped off the bed and opened his door to find an old life sentence prisoner cleaning up.

"You okay George?"

"Not bad boss, how can I help? You never speak to me unless I can do something for you." Kevin laughed, that was true. He kept his business close to his chest.

"Is the gym screw Gary on duty George? If he is go fetch him for me."

George shuffled away leaving the broom leaning against the wall, returning five minutes later, Gary in tow.

"Step this way Gary," Kevin held the door open to his cell. "I have a favour to ask and another pile of cash to give you for doing it."

"Leave it out, you will get me arrested Kev. I told you the last time, I'm out of that game. I nearly got caught bringing the last load in and the risk isn't worth it any more. No more favours." Gary started to turn to leave but before he could move, the back of his head cracked against the wall as Brood grabbed him by the throat and pushed him backwards.

"That is not how it works, if you jump into business with me you only get out when I say, do you fucking understand?" He didn't wait for an answer. "And let's not forget that I have your bank account numbers and proof that I have been paying you. Along with the address of your lovely little wife and kiddies. You still want out? It's your choice."

"No."

"No fucking what you lump of shit?"

"No Mr Brood."

"Good boy, now I want you to do me a little favour." He lay back onto the bed and lit a cigar. "I want you to get me out of here for tomorrow night, let's just say my work placement at the leisure centre are having an open evening and I am needed. Then I want you to drive me to a little meeting that I need to attend in Orpington. Understand?"

"Yes Mr Brood, I can do that easily. Your release license will be ready in the morning." Gary knew he had no choice and was totally owned by Brood.

"Shut the door on the way out Gary, I have a couple of calls to make."

# CHAPTER SEVEN

Terry was woken up at 2am in the morning. A calm voice greeted him as he answered the ringing phone.

"Sorry to wake you up sir. The Night Orderly Officer needs to speak with you. I will put you through."

He heard the phone ring for a second before it was answered. Terry knew that this was bad news.

"Morning Terry, Mike speaking. We have had a prisoner hang himself, staff found him unresponsive ten minutes ago. Health Care staff have managed to get him breathing again but he's been blue lighted out to hospital. It doesn't look good."

"Okay, I take it the Duty Governor is aware?" Terry was already getting out of bed as he spoke.

"Yes sir, she is on the way in."

"Give me an hour and I'll be there." Terry hung up and hurriedly got dressed. Fifty minutes later he walked into the duty governor's office. "Any update?"

"Life support at the moment. The consultant has asked for the Next of Kin to come in. It sounds grim," the duty governor explained. Terry looked through the paperwork on the desk. This lad was only twenty-two years old. Recently convicted of murdering his mother, he had received life with a recommendation of twenty-four years. He had attempted the same thing twice within the past five weeks, yet he wasn't even considered a risk for ending his life. Scanning the documents Terry had a sense that this one was badly managed.

The phone rang, an external call. Terry picked it up and listened to the message, replacing the receiver before passing on the news.

"The boy is brain dead, the life support is going to be left on while organ donors are found. They will be turning off the machine at some point today, dreadful news." He took a deep breath. "I am going out to see his dad. Where do you start to explain that he died in our care?" Turning his back, he zipped up his jacket and left for the hospital.

The following day saw the start of the inquiries. Area Office had sent in the Safer Custody Lead and the ombudsman's office had dispatched an investigator to establish the facts. Terry knew what would be found, a series of mistakes culminating in the boy's death.

Late morning, the Area Lead knocked on Terry's door. Her face was stern and turning down the offer of a coffee she launched straight in.

"Terry, what the hell has happened here? I am struggling to find anything which can dig us out of this mess." She looked exasperated. "Nothing has worked as it should. This boy has been allowed to die in your care without anyone preventing him from doing so. How many warnings did the staff need? I can't believe what I have seen. Terry, heads are going to roll."

The ombudsman's investigator knocked on the door two hours later, and although a great deal more diplomatic, the message was the same. Once left alone, Terry pressed his hands onto his forehead and phoned the Deputy Director of Custody who was Stephen's manager. The evidence was discussed and it was agreed that a full external investigation would be held led by a senior Governor.

First a riot and the next day a death, what a time to be left in charge. There would also be a separate police investigation looking for any criminal actions. Terry knew that this could lead to man slaughter charges if blame could be found, so these were really worrying times. He rang Stephen and talked him through the events, Terry just wished that he were here. Stephen was a great Governor and would know how to handle the coming flack; he had been away for a few days but would quickly get back into the stride of things. Stephen was quick to reassure his deputy, "Terry, I will come in. Hold the fort for today and I'll be back tomorrow."

"Thanks boss," Terry said with some relief, "there are a lot of politics floating around and this is a bit over my head."

"No problems mate, see you in the morning."

Stephen's alarm sounded at 5:30am. He really didn't feel like returning to the prison as he was enjoying his time off, but as Governor, he was ultimately in charge, on holiday or not, and he needed to get back to the normality of an abnormal occupation. Stepping into the shower, his stomach took a spin as he worried about the events that had happened, but knowing Terry needed his support at this time, he told himself firmly to get a grip. His words were lost under the cascading water in the shower.

"Sorry, did you say something Stephen? I couldn't hear you," Tanya called from the bedroom.

"Nothing sweetheart, just moaning to myself." He finished getting ready, kissed Tanya and the children goodbye, and climbing into his car he took a deep breath before heading on his way.

Driving in was normally a joy, he loved the scenery and the way in which nature changed the backdrop before it could become the norm. Today however he was not in the frame of mind to appreciate it. Swinging into his car park space he grabbed his bag and walked through the gate area. The familiarity of the routine eased Stephens's anxiety about the situation and taking his security keys, he walked through the open courtyard towards his office. It was still early and he figured that Terry was not in yet.

His office was as he left it and turning on the computer, he guessed that he would have hundreds of emails that would need his attention. Clicking the mouse, he was delighted to see that he had less than fifty. Obviously Terry had kept on top of things in his absence. It always amazed him how peaceful a prison was at this time of the morning, a few night staff getting on with the business of handing over to the day shift, other staff drifting in, still lost in thoughts from home until the day kicked in and distant piss taking about one pointless thing or another. It was the same in every prison he had worked in.

Twenty minutes later Terry came into Stephen's office. Sporting a North Face jacket and carrying his gym bag he could have passed for someone on their way to the leisure centre. Terry had cracked the look of casual down to a fine art. He never looked rushed or flustered which was a miracle given the shit storm that had hit him during the past few days.

"Hi Terry, thanks for taking care of business for the past few days," Stephen greeted him, and after a quick catch up regarding family life, he got down to business. "Can you show me the details regarding the suicide and the disturbance on B Wing? You handled that one well by the way but we can discuss it further when we get to the bottom of the Death in Custody." Terry had everything to hand and Stephen studied every detail.

"Bad decision making for the death Terry. The Duty Governor and Orderly Officer have dropped the ball badly. We will need to investigate this quickly. Give me ten minutes and come back. I need to take some advice."

When he returned Stephen had a number of documents printed out on his desk. Terry recognised them, he had dealt with them a number of times, letters of investigation and suspension. Stephen talked Terry through what had been discussed with the HR department before asking him to fetch Tracy Edwards, the Duty Governor when the suicide occurred and Mike Green who was the Orderly Officer, giving it ten minutes between each appointment.

Governor Edwards sat on the sofa in the waiting area outside the office. The door opened and she was called in.

"No easy way to do this Tracy," explained Stephen. "There is an allegation that you failed to perform your duties in the lead up to the recent suicide which is seen as gross misconduct. Do you want anyone in here to assist you?"

"No," Tracy replied. She knew as soon as the suicide occurred on her watch that there would be repercussions.

"Okay, I am asking for this to be investigated and as part of the process, you will be suspended on full pay pending this work.

Do you understand?" Stephen looked at her, checking her understanding that this was a process he was obliged to follow. She looked shocked but nodded.

"Please give Terry your keys as you will be leaving right now. Do not discuss this matter with anyone until asked to do so by the investigators." He handed her the documents outlining her suspension and turned back to face his computer screen while Terry escorted her from the prison.

Mike Green came into the office, attitude written all over his face. Having many years in the prison service behind him, he was aware of the process about to take place and was not going to take it lying down. Before Stephen could open his mouth, he went on the attack.

"I know that you are going to kick me out and probably sack me so you know what? Fuck You, I quit. The Brood boys are going to take care of you, you smug bastard, mark my words." He threw the last sentence at Stephen's astonished face.

"What the hell are you talking about Mr Green?" Stephen asked, trying to remain calm in the face of the verbal attack.

"Trust me Byfield, I know what storm is coming your way and I hope that it rips your heart out." With that final spit of venom, he took his ID card and keys and threw them at Stephen, "Good luck Governor, you are going to need it." With that he turned, pushing past Terry as he headed down to the gate, Terry following to ensure he had left the prison.

Stephen sat stunned, contemplating what he had just heard until Terry came back into the Office and enquired,

"You okay Stephen? Bloody hell, he's been harbouring some hate for a while, that's for sure."

"I'm fine Terry," he replied thoughtfully, "but how would Mike Green know about the Broods? And how would he know what they are up to? I don't get it, the cheeky bastard. I felt like knocking him out." They both laughed, relieving the tension somewhat.

"There have been some rumours around for the past few weeks about him, nothing concrete but he may have just played his hand," Terry pondered. "Evil little bastard anyway so good riddance." Terry left, heading back to his own office leaving Stephen to dwell further on the threats he had just received. The worm that had just been inserted into Stephens head spun around again and again, what did he mean, rip my heart out? Giving himself a mental shake, and finishing off a few last bits of work, he closed down his computer and popped back into Terry's office.

"Okay Terry, that has taken care of that. If there is nothing else at the moment, Tanya and I have a few things to catch up on so I'll see you in a few days buddy, once my leave is over." He mulled over what Green had told him for the entire drive home. It had sounded like the guy knew a storm was coming his way but what form it would take, he had no idea.

# CHAPTER EIGHT

Stephen and Tanya were sitting chatting in the lounge, the children were in bed and Chris was relaxing in the annex. It had been a perfect few days at home. He had taken the unusual step of taking an extra week away from work despite the trouble of the past few days. That was all dealt with and there was little that needed to be done that couldn't wait for his return. He was starting to feel the need to become involved with the cut and thrust again, his mind itching for action.

It was coming around to the twins' birthday and at four years old, they were old enough to have playschool friends around. This would be the first real party and planning it would be a lot of fun although they had left it late with only one week to go. Now Chris seemed to be moving forward with his life, it had encouraged them all to do the same. They sat discussing what they should go for and the obvious option was to hire in some form of entertainment, a clown or puppet show seemed popular according to Google. The other options involving burger bars or bouncy castles seemed more trouble than they were worth with a group of over excited four-year-olds and the house was big enough to cope with inside entertainment anyway.

"I think I've got it!" Stephen exclaimed, glancing up from his phone. "There's a party company here who will provide everything, a clown, puppets and a magic show. Perfect Parties seem to cater for everything."

With Tanya in agreement, Stephen phoned the number and a hundred and fifty pounds later and thanks to a late cancellation, all the arrangements were made.

Tanya wrote out invitations for Harry and Ellie to take into school the following day and then they both relaxed imagining the delight on the twin's faces when they saw what had been arranged for them.

The domestic side of Stephen's life was coming together again, a loving family, the new edition, Hector, bringing joy to them all as he headed for eleven months old. But he still had a lot of fire burning in his belly. Stephen was a hard man, he had seen a lot and could handle himself mentally and physically. He was a handy guy to have by your side in a fight with a lot of courage and, as many had discovered who had crossed him in his past, this boy could hit like a mule. Maybe it was time for him to show a bit more of this side to his management team, they needed to understand his drive.

The following morning, fully rejuvenated from his break, he picked up the phone and dialed Terry's office number. Terry answered quickly and instantly Stephen felt the camaraderie between them and the urge to get back to work increased. Although he had briefly returned to the prison to sort out the young lad's death, Stephen felt that he had not taken ownership of the riot and suicide, and had really left Terry to deal with it. This would stop today when he would return and take responsibility.

Having discussed his return to work with Tanya the previous evening, he collected his things together and sprang into the car. Head buzzing with exciting projects he could implement to get the prison moving forwards, whatever threats made against him were cast aside as minor irritants and he would ride straight at them. Bring it on.

He felt a relief as he entered the gate area, he had been on annual leave during the riot and had not played any part of the heroic acts in getting the prison back on track. In fact, he felt a bit surplus to requirements. But the look on the staff's faces said it all. They were happy to have the boss back in at work. He had seen this before and appreciated the feelings of goodwill. They had stuck with him through the torture of last year and had given him the strength to battle back. He would run through walls for them and they for him.

He stuck his head into Terry's office and seeing the familiar jacket and sports bag which were placed on a small coffee table in the middle of the office, Stephen knew Terry was around. Turning to go on to his own office, he almost bumped into Terry coming up the corridor behind him.

"Hello stranger" Terry greeted him, "I've tried not to cause any more havoc while you have been away. Good to see you back, you look well."

"Thanks Terry, I feel ready for action," Stephen replied, shaking Terry's hand warmly whilst giving him a bit of a man hug. These two would always be more than just work colleagues after the horrors they had shared together. As they walked through into Terry's office, he continued, "I'm looking forward to chatting with you about some new ideas to sharpen up our Safer Custody processes. We need to move forward and we need to do it quickly. There will be a lot of questions asked during the inquest into the lad's death so let's get ahead of the game while we still can."

"Good idea, a review into our processes is long overdue," Terry agreed.

"Brilliant, now what happened during the disturbance on B Wing?" Stephen asked, eager to get to the bottom of the cause for the riot.

Terry handed Stephen a mug of coffee from the machine in the corner of his office before replying. "Although it was a pretty big event, there has been minimal damage. A few office doors were kicked open, a lot of documents were set on fire and the obvious damage to the cell wall where they tried to get to Jenny. The staff, or damage to the wing, had not been the original goal but simply a byproduct of the primary aim which was to get the North London boys."

Stephen took a sip of his coffee. "What shocks me Terry, is the violence offered to those five or six prisoners, one dead and the others with multiple broken bones. Was this just a vicious excuse to hurt and kill?"

Terry nodded. "We have had a stack of information since then, people were paid a lot of money to get involved. The guys who actually committed the murder were paid five hundred pounds each. Payment on death. We have bank records where transactions were made on the Sunday."

"What?" Stephen was starting to get a feel for how premeditated the whole event had been.

"This was so pre-planned it is ridiculous." Terry continued. "The wing was swamped with heroin in the week before. Anyone volunteering to be involved had free gear all week. The plan was nearly scuppered the week before when we rumbled what was happening. That was just down to good old-fashioned prison officer work but then a big fight in visits brought it all back on and then there was no stopping it."

Stephen shook his head incredulously. "How is Jenny?"

"Tough girl, she was back on duty the next day, not a scratch on her." Stephen made a note to put her forward for a commendation. "Terry, I want all of those staff involved in the rescue to receive a letter of commendation. They showed massive bravery. How are the injured staff?"

"Mike Harper has a broken arm, he was hit with a brick but he will be fine. The other injury was Kate Wilson, she just has a bruised head where the metal pipe played a tune on her helmet."

"I'll give them a call and arrange a visit. Leave the staff to me." Stephen got up to return to his own office to face the rest of the day's work. "Thanks mate, you've had a fair bit to deal with in my absence, and I appreciate it."

Later that day as Stephen left for the drive home, he phoned both staff as he sped along the country lanes. They seemed fine and they made arrangements to meet next week. He was moved by their attitude, it was all about team, and saving the life of Jenny. True heroes.

# CHAPTER NINE

The party people were there early setting up and it all looked like it was going to be amazing. Puppet shows and magic equipment were unloaded into the large dining room. The kitchen was in full flow as Tanya prepared all sorts of tasty nibbles favoured by four-year-olds. The smell of mini sausages and pizza bites wafting from the oven was delicious.

The children began to arrive and the hustle and bustle of the party got underway. Chris was looking after Hector who had just started taking his first steps and was into everything. He seemed as tough as his parents and there would be no stopping him once he got going, a total bundle of energy.

The puppet show was a real crowd pleaser, the children laughed all afternoon and even little Hector was joining in with the party spirit. He giggled with the girls and wanted to play rough and tumble with the boys in between babbling at the puppets who he was convinced were talking to him. Stephen looked at the clock. The other parents would be due to collect in twenty minutes much to his relief as he was running out of steam.

A white painter and decorator van pulled into the driveway, there always seems to be one parent who arrived early and got in the way. However, they seemed content to wait in the van which suited Stephen just fine as he looked out through the window. He saw a young man and a woman obviously taking a call on the phone. He didn't recognise them from dropping children off but it had been hectic and he had probably been talking to other parents.

He turned back to the magic show now taking place. The magician's assistant was also in the process of taking a call behind the makeshift stage, Stephen noticed that she looked shocked, in fact she dropped the phone before quickly picking it up and disappearing outside briefly. She returned and spoke frantically to her partner as he prepared for the final trick. He looked around and nodded to her as the grand finale was prepared.

"And now ladies and gentlemen, girls and boys, one last spectacular trick," he announced. The children cheered and clapped as he continued.

"This is a trick so amazing, we only do it at special birthdays, but we need you all to help cast the spell. Will you do that?"

As the children all screamed their assent, Stephen looked up at the assistant. She was crying, trying hard not to be noticed but something had upset her. It worried him as he watched her wipe away the tears, possibly a domestic or some bad news, but either way it was odd and not at all what he expected to see in the middle of the show.

"Now I need special twins for this last trick, do we have any?" the magician asked the enthralled children. Ellie and Harry jumped up, "Us! Us!" they shouted, "We're twins." Everyone laughed as they were led up to the stage area by Tanya, pulling on her hands in their eagerness. Stephen tapped them on the head as they walked past him.

"You stay there Mum, you can't see the magic happen," chanted the magician, stopping Tanya from entering the stage area. Tanya did as she was told and laughing, took photos as the children were led away. A gigantic multi-coloured sheet blocked off the end of the room and the twin's silhouettes could be seen behind it, waving and giggling. The children in the audience chanted the magic words as directed by the magician and the lights went out followed by a puff of smoke as the lights came back on. The sheet was pulled back and Harry and Ellie were gone. The children roared with laughter, as Tanya and Stephen clapped. "Can you keep them for a few minutes longer?" shouted Stephen. The assistant standing to the side of the sheet continued crying.

"Where have you put them, this is the quietest they've ever been," laughed Tanya.

"I am so sorry," sobbed the assistant.

"What do you mean sorry?" asked a confused Tanya.

"They told us that we had to do this and if we didn't, they would kill us."

"Who told you to do what?" Stephen demanded.

"Help kidnap your little children." She sobbed even louder.

Stephen leapt to the front door, just in time to see the young couple in the van pulling out of the driveway. He raced outside and was just able to catch the rear door handle. The door swung open and he could see the children cowering at the far end, a large figure looming over them. He threw himself forward and managed to get into the back before a hefty kick sent him half out but he clung onto the door and slammed a punch into the chest of the oncoming man. He staggered backwards before grabbing a metal bar and crunching it down onto Stephen's arm making him fall backwards onto the driveway as the door was pulled shut. Leaping back to his feet, Stephen lunged back at the van but it was too late, it roared out into the lane and was gone. Rushing back into the house holding his battered arm, Stephen yelled at the magician. "What the fuck is going on, what the hell have you done?" before turning to Tanya and shouting at her to phone the police quickly. She rushed to find the phone, hunting through piles of children's clothes that were thrown on top of it.

Other children wandered around confused with what was going on. Some still sat cross legged looking at the magician who was franticly packing his stuff together. The terrified assistant held out her shaking hand, and passed an envelope to Stephen. It was sealed and inside was a hand written note, which he unfolded, terrified by what he would read.

"Who gave you this?" he demanded.

"The young woman who was sitting in the front of the van," she replied with another sob. Stephen frantically read out loud the words on the page.

*Dear Stephen and Tanya.*

*Your children have been taken. They are in the process of being moved to one of our safe locations.*
*Please remain calm. Any panic will result in their death. Police involvement will also ensure harm to Ellie and Harry.*
*Should you choose to keep them alive, phone the number below within the next five minutes.*
*We have your home under electronic surveillance so what you decide to do next will be observed and acted upon.*
*You now have four minutes.*
*07898 25261234*

Tanya found her phone and handed it to Stephen who quickly dialed the number, which was answered after less than two rings by a female voice.

"Hello, well done for following the instructions."

"Stephen Byfield speaking what the hell is going on?"

"Mr Byfield thank you for the prompt response. Allow me to explain the rules which you must follow if you want to see your children alive again. Firstly, I will tell you who we work for, I know that this is a strange way for negotiations to start as normally the police would do that, but let's just skip the middle man.
We are employed by the Brood family who you have cost over half a million pounds in revenue during the past two years. You will pay this back."

"I don't have that type of money, I could never get that amount," Stephen replied incredulously.

"We know that Stephen."

"So why ask for it? I don't understand. Give me my children back or I will fucking take you to pieces." Stephen yelled in frustration.

"You are in no position to threaten us, and you will earn it back for us, every penny. We will explain how in time."

The phone went dead, he tried to phone back but the number was unobtainable. Pay as you go phones, easily changed and untraceable he subconsciously thought.

"Tanya what the hell are we going to do?" he asked as they stared at each other in disbelief and the pain started to thud along his arm.

"Oh my God, where's Hector?" Tanya suddenly shouted in panic. She spun round to see Chris walking towards them holding him in his arms. She grabbed him and held him close, her head spinning while she cried uncontrollably.

Almost on automatic pilot, Chris and Stephen saw the other children off to their somewhat bemused parents who wondered why they received such curt replies to their queries as to how the party had gone. With the twin's lives in peril, there was no way they wanted to risk anyone talking before they knew quite what they were dealing with.

# CHAPTER TEN

The chloroform had worn off and Ellie and Harry both woke up at the same time. Their hands were tied and sticky tape had been fastened over their mouths. Ellie panicked as she struggled to breathe through her blocked nose. The back of the van was cramped and cold and the dirty white metal interior vibrated their bones as the van dashed through the countryside with the wheel arches making an uncomfortable back rest and the filthy spare wheel adding to the stink of oil. The young woman had swapped places with the large man who had taken the children. As she climbed into the back of the van when they stopped in a country road lay-by, she noticed Ellie's discomfort. Leaning forward and pulling the tape from Ellie's mouth she warned,

"If you stay nice and quiet, I will keep it off." She then did the same for Harry. "And you too. Any shouting and I will put it back on, understand?" The twins nodded in terrified silence. They were four years old today and having spent every minute of their short lives together, a telepathic understanding had grown between them. They had also inherited the toughness and guile of their parents but they were too young and frightened to realise this.

Ellie was the first to talk. "I'm cold and I want Mummy and Daddy. I'm frightened." She began to sob gently. She got the woman's absolute attention.

"Listen kid, think yourself lucky that you can still breathe so keep your mouth shut or else," she snapped. Twenty-seven years old and hardened from the streets of Belfast, a top education had given her a brain as sharp as her toned body. Beverly McCullock was as callous as they come. She had watched grown men from her childhood streets being torn to pieces in front of her eyes just because they had spoken to the wrong person. Two snotty kids were just an inconvenience. It was tolerable because she had been promised that it would be no more than one week. Either they would be dead or Stephen Byfield would be sensible and do as he was told. The twins got the message and kept very silent.

One cold hour later the van pulled into a farm yard. A small group of men came from the house to meet them. A large set guy with a full beard limped over to the back door of the van. Opening it he cast an eye over the prize before holding out a hand to Beverly. "Come on, jump out and come and get warm with me in the house."

He beckoned a scruffy man over who looked as though he had been working on the farm with filthy overalls and muddy boots.

"Take the kids into the basement and make sure that they have something to eat and drink. This could be a restless night." The bearded man turned and went into the house with Beverly. The scruffy man untied the twin's feet but left the plastic pull ties in place to secure their hands. Taking hold of the straps he pulled them out of the van and onto their feet.

"Follow me ya little bastards," he growled, and took them down a small flight of steps that were on the right-hand side of the house. He smelt like he looked, horrible, the type of man that a four-year-old child was terrified of. They reached an old blue wooden door, the paint peeling off it and with a rusty handle hanging half attached to the door.

After knocking twice, the sound of a heavy bolt could be heard sliding back. Slowly the door opened and a youngish male face peered out.

"How ya doing old fella? Bring them in." Harry walked in first, his head down facing the floor. He was almost too scared to see his capturers but Ellie on the other hand took in every detail. One small window was very high up on a bare brick wall and there were three camp beds all with sleeping bags on top of them against the wall with the window. A single light bulb hung from the ceiling beaming a harsh light into the room. She could see that there were two other men waiting in the room, both standing and staring, both looking very frightening to the scared little girl. A cooker and a fridge, and a curtain hiding a small area were on the other wall. She could see no more, she didn't want to see any more. It was a scary cold place.

The twins both started to cry. It would appear that child care would not be on the agenda. The sticky tape was re applied to stop the noise and thrown onto the camp beds, they knew that they were very alone.

"Lay there you little brats," the younger man ordered, "make a noise and I will kill you down here in this very room." They cowered, bulging eyes not leaving the horrid man, their tears making tacks down their dusty faces. A cold takeaway burger each was thrown onto their beds with orders to wait a minute and they could eat. To the children's total horror, a large hunting knife was pulled from the waistband of the jeans of one of the men. He walked over to the children and cut off the plastic restraints and pulled the tape back off from their mouths.

"Mess me about just once and you will get this," he showed them the blade. "Now eat your food." The twins looked at each other and neither took a mouthful.

"Every time you need the toilet ask me, it is over there." He pointed to the curtain which one of the other men pulled back revealing a metal bucket sitting on the floor.

Two of the men left, whispering briefly to the remaining man before he shut the door. He pulled his camp bed over in front of the door.

"I am turning this light off in two minutes, so get in your sleeping bags. and lie down."

Harry and Ellie did as they were told before the plastic cuffs were reapplied only this time their little hands were fastened to their bed frame. The lights went out and so did any hope in their little hearts.

# CHAPTER ELEVEN

The black Audi TT pulled up outside of the sports bar in Orpington. Gary looked at the clock on the dashboard, it was six thirty, bang on time.

"There you go Mr Brood, right on time. I will park up around the back and wait."

"Oh no you won't my old son, you are coming in with me. I want to introduce you to a couple of associates." Kevin patted him on the shoulder, "Leave the keys with the doorman, he will park up for us."

Feeling flattered Gary handed the keys over and walked in the club, shoulder to shoulder with the boss. The lack of respect was not lost on those waiting inside, nor on Kevin. He would extract revenge for this over familiar behaviour at a later date. The pair of them were ushered through the packed bar and into the back room where things were in full swing and pretty girls were everywhere. The chair in which Green Mile had met his end was long gone. Gary felt like a million dollars, this was VIP treatment indeed. Kevin opened his arms and embraced his brother.

"David, this is Gary who I spoke with you about, can we make him comfortable while we meet?" David nodded and a young lady walked over and took Gary's arm.

"One minute Gary, just before you go," Kevin reached in his pocket and handed him a bundle of fifty pound notes. "Have fun, we will be done in an hour" Kevin told him before he and David disappeared into a meeting room that already seemed full.

Gary was led to a roulette table. It was a private table set aside for high rollers and only five people played in this area specially cordoned off from the rest of the punters. The green baize of the roulette area was covered in chips, and as he exchanged one thousand pounds in notes, he noticed that he still had at least another two thousand to play with.

He hit his lucky numbers 17, 18, 19, 20 and 21. The wheel spun and the ball settled Black 20. Tom had more than two hundred pounds in chips on this number and a massive pile was handed over to him leaving the original bet on the table. The wheel spun again Red 18. Another winner.

"It seems as though this is your night tonight sir," the croupier commented.

Gary smiled back "You can say that again." The winning streak seemed to go on; gambling was easy with other people's money, so was drinking the whisky that flowed and his glass was never empty. The line of friends wanting to entertain Gary was endless.

The small blonde girl was only nineteen, her name was Zara and it appeared that she had a thing for older men. Her attention to detail was exceptional, as was the constant inflating of Gary's ego as they sat and chatted during a lull in the gambling. She had a small apartment above the club and they soon found themselves falling through the door as she tore at his clothes while he undid her buttons on the flimsy black silk shirt. They stumbled into the dimly lit bedroom where she fell onto her knees and took his erect penis into her mouth. Gary closed his eyes, his brain foggy from whisky and overcome with anticipation and excitement. She stood and led him to the bed. "Do you want a livener before I fuck you silly?" she giggled before quickly making two big lines of cocaine.

"I've never taken the stuff," he stuttered before sniffing a long line up with one of the fifty-pound notes.

"Well enjoy," she instructed as she took the second line and mounted him.

For Gary the sex was terrific, and although he had never cheated nor lived this gangster lifestyle before, from that moment he wanted more. For Zara, it was a night's work. She had been well paid for fucking this boring ape, and the cameras filming every little detail provided a guarantee of future cooperation with the Brood family. However, the agenda for the meeting taking place downstairs was the real pay day.

"Good evening ladies and Gentlemen, thank you for attending at such short notice." Kevin brought the gathering to order.

"If I can just bring your attention to the agenda for tonight's meeting. Given that I am slightly pressed for time this evening I wondered if I could bring item seven forward and leave David to take the finance report and the overview from Heads of functions in my absence. Any objections?" Of course there were no objections.

"Item seven, Stephen Byfield. Where are we precisely?" Kevin Brood's Head of Operations opened her briefcase. She was a bright, young lady with a degree in law from Oxford.

Susan Turner had been recruited to the business after representing David Brood during a court hearing in 2007. While it seemed to the legal team that David would be spending a long time in prison, she noticed a discrepancy in the collection of police evidence. Even the ten thousand pounds a day barrister had missed the clues. Her attention to detail along with the endless hours she gave to her profession had discovered it. The barrister had the case dismissed and he was well paid with an enhanced reputation. The real hero however was spotted by the family. Her love of money and the dangerous lifestyle seduced her and made her a valuable member of the board.

"Thank you Kevin, I have a detailed report on Mr Byfield." A folder was passed to each board member before she continued.

"Enclosed within the report are bank details and transactions, address details and all phone numbers along with every phone call made within the past six months on the family's mobile and land lines. I also have details of every club that they are associated with along with the addresses of friends which thankfully the golf club kindly supplies to new members.

I have a breakdown of events concerning the prison riot at Marwood in which we eliminated a number of threats, plus the list of those staff who are on our payroll. At present we have fifteen prison staff which include one 'In charge' Governor from an undisclosed prison and a number of Senior Prison Service managers who will remain anonymous at present due to our security measures. We also have senior police and military personnel available as and when needed.

We are currently paying out on average twenty thousand pounds per month at a profit of seven hundred and forty thousand through the smuggling of contraband across the country's prisons.

This afternoon we kidnapped the Byfield twins, they are at present being held in a secure location within the UK. This was an opportunist acquisition but one which I sanctioned as the situation presented itself during surveillance and we were in a position where we could manage it. We have contacted the Byfield family already and will do so again this evening with details of our proposition."

She stopped and waited for people to catch her up. Kevin cleared his throat. "And what are we proposing?"

"We want our money back, Byfield has cost us a great deal in lost money and reputation." Susan replied. "I want both restored and if he does what I have in mind to get his children back, then this man will be destroyed."

The room was silent until Kevin spoke. "Brilliant, absolutely brilliant. I am looking forward to seeing how this develops."

"Oh it will develop," she affirmed, "if he loves his children he will be so far in bed with us that it can't fail to develop."

"Susan Turner, you turn my blood to ice sometimes. Keep me informed please. Just one point, I want the kids out of the country, can our Irish friends help us?"

"All in place Kevin, they will be gone by the end of the week. On another topic, we are also developing links with a North African criminal gang who have acquired a great deal of weapons and ammo. This potentially could be worth a great deal of money, in fact a game changing figure." Susan concluded her report and sat down.

"Keep me updated on this one," Kevin instructed, "I would

like David to oversee this deal, if that's okay with you David?"

"No problems Kevin, I'm on it," replied David.

Kevin got to his feet. "Sorry that my stay has been brief this evening, unfortunately I will be missed back at the prison if I'm late back." He collected his papers and handed them to David before shaking a few hands and leaving the meeting room.

Sat alone at the roulette table, the euphoric figure of Gary presented a pathetic sight. Pumped up on sex and cocaine he stood and patted Kevin on the shoulder, "Ready for home boss?" he slurred.

"Not with you in that fucking state, you stupid bastard," Kevin answered, looking at him in disgust. He looked up and summoned the bar manager over.

"I need a lift back to the prison, this idiot has overdone the whisky and coke, any chance Gerald?"

"No bother Mr Brood, I can be ready in two minutes." Gerald knew it wasn't a request but an order.

"Perfect, I will make it up to you." He took the staggering Gary into the car park, "I have arranged a lift for us, you will need to pick your car up at a later date." The slurred thanks from Gary was lost as Gerald pulled up and opened the doors. Kevin sat in the front as Gary sat reflecting in his glory on the back seat.

"How much have you won Gary my old son?" asked Kevin.

"Twenty-five grand, I have the cheque in my little old pocket here," Gary replied, tapping the pocket of his trousers.

"Oh well played, I expect I have signed that one.'"

The rest of the drive was spent in silence, Gary tried to make small talk but was dismissed so he spent the rest of the journey dozing in and out of inebriated consciousness.

The car swung into the dark prison car park where night staff had started their shift as others had left at nine o'clock. His licence details stated that he had until nine thirty to get back so he was nice and early with another ten minutes to waste. Kevin turned around to face the now deflated Gary.

"Now, I trust that you enjoyed your evening?" he queried. Gary nodded.

"All I need now then is my cheque back."

Gary sniggered, "Not a chance, I earned this, I got you out for the evening."

"And I got you a girl, whisky and Coke. I think we are even."

Gerald turned around and prodded the barrel of a pistol into Gary's now sweating forehead, "Pay back." The cheque was handed back with a trembling hand.

"Good Boy. Now fuck off and find your own way home. Oh, and one last thing Gary, don't bother picking your car up, it has been sold already, call it Karma but that's what you get for shagging my sister." With that parting shot, Kevin opened the car door and climbed out.

The car lights disappeared back into the lane as Gary turned around and headed on foot back in the direction of home. He could hear Kevin Brood laughing all the way back to the prison gate.

# CHAPTER TWELVE

Karen Mathews checked on the time. It was nearly eleven o'clock and she was shattered, she'd had a long day at the vets followed by writing a training course she was expected to deliver in a couple of weeks-time. She had ended her shift in the veterinary surgery at seven with another four hours studying. It had been a busy day. On top of helping out as a theatre assistant with two operations she had also assisted some trainees prepare for forthcoming exams so all in all she was ready for her bed. Her phone bleeped telling her that she had a text waiting, she slipped into the rest room and opened the incoming message. It was from her boyfriend David, David Brood.

It simply said Ring me, we need to talk quickly. She dialed his number and the phone was answered immediately.

"Hi darling, what's wrong?" she asked him "Your message sounded urgent."

"Hello Sweetheart, nothing's wrong, I've just come back from a meeting where we discussed moving some items from England to the Irish Republic. Can you help?"

"Of course I'll help you," Karen replied with a smile in her voice. The vets she worked for specialized in equine surgery and they often moved horses backwards and forwards in and out of Ireland.

"Call round here when you finish, I can't chat on the phone, see you in a bit." David rang off, and quickly tidying up her desk, Karen locked up the long empty surgery and rushed off into the sleeping streets. Thirty minutes later she pulled up outside the electronic gates of David Brood's home where the intercom crackled a greeting and the six foot high black solid metal gates slowly swung open revealing a gravel driveway stretching one hundred yards towards a mock Tudor house.

As the car wheels crunched to a stop, she looked up and noticed David standing in the doorway. He was wearing a sharp black suit and looked every inch the business man. Taking her hand, he led Karen through the marble hallway and into a large lounge. An eighty-inch television looked small in the vast expanse of a room, where large black sofas were positioned around tastefully. Beautiful works of art hung from the immaculately painted white walls and soft music played from an invisible sound system enveloping the room with a relaxing ambiance.

A piano sat in the left corner, black and shiny. The lid was raised and it was obvious that someone had just been playing, the music sheets scattered on top.

David poured her a glass of wine from an already opened bottle and kissed her before they slipped into the luxury of the leather sofa. He had two lines of cocaine already cut onto a large glass coffee table. Karen bent down and took them both, tossing her head back allowing her long blonde hair to fall back, away from her face. Taking drugs was something she had never been part of before meeting Brood but she had allowed herself to be seduced over the last few months in his company, and found the odd line a great relaxation tool. She let out a long sigh and kicked her shoes off revealing bare feet. Curling up on the sofa and placing her head onto David's lap she melted into a cuddle, closing her eyes and enjoying the rush of the drug.

"What can I do for you sweetheart?" she murmured as she felt the cocaine sweeping through her body.

Stroking her hair, David replied. "I want two children moved from the UK to a farm in County Cavan. Can you help?"

Opening her eyes and half sitting up, Karen exclaimed "What do you mean children? That sounds very wrong to me, where are their parents?"

"Don't worry, the parents are in a spot of trouble, we just need to deliver the kids to a safe place until the family can get back together again. It's definitely life and death kind of trouble, not at all pleasant but we can help," he reassured her.

Lying back down, she asked "What am I supposed to do?"

"I thought that they could come with you on your little trip to the republic tomorrow."

"Oh, that sounds okay," she sighed and cuddled in deeper. "We have the big horsebox with a large sleeping area going over. It's an early start though, this is all a bit last minute David."

"Can't be helped, we need to act quickly, can you do it?"

"Suppose so. If it means that I'm saving these children, of course I can help. I looove kids," she murmured, stretching her body out further.

"I have sorted out the details already Karen. I have the same driver as last time you guys made the trip. Just phone me when you are in Wales."

"Will do, now honey, can we go to bed? I am feeling very ready for what you have in mind for me." David smiled, he stood and took her hand again but this time he led her to the bedroom.

# CHAPTER THIRTEEN

The twins sat on the grubby bed, confused and looking at each other. The lady had come back and woken them almost before it was light. They had not enjoyed the lady filming them on her phone. They had been told that if they spoke even one word a nasty man would kill Daddy. This had made them both cry, only stopping when the lady who always seemed so cruel hit Harry across the face. It left a stinging red mark on his cheek and made Harry stop crying, not because he was scared, but because he had become angry.

"Don't do that," he shouted, "I am telling my Dad." When he spoke to his dad he would tell him what had happened and she would be in for it he thought. Beverly hissed back, "Any more tears and I will phone the bad man to come back and get you, you little bastards." They stopped crying because they knew that she would, she was a horrible lady. Her phone rang.

"Right you two, I am going outside for one minute, I will be listening at the door. Any nonsense and I will be back in to give you another slap, understand?" Without waiting for them to answer, she left, closing the door behind her. Listening intently, they heard her walk up the stairs talking on the phone. They continued to listen until they could no longer hear her. For the first time since they were imprisoned in the dark basement they were left alone. Too scared to move around, they sat and whispered, rushed conversations that only another child could understand. Ellie looked around before climbing off the bed and quickly, on tiptoes, she ran across the room to the wooden table. Looking on top she could see a sandwich and a partially drunk can of coke. Grabbing it she darted back to the grubby mattress hiding the food but sharing the drink with Harry. Still no one came so again she rushed back to the table replacing the now empty can her bright little eyes looking for danger, hardly daring to look away from the door.

Ellie reached the safety of the mattress just as the door opened and the horrible lady came back in again. She sat back at the table and reached for her drink. She looked confused and then over to the seemingly sleeping children. She placed the can back down and continued tapping away on her phone. To the twins it seemed like a small victory. At least they would have something nice to eat when all the grown-ups were not watching.

Her phone vibrated and was quickly answered. It was a whispered conversation and her eyes kept darting towards the children. After only a minute or two she placed the phone back onto the table.

“Okay you two, time to get busy.” She stood and walked towards them. “And don’t think that I haven’t realised that you stole my lunch.” She strode over and reached under the mattress grabbing the sandwich pack.

“You two must have thought that I had just come down with the morning rain,” her Belfast accent was thick with sarcasm.

“You,” she looked directly at Ellie. “You are going on a holiday.” Grabbing her little arm, she dragged her onto her bare feet. “Put your shoes on, we’re going.” Ellie sobbed in terror at the thought of being separated from her twin. “Harry, Harry. I want Harry to come,” she begged.

“Oh don’t worry, I don’t want the brat here, he’s coming with you alright.”

The sound of a large truck crunching across the farmyard ended any further conversation as the smell of exhaust fumes filled the basement and caught in the back of the throat. To the twins it felt like the end of the world had arrived and then a loud knock on the door heralded the grim reaper.

“Here they are,” the horrid lady said to the driver of the truck. “Just watch her, she’s a crafty little bastard. She will steal your fucking eyes if you give her the chance.” She looked at Ellie once more, not one ounce of compassion in her cruel brown eyes.

Ellie stared back, just hoping that someone would take pity. Not a chance.

They were led outside. A large horse box stood in the farmyard, the lorry doors were open and a sleeping compartment behind the seats was exposed. The man leading them to the van picked them up one at a time and stood them on the driver's seat. He had a kind voice which was the first they had heard since they had been taken.

"Try not to be scared. Climb onto that bed. I have left you some sweets and a drink up there for you both to share. My friend here has also got you some clean clothes. They're only track suits but I hope they fit." Ellie felt the kindness and looked across at the blonde-haired lady sat across in the passenger seat. She looked nice and not the type of person who would hit a child.

She smiled at them and said, "Hello Ellie, hello Harry, my name is Karen. We have been told to take you on a little holiday until your Mummy and Daddy can come and see you again, would you like that?" They nodded, Karen smiled again and ruffled Ellie's hair.

"Jump up then, we need to close the door so that nobody sees you. Is that ok?" Again they nodded although not believing a word of what was said. They knew they had no choice but to do as they were told, and at least they were getting away from the horrible lady.

"I am going to leave a little light on in your room, just don't make a sound, okay?' Karen continued.

"Am I going to see my Mummy and Daddy soon?" a tear trickled down Harry's dirty face.

"Yes, you are going to see Mummy and Daddy, they will be along later." Karen gently closed the compartment door and started programming the satnav. She felt really sorry for these two little kids, they looked scared to death.

Ellie looked around her new surroundings, a single makeshift bed with a small table beside it. There was a light on the low ceiling. Even at her height she was unable to stand up and had to crawl onto the bed where two small blue sleeping bags lay on top of a thin mattress. Harry found a plastic bag on the table top and looked inside, two small packs of sweets and some cartons of orange juice. At least that part of the story was true. Feeling very afraid, they hugged each other and sobbed again. Ellie was missing her parents, but even at her tender age she felt that she needed to look after Harry. She was the older twin by five minutes and took her role very seriously. They could hear the people in the front talking and straining her ears to find out what they were saying, she was desperate to hear if their parents were there.

"Come on then, get driving. Time is a bit tight and we still have a long drive. We must get there by ten o'clock." Karen looked at the driver, "Chop chop!" The engine revved and the horse box drove out into the country lanes as Karen pulled out her phone.

"Hi David, we have picked them up no problems. The children are lovely. I will give you a ring when we get to Holyhead." Placing her phone back into her pocket Karen settled back into her seat. Eyes closed she thought about the trip ahead. She had taken things into Ireland for David before. Things that she hadn't even bothered to ask about, but this was the first time that she had been asked to take a person. Not just any person but frightened little twins. Ellie and Harry were so young, how could their parents have just let them go? Where had the kids come from? A million questions buzzed around. This felt wrong, so very wrong and she was starting to feel very uncomfortable with this. She half turned in her seat and called through to them,

"Are you okay in there?" There was no answer so opening the door between the cab and the bunk section, she glanced in and saw two very frightened pairs of eyes looking back at her.

# CHAPTER FOURTEEN

Kevin Brood lay back on his prison bed. It had just crept past lunch time but today he was not hungry. His head buzzed about last night's meeting. He was angry with Gary's lack of respect during his big night out. The boys back in Orpington had a full homemade DVD, every very gory detail recorded. But Kevin was uneasy, he still thought that this idiot had an attitude and an idiot with an attitude could be a dangerous bastard. His door pushed open and Gary stood leaning against the frame, confidence oozing now they were back on his home turf.

"You are a liability Brood. You think that you can fuck me over. You took twenty-five grand from me and I want it back."

"Shut up, you stupid mug. Shut your fucking mouth and do your job." A demonstration of exactly the attitude he was worried about.

Gary left and the door closed, but only for five seconds. It flung open again, hitting the wall behind and three staff unknown to Brood came in.

"Get on your feet Brood, you are on your way out of here. Don't bother packing."

Kevin remained sitting on his bed. "I ain't going anywhere till I see the Governor, did your little mate tell you that he is a bent screw?"

"Not a chance of you seeing anyone old son. Bent Brood? You fucking prove it." The larger man at the front lunged forward and took Brood's head smashing his nose into the bed frame. A trickle of blood ran down his chin and dripped onto the floor. The other two staff took his arms and there was nothing Brood could do other than comply. Five minutes later he was sitting in the back of a white minibus handcuffed to a young officer.

"Where are we going?" he hissed even though he knew that he wouldn't get an answer.

"Wait and see, but one thing's for sure, you can say good bye to your phone and any other perks you had in there." The officer laughed as they drove through the gates.

Brood sat in silence for the entire trip, thinking and planning. He had been stitched up good and proper by that corrupt little screw. He could report it and have him locked away but that wasn't the Brood style. He would just sit and listen for now, prison staff had big mouths and he could find out a lot by just listening.

Just as he hoped, the conversation between the driver and escort soon turned to prison matters. Apparently, Brood was running the prison and had to go. It was thought that he was still running his empire from inside and this would no longer be tolerated. He sat and pretended to fall asleep. He didn't catch many more details other than the man who broke his nose was called Ray but that was a good start. Although they may have looked a bit dense, they were a tight unit and for all his guile they had dealt with him quickly and effectively. In fact, he had had no chance to sort out any unfinished business back at the jail so these were not boys to be played with. Three hours later they pulled into the courtyard of a dingy Victorian local prison. The place oozed 1880's charm as Brood looked out of the van window at the brick faced building.

Fucking great he thought. HMP Woodlow in deepest, darkest Norfolk. Back into the land of dirty shared cells and plenty of time locked behind his door. It was like moving out of the Hilton and into a backpacker's doss house. No cushy job, no special deals with the staff just yet, although he would sort that out within the first week. No room service and certainly no special trips outside of the prison. Life would be a bit baron again until he could exercise his influence. He climbed the worn stairs into a harshly lit reception building where the duty Governor was waiting.

“Welcome Mr Brood. I am sure you have worked out where you are?”

“I fucking know where I am, I was here before you were born.”

The young governor blushed but carried on. “I see that you have a damaged nose, the nurse will see to that.”

“The nurse can mind their own fucking business. I slipped when I got into the van, it’s fine.”

“Do you have any complaints about my staff?”

“I take care of my complaints Governor, you just worry about yourself.”

“Have it your way.” He spun on his heels and marched briskly away.

Brood sat back in the holding room. Two things were certain. Gary was a dead man walking and the bastard that broke his nose would be in hospital within the week. That was the guarantee which Brood money could deliver.

Later, on the wing, the cell door opened with a metallic snap as the bolt shot open. All staff members ‘shoot the bolt’ which prevented the door from locking shut behind them. Brood had witnessed the embarrassing moment when an officer had discovered that he was locked in a cell with a prisoner, the joys of only having a key hole on one side of the door. Kevin looked up to see who was about to bother him. He had been lucky to get a single cell and hoped that they were not giving him a cell mate. Seeing an officer he recognized from a past stay, he greeted him.

“Bloody hell! Mr Jenkins, I haven’t seen you for years. How are the family?” He knew full well that the greedy little corrupt officer would sniff out an opportunity.

“Very well thanks Kevin. What are you doing with us? I had heard that you had a nice little number at Blandford House?”

“Well that’s a long story Mr Jenkins. When it’s a bit less hectic tonight why don’t you pop in? I think that we can still do some good business. I take it that Mrs Jenkins still has expensive tastes?”

“She does Kevin. I will pop in later. I hear that you have lost your phone?”

"You hear right Mr Jenkins, such a shame. My old mum loved her late-night calls."

"Worry no more Kevin," he said as he reached down into his pocket and stepped well inside of the cell ensuring that the two of them were alone. "How about a nice little Samsung 5? Would that keep her happy for a while. A snip at five hundred pounds."

"Fuck me your prices have risen you dirty old fox. I will take it and a charger, five hundred quid and not a penny more. Meet my people in the usual Tesco car park at ten thirty tonight. They will sort the cash out."

"Nice doing business again Kevin." He tossed the phone onto the bed.

"Piss off you greedy git." Both men laughed and the door was shut again. The following days would be busy times for Kevin Brood. He was in a new prison and needed to establish himself as top dog again. His reputation and pull sorted this one out almost before he was unlocked the next morning. A line of prisoners waited to greet him, it was like an audience with the pope. All areas of the jail were his, such was the fear supplied free of charge by the Brood name. He would allow other smaller gangs one week's grace before their drugs rackets were put on ice. He was the master of HMP Woodlow and wasted no time proving it, first dealing with the screw who had given him a bloody nose.

Ray Moore, a thirty-two-year-old prison officer, had seven years' experience and had the reputation of being a hard man. Most prisoners didn't like him, mainly because he wouldn't raise a finger to help anyone. Staff were scared of him, he was lazy and bullied all the new officers. On this day he was detailed to work on B Wing. Prisoners on here were all on remand and the landing which he was unlocking today was the detox landing, full of smack heads and old drunks. Kevin Brood sat in his cell on C Wing looking at his watch, looking, smiling and waiting.

"Any more for exercise?" shouted Ray. A muffled response came from a locked cell. A cell bell light came on from number 28. He strode along to open the door cursing the occupant. He had unlocked him less than five minutes ago. Why had he shut the door again?

"Sorry boss, my door was kicked shut, let me out for exercise," pleaded the occupant. Ray unlocked the door expecting to see the same old man who had been sitting in there alone for the past three days.

"Go on then, get out quick. Fuck me about again I will give you a dig," Ray threatened as he held the door open. What he saw next seemed like a blur, as a stocky figure using a pillow case as a mask over his head exploded out from behind the door. A plastic toothbrush with two razor blades melted into the end of the handle and covered with excrement slashed and cut deeply into his face opening a ferocious looking train track cut. Screaming in pain, he tried desperately to avoid the second slash but was too slow. The blade cut through his right eyelid and across his nose. The hooded figure barged past leaving a screaming bloody officer kneeling on a sticky dirty floor, and quickly joined a group of cheering prisoners hiding in the shower area unseen by CCTV. The blade was wiped clean and thrown back onto the landing, a burning hood following it. No evidence and therefore no police action. Twelve triumphant prisoners spilled onto the landing as the alarm bell sounded and staff and medics rushed to the scene. Kevin Brood lay back on his bed, a smile playing across his lips. Fuck with the Broods and we fuck with you was a clear message to all willing to listen.

At the same time in a grubby semidetached two up two down in Ipswich, Gary Hardy sat in his lounge watching mind numbing TV while his wife was out working in the eight till late store. It was his first afternoon off for a while and he intended to waste it, and himself.

He dropped another empty larger can onto the floor, which bounced on top of the other ten until it rolled under the coffee table joining a thick layer of dust and grime. Letting out a volcanic belch, he staggered into the kitchen looking for more crisps. His dark blue Adidas tracksuit bottoms were starting to get a bit tight around his middle and his white T Shirt backed up the fact that he had let himself go as a real beer belly was starting to grow. He lit a cigarette and blew the smoke towards the ceiling as he cursed his error in not buying more junk food during the last shopping trip. They were broke anyway so it was probably for the better he reflected. Taking a cereal box, he poured some into a chipped bowl before sniffing the milk which, making him gag, he tipped away over the sink full of dirty dishes.

He was still angry that Brood had taken the twenty thousand pounds from him, he would have been able to pay off the credit cards and get himself another car. On top of that, due to his insistence that Brood be moved back into a secure prison, his grubby little agreement that he had with Brood had stopped, costing him another five hundred pounds a month at least. Now he just hoped that he hadn't been reported for corruption, though he didn't think that was Brood's style.

The door bell ringing caught his attention and closing the cupboard door, he went back into the lounge to see who was outside. Peering from behind the graying net curtains, he saw a motor cycle courier standing on the doorstep holding a small rectangular box wrapped in white paper about the size of a medium box of chocolates. Pushing the mail on the floor to one side with his foot he opened the door

"Yes mate, what have you got for me?"

"Don't know bud, I just deliver the small stuff, you are Mr Hardy?"

"That's me, I don't remember ordering anything."

"Just sign here sir." A clipboard was handed to him, as Gary thought that it always seemed a bit spooky talking to someone who was wearing a crash helmet where you could only see their eyes. He signed and looked up to hand it back. The last thing he saw was the blackness of the gun pointing directly at his face. He understood the position immediately and thought he recognised the eyes as those of Gerald, Brood's trusty barman.

Head exploding, he fell directly back onto the dirt stained hallway carpet, blood and brain matter splattering over the banister railings, the magnolia painted walls and the cheap

Argos light shade that swung above his bloodied body. He crumpled twitching in the bizarre dance that signaled his death.

"Special delivery sir, courtesy of Mr Brood with a no returns policy," the killer delivered before dropping the box on the dead body and driving off on his motor bike. When Gary's wife returned, she would find it contained nothing at all.

# CHAPTER FIFTEEN

Stephen and Tanya sat at the kitchen table, eyes red and gritty from lack of sleep. This was a living hell, the feeling that no parent should ever have to face and Tanya had not allowed Hector out of her sight since the twins had been taken. Her body hurt through every sinew and the pain that her heart felt was intense, as though she had a lead weight sitting in her chest. She would have died to get the twins back, gladly offering up her own life. Desperation didn't even get close to her feelings of despair.

They stared unspeaking at the phone as it began to vibrate on the solid wood kitchen table. Stephen grabbed it, turning it on to speaker mode so they could both hear it.

"Stephen Byfield speaking."

A youthful sounding woman spoke. She sounded educated.

"Good morning Mr Byfield. Firstly, let me reassure you that the children are safe with us. No harm has come to them. That situation can however change."

"Okay, well obviously I don't want that to happen. We will do whatever it takes, please just return them to us, safe and unharmed."

A second of silence was broken by the recorded voice of a small child.

"Please Daddy, please can we come home?" Tanya let out a gasp followed by a sob at the sound of Ellie's voice. Another second and the voice of the woman came back onto the line.

"Stephen, we would like to meet you. Can we trust that you will come alone?"

"Yes you can, you can totally trust me."

"Let me just explain one point. Your children will not be separated and should anything happen to any of my friends, one or both of the children will suffer the consequences. Do I make myself clear?"

"Absolutely, when and where can we meet?"

"I will be back to you within an hour. Should you phone the police or report this conversation we will know. Just wait for my call." The line went dead as Stephen and Tanya looked at each other in confusion and terror.

"Oh my God!" exclaimed Tanya, "Ellie sounded so scared. I can't bear to think how terrified they must be. We've got to find them Stephen."

Stephen grabbed her in a hug before jumping up and pacing the length of the kitchen and back. "It's this bloody inactivity that's killing me, making us wait for every instruction. Why can't they just tell me what they want and be done with it?" It was almost thirty minutes later when the phone rang again. There was no introduction, just instruction.

"Grafton Hotel, Tottenham Court Road. Be there at 22.00 this evening. Remember any surprises for us will result in serious consequences for you and your children."

"Okay, Okay, I will be there alone." The phone cut off before he could say any more. He turned to Tanya. "Looks like I'm going up to London. Will you be okay here? I'll get Dad to come in and sit with you otherwise he'll insist on coming with me."

"I will never be okay until they are safely home." She broke down again, "Bring them home with you, please."

"I can try, I will die trying Tanya," he promised.

Stephen checked the train times, which involved changing trains at Reading where he would take the train into Paddington station. He would need to leave in a couple of hours to ensure that he would get there in time allowing for the usual delays and cancellations. This was one meeting he could not afford to be late for.

The journey from Reading took thirty minutes before pulling into the busy London station. He strode straight through to the underground and found the line for Tottenham Court road. He had fifteen minutes still before the meeting time. Leaving the tube station, he turned right and found the hotel only a few paces away.

The sign outside advertised Steak or Lobster meals for £20, a specialty of their restaurant. This was the last thing on his mind. Checking behind him for any signs of being followed, he rushed through the door. Turning right he spotted the bar area, and taking a seat he grabbed a paper and ordered a soft drink whilst his brain buzzed with second guesses. He knew that it was useless to even attempt to predict what may come next but he couldn't help himself. The waiter arrived two minutes later with a cold coke and a bowl of assorted nuts. It looked as though they were cleaning up ready to close and could have done without any other guests

"Excuse me sir." Stephen looked up at the waiter who had reappeared. "The lady who was sitting at the bar earlier has asked me to hand you this note." The letter along with his bill were positioned on the table. He allowed the man to walk back to the till before opening the note.

*Dear Stephen.*
*There is a bag waiting for you behind the reception desk. Please take the bag and follow the instructions provided.*
*Kind Regards.*

Leaving his drink and payment for the bill, Stephen rushed to the reception desk. After a quick discussion with the young receptionist, a sports holdall was retrieved from a back cupboard.

Stephen took the bag without thinking of what it may contain and headed back to Paddington. He stopped at a KFC on the main road and took a seat at the back where he could not be overlooked as he sat with a three-piece variety meal going cold in front of his eyes.

He unzipped the bag. The first item that caught his eye was a dirty tee shirt belonging to one of the twins, but racking his brain he couldn't remember which one. He pressed it against his face, hoping to get a faint waft of his child. After a few moments, he looked back down into the bag. Under the shirt was a further note which was resting on what looked to be packages of drugs. Sweat dripped from his forehead and his hands became clammy and shaking as he felt the grip of blackmail choking the life from him. Ripping the envelope open, he read the letter inside.

*Dear Stephen,*
*Within this bag is £20,000 of cocaine. We would like this delivered into your prison and given to the kitchen manager. He is expecting you. Failure to do so will result in sanctions.*
*Kind Regards.*

Rushing to the toilet Stephen vomited. Never before had he considered taking anything into a prison, he had spent his working life fighting this very thing. He hated corruption and felt furious that he would be forced to do this act. He also wanted to tear the kitchen manager limb from limb at the earliest opportunity.

Cleaning his face, he made his way back to the station where he boarded the last train home. His head numb, he fantasized about being mugged and his problem taken from him or better still a train crash where the bag was destroyed. Of course, neither happened and he arrived home three hours later.

His ashen expression told Tanya all she needed to know. Stephen was furious that these bastards could take such liberties, and he paced up and down as he told her the story.

"Did you even see the children?"

"I didn't see anyone, just had this package left for me that spells trouble. If I get the chance, I will rip them to bits Tanya, I swear to God I will get my revenge." He banged his forehead with the palm of his hand, "What do they want, what do I have to do?" he shouted and clenched his fists before dropping into a chair in despair.

"Stephen, you will never take those drugs into the prison. I will not allow it. This has gone far enough and we must take a stand regardless of what may happen."

"Tanya, I have no choice, they are holding all the cards." He stood up again, "Is Hector asleep? I have a need to check on him, and give him a cuddle. I can't bear the thought of not being able to hug the twins so the least I can do is feel his little warm body in my arms." Tanya put her arms around him, sharing his anguish but also not wanting her youngest child disturbed.

"Stephen, it's bloody two in the morning, where do you think he is going to be? Just let him sleep and let's try and get some sleep ourselves before facing tomorrow."

They went upstairs and Stephen paused in the doorway of Hector's bedroom, and stood there in the dark, listening to his breathing. He then opened the door to the twin's room which felt cold and empty. "Keep strong children, I'm coming for you," he whispered before quietly shutting the door.

# CHAPTER SIXTEEN

Kevin Brood's phone vibrated quietly under his pillow. He checked the time, 02.00.

"Speak," he said softly.

"Byfield has the package, we followed him home. It is in the house. I think that we have him in our hands."

"Good work. Keep your eyes on him and as soon as our men on the inside tell you that it is in the prison, I want you to phone me. That should happen before breakfast. Keep me posted." He hung up and slid the phone back under the pillow. This would be a long night for everyone involved. The hum of the wing and the constant movement of prison staff working on the night shift kept Brood company as he worked on all possible scenarios. Every minute seemed like an hour, excitement and anticipation pulsed through his body. He couldn't see any way out for Byfield he mused as the milky light of dawn crept through the high cell window. Only a couple of hours and this would be over, Byfield would be his.

The observation flap opened and closed as the day staff accounted for the prisoners, the prison buzzing back to life as the early court appearances were unlocked. He felt another tinge of excitement as he visualised what would be going on at HMP Marwood. Envisaging Stephen Byfield carrying a large shipment of cocaine into the prison was totally surreal. After all, it was stopping this very thing that had got Byfield into this position in the first place. The very irony of the situation filled Brood with great satisfaction.

His cell was opened up, it was time to get out and about. He would make a couple of phone calls on the public prison phone knowing full well that every word was listened to and then have an hour in the gym. Any news would have to wait for him to get back.

Stephen had not slept all night. Sitting at the kitchen table they discussed the options and Tanya was trying to persuade him that they should involve the police. He grew angry as he spoke.

"Tanya, what choice do I have? For the sake of the children, I have to do this. We have no fucking choice, just trust me please."

A knock at the door jolted the pair of them back into the present. Tanya looked at the clock, 08.25, and Stephen was already late setting off. She opened the door to find an attractive lady standing on the doorstep. Looking in her early fifties and dressed as though she were about to attend a powerful business meeting, her blond hair was pulled tight to the rear of her head, an Essex face lift thought Tanya uncharitably as she continued to stare at the woman. It was obvious to her that she was involved and thoughts whizzed through her mind between spitting in her face or dragging her to the nearest police station.

"Who exactly are you?" she demanded.

"My name is Sandra Brooks. May I come in?" Before Tanya could answer, she pushed past into the hall way and walked directly through into the kitchen. Sitting down opposite Stephen she took her phone from the pocket of her black jacket and selected a video for him to watch. Looking towards Hector covered in breakfast she laughed. "He looks like you Stephen." She pressed the play button as if it would show Hector's favourite cartoon show.

Stephen froze, mesmerized at the sight of their two darling children sitting on a mattress in what looked like a cellar type room. They said nothing but appeared to be looking at the person who was filming them. Their cloths were dirty and it was clear from the lines running down their dusty little faces that they had recently been crying. It tore Stephen and Tanya's hearts out, and he wanted to kill the woman but held his emotions in check. She took the phone back, turned the video off and placed it back into her pocket.

"What sort of monster are you? They are my children you evil woman." Stephen spat at her in disgust.

"I am a monster who is as dead as you, should I not do my job, but trust me, I don't care if I live or die. I am in as much trouble as you could ever imagine. However today, yes today, is all about your little problem. Grab your bag Stephen, I am driving you into work today. Oh and of course don't forget the little present we gave you."

"Fuck you. I am not getting into that car with you. Nor am I taking that bag of filth into my prison."

"Fair enough, I can't be bothered to argue. Life is too short. Which one of your children would you like to die? You pick or we will pick." She stood and made her way to the kitchen door before turning back to face him.

"Five seconds sweetheart." She took her phone out and hit a number.

"Hi, Sandra here." She looked back at Stephen. 'Five, four, three, two, one. Game over. Kill the girl." She reached the front door, phone still in hand before she heard Stephen's frantic voice behind her.

"Wait! Wait!" Stephen was stood there with the bag.

"Hold the killing," she ordered, "just spare her until I phone back." She hung up and again the phone slid into her pocket.

"I take it that you are coming after all, I'll see you outside."

Kissing Tanya and Hector a quick good bye, he climbed into the car throwing the bag onto the back seat. The familiar drive seemed to take an age, and the couple did not exchange words until the car pulled into the prison car park.

"Okay Stephen, take the package in. When I receive the call telling me that it is safe hands, I will phone my boss. You will then get your daughter back."

"What about my son?"

"Later sweetheart, you may have more work to do in order to earn that little present." Stephen climbed from the car, holding the bag nervously as sweat formed on his forehead.

"Stay calm pussycat. Do this right and we all live to fight another day. Mess it up and it's curtains for everyone concerned." She selected reverse and backed the car out before gracefully sweeping out of the car park and onto the main road.

The bag felt as though it was twenty feet wide and had drug stash written on the side of it in florescent paint. He just hoped that the search teams would pick him out, find the package and allow him to explain everything but not a hope. The search team on the gate waved him through, and the drug dog, so often interested in sniffing around Stephen's bag, was in the yard playing ball. Apparently, it was his ten-minute break.

Nothing, absolutely nothing Stephen fumed to himself, angry about how easy this had all been. He took his keys and walked through to his office. His PA had not arrived yet so Stephen sat at his desk for a second, thinking about what he was about to do. Terry stuck his head around the door, startling him.

"Are you okay boss? You look shattered."

"I'm okay Terry, I just need to speak with the kitchen manager, I'll be back in five minutes."

He took the bag and walking back out into the courtyard, he decided to take the longer, outdoor route to the new kitchen building. Opening the first barred gate he walked through a small passageway until he reached the kitchen managers office. He pushed the door open and saw the man sitting in front of the computer screen ordering food for the coming week. Nigel Larkley. Stephen had employed him two years ago. He came from Long Lartin with a great reference, he had interviewed well and had impressed him with his operational knowledge. In fact, Stephen had considered him for further promotions. Not any more, the dirty bastard.

"Morning Governor." It was so matter of fact that Stephen thought that it must be a mistake. He didn't answer but just entered the office and shut the door.

"Are you okay Stephen?" again he spoke in a very matter of fact way.

"Yes, I am, shall we get this over with?"

"Get what over with?" He looked at Stephen. "Boss, if I have done something wrong can you just tell me and mess my day up now? You're scaring me."

The sense of relief that flooded through Stephen's body was vast. He honestly knew nothing about what was sitting in the bag by Stephen's feet.

"No, you're fine Nigel, I just wanted to have a quick look around. Shall we get on with it?"

"Sure boss," the manager replied getting to his feet giving Stephen a bemused look. The bag was left in the kitchen office while Stephen pretended to examine the cleanliness of the kitchen. After he had made enough of a pretense, he returned to the office, picked up the bag and left heading back to his own office with his head spinning. He sat in his chair for no more than a minute when the phone rang. It was a call from outside the prison.

"Morning, Stephen Byfield speaking." It was Sandra and she was laughing wildly.

"Well done Stephen, you did it, or should I say would have done it. My boys have been watching you, I even arranged for the dog to be on playtime. See how easy it is? Now bring the bag back to me, we have a proper job for you."

Stephen walked through the prison gate and back into the car park where he noticed that his car parking space was taken. He felt sick as he saw the woman sitting in the car painting her fingernails. He threw the car door open.

"What the hell do you want from me?" his voice was raised, on the verge of shouting. Carefully finishing the last nail she looked up.

"Don't make a scene Stephen, people may be watching. Just get into the car and come with me." Taking a seat, he placed the bag between his feet.

"I just don't know what you expect of me." He bent forward placing his head into his hands, before rubbing his eyes wearily and regaining his composure. "I have done what you wanted, yet all you seem to want to do is play games with me."

The car continued through the busy roads until pulling into a much smaller side road. It seemed that the only traffic that used this road were farm workers where large muddy tyre marks were the tell-tale signs of tractor use. They continued for a further ten minutes before reaching a public woodland beauty spot where they pulled up in a wood chip car park. Sandra opened the car door and climbed out, she sprung the boot and pulled on a pair of wellington boots. To any observers it seemed like a couple of friends preparing to take a walk through the woods.

"Stephen, I have a pair of boots for you. I have taken care to get the right size." She noticed the incredulous look on his face as she spoke.

"There really is very little that we don't know about you. You have been our project for so long."

"Oh have I? How touching." He pulled the bag of drugs from his holdall. "Then this shouldn't come as any shock." He ripped the package open and emptied the powder into a shallow ditch, shaking the bag out to waste every single grain before slam dunking the empty bag into a nearby bin.

Turning victoriously, he declared "That's another twenty thousand I owe the Broods, put it on my tab."

"You are such an idiot Stephen. Johnson and Johnson will be miffed that you have wasted a whole bag of baby powder. Do you honestly think that we would be so stupid as to trust you with such a job? We have so many of your staff who would gladly have taken it in for us." Again, she chuckled. "It was never about the drugs, we just wanted to know how far you would go and you showed us you will do anything. I like that, it makes the next job far easier for all of us."

"What do you mean? You promised me my daughter back. All I had to do was that one job and I did it."

"If only life within the Broods were so simple. Let's walk and talk, I have a proposition."

Stephen snapped. He twisted and grabbed hold of Sandra, dragging her towards the rubbish bin. She tried to kick out but the pace and the power of Stephen overwhelmed her efforts as he thrust her well-groomed head into the top of the stinking bin.

"This is where you belong you evil whore," he hissed at her before remembering that she held all the cards and releasing his grip. She flopped backwards but managed to keep her balance before regaining her composure.

"That sort of aggression towards me will get your children killed Mr Byfield. Calm down, keep your hands to yourself and follow me."

They walked in an uneasy silence along the path into the woods. The earlier rain had set small puddles on the trail as the sun shone through the tree canopy casting shadows and sun beams. Sculptures from local artists dotted the scene and in any other circumstances it would be a pleasurable stroll taken by people every day. Today was not one of those days.

Reaching a wooden bench, she sat down. Stephen joined her, feeling the bizarreness of the situation he found himself in, sitting with a gangster's moll discussing the fate of his family.

"Sandra, where do we all fit in? I realise why I am on the hit list and I can live with that but just bloody take it out on me and leave my family alone, it has nothing to do with them."

"Stephen, you have become a million-pound investment that we are determined to get our return on. We have a special role for you but I do have to warn you that after you have helped us you will die. The speed and style of the death will depend upon you. If you help, I do promise that it will be quick and relatively pain free."

Stephen gave a short laugh. "I have died a thousand times in the last year and I couldn't give a shit about myself. But what about my family?" he demanded, looking straight into Sandra's eyes trying to gauge a reaction.

"Then the debt will be paid. They will be free to live with no further concerns of us. You have the Brood's word on that."

Stephen gave another laugh of disbelief. "The Brood's word is nothing, just vile crap. I wouldn't trust the Broods one inch. Why are you involved with this scum anyway? Where do you fit in, who are you?"

"Just another pawn, I suppose. I have a high-ranking job within the business, I choose who lives or dies, an operational field manager I believe it is called." It was her turn to give a somewhat wistful laugh.

"My husband was one of the most feared members of the family until he was shot by government agents who thought that we were a threat to national security. What a joke. He died on a South London street in a hail of bullets and I was promoted as a debt of gratitude in order to pay the bills. The ironic thing is that I have proved my worth." She sat silently for a few moments, as her thoughts drifted back to happier times. "But enough of that," she continued. "I'm taking you home Stephen and we will be in touch." She got up to walk back to the car, a coldness returning to her voice.

The drive back was in silence but Stephen's thoughts were far from silent. This had to end, he had to tell somebody before the story reached its bloody conclusion. As a child Stephen disliked anything ending, he always liked to be in the middle of the story, always looking forward to events, always trying to shape what would happen. He felt very much in the middle of this mess and he didn't want this ending in the way Sandra had suggested. He had too much to offer, too much to live for and he wasn't ready to die and he certainly wasn't ready for his children to die. If the ending was as grim as Sandra had promised then he might as well go down in flames. It was time to share the burden and get help in finding his children. Terry was about to get an invite over to the Byfield's.

Pulling the car into the driveway, Sandra waited for Stephen to climb out. He didn't look back, even when Sandra commanded "Wait for the call and don't try any heroics, remember, lives are at risk." The car sped off leaving him ringing the doorbell. He saw Tanya's silhouette walking towards the door before she opened it and fell into his arms. He hugged her tightly as he told her,

"Tanya, enough is enough. Let's get our children back."

# CHAPTER SEVENTEEN

Sitting in the truck in the darkness of a Holyhead evening, Karen thought hard as she played with her phone. Something felt very wrong and this wasn't how she expected to feel. Finding the number for Avis car hire she quickly made arrangements and payment. Unsure about what would happen next, she flipped open the sleeping compartment door.

"Come with me you two, we need to find your mummy." Taking hold of the little hands reaching out for her she helped Ellie and Harry down and out of the cab into the chill of the evening air.

"We need to be quick, and very quiet," she told the frightened pair as she led them away from the truck. They swiftly reached the Avis office and entered into the harshly lit prefab building.

"Thanks for waiting for me, we are in a dreadful rush," she explained, handing over her driving licence before being shown the basics of the four-door silver Ford Focus.

With the documents completed and the children strapped in, they soon found themselves heading out of the town and into the countryside. One thought was in Karen's mind, to head south and find her friend in Cheltenham to pass the rest of the night. Ten minutes into the drive her mobile lit up, jerking Karen out of her thoughts. The name shone out ominously, David Brood.

"Hey David, everything ok?" she asked, trying hard to make her voice sound normal even though her heart beat loud enough to be heard down the phone.

"I do hope so Karen, where are you sweetheart?"

"Just had to take the kids to the toilet, we are getting a burger and then back to the truck. Sorry, have we given someone a shock?"

"You could say that, phone me when you are back." He hung up without another word. They drove for another fifteen minutes before the phone flashed again. This time she ignored the call. A text flashed up,

*If you have done what I think you have, keep running.*

Her stomach churned. Glancing in the rearview mirror at the children, she noticed that Ellie had fallen fast asleep, looking very little and vulnerable. Harry was sitting with his arms crossed, staring out of the window into the darkness.

"Got to get you home little fella. Then we will see what becomes of me," she muttered.

The texts and calls stopped, and she assumed that everyone now knew what she had done. Karen pulled over into a brightly lit petrol station to fill up with fuel. Taking her phone, she scrolled through the contacts before finding her friend, Judy. She didn't have to wait long before it was picked up.

"Hi Judy, it's Karen. Sorry to impose but I wondered if you could do me a big favour? Long story but I'll explain all when we get there."

A full tank and a bag of goodies later, they pulled back onto the road heading south as she checked the satnav. Two hours and ten minutes until they reached Judy's farm, get there and they would be safe for what remained of the night. David knew nothing of the farm, the Broods would not have a clue where to start to find her, but start they had.

The young man behind the Avis counter looked terrified as the two large men asked him a lot of questions regarding a lady and two young children. He had neither the will nor the inclination to withhold any information. They had hired a silver Ford Focus and a full registration was provided along with the final destination, West Midlands Airport. Apparently satisfied with these details they made their way out and phoned back to David.

"Got some information boss. We have the car details and destination. It looks like they may be bolting the country."

"Have they fuck, her card has just been used in a petrol station at Lymm services. They are heading south." Gunning the engine in the car they screeched off in pursuit.

Karen had a two-hour head start, but a sixth sense told her that she had slipped up by using her debit card. A cold shiver flushed through her body as she cursed her carelessness. The clock was ticking. She pressed the accelerator with a bit more urgency and pushed on through the night. Two hours later the comfort of the country lanes wrapped around her like a snug blanket. She couldn't be found here, nobody could locate them, so no more mess ups, no cards and the phone turned off.

Pulling quickly into the driveway of Holly Farm, Karen hid the car out of sight from the road. Judy opened the house door allowing two Jack Russell dogs to run over to the car.

"Karen, what on earth is going on? Come in quickly. John is away this week luckily so we have the house to ourselves." She gave Karen a big hug before noticing the two little faces staring at her from the back seat. "Who have we got here?"

"Thank you so much for helping us out, this is Ellie and this one is Harry. I will tell you everything once we have them settled down. I am so sorry to impose upon you like this." Karen helped the twins out of the car.

"Don't be daft, isn't that what friends are for? Let's get them a good hot bath and some supper, they look like they need it." Having shown them upstairs into the bathroom, Judy disappeared into the kitchen and got to work on some supper while the twins sat in silence washing themselves in the mass of soapy bath bubbles. Karen blew bubbles from the palm of Ellie's hand and wondered how anyone would want to cause a little child such harm. She was saddened that the man she thought she loved would be involved in something like this. She knew he was no angel but this was a different league altogether and one she wanted no part in. Drying the twins off and watching them eating a lovely plate of fish fingers, beans and chips that were gone in seconds, it only took minutes before they were ready for bed. Sleep came as quickly.

Judy poured two large glasses of wine while Karen tucked them up in bed, leaving the hall light on to provide some comfort to the shattered pair. Karen slid into a soft chair in the lounge. Lifting up the glass to her lips she muttered, "God, what have I done?" before taking a large gulp and filling Judy in on all that had happened.

The phone buzzed three times before a large hand grabbed it from the cup holder in the car.

"Where are you?" David Brood demanded.

"We're at a service station just outside of Bristol boss. Any news?"

"Yes, I think that I have a lead. She has a friend near Cheltenham, I have got her Facebook account open. Not sure of the address yet but I am going to check the electoral roll in a minute. Book into a hotel and get some sleep. Tomorrow will be a busy day." He hung up.

# CHAPTER EIGHTEEN

Karen awoke at 5.30am, she knew that David Brood would find them eventually, even given her previous optimism about her safety. There were enough clues in her past to lead him to the farm house door. She had endangered her friend's life but dare not tell her that part of the story. She also knew time was not her friend and if she did not move quickly, they would all be dead.

Waking the twins, she whispered. "Come on you two, let's get you home," as she lifted them one at a time from their bed. Urgency was overpowering all other senses as she could smell the hunters closing in.

"I haven't cleaned my teeth yet," Harry protested, as he pulled on his track suit bottoms.

"We will do that later darling, let's get going." Ellie sleepily pulled on her clothes and trainers and followed Karen to the car. It was starting to get light as she scribbled a note to Judy. She couldn't risk giving her anymore information as she knew it would get out one way or the other. Starting up the Focus, the trio disappeared into the dawn light.

Heading down the M4, Karen turned the radio on, it was 6.30am and Zoe Ball had just started her breakfast show. The children had dosed off again which gave her time to focus on her next move. She knew she had to stay one step ahead or they were all in trouble.

At the same time a car crunched into the driveway of Holly Farm. Two large men climbed out and kicked the house door off its hinges. Hearing the commotion, Judy leapt from her bed and out into the hall way. Still in her pajamas, she raced down the stairs where she stopped dead, eyes bulging as she saw her two dogs laying stabbed to death on the kitchen floor. The two brutes were searching the rooms but seeing her, they stopped their search and grabbing her they dragged her into the lounge and threw her down on the sofa.

"Where are they?"

"Who?" Even though she was terrified, she didn't want them to know Karen and the twins were in the house. Her arm was pulled across to the side of sofa and the edge of the biting blade of a large hunting knife was pressed against her index finger.

"One more time lady, where are they?"

"They must have left this morning," she whimpered. "I don't know where they have gone." Pushing the blade to her throat they dragged her out of the back door of the house before handing her her mobile.

"Phone her. I want to know where she is." Before she could call, the phone rang, and seeing it was Karen, her heart sank as she answered it.

"Hi Judy, sorry we left without saying goodbye, I will explain later," Karen greeted her before she could say a word.

"Where are you Karen? I need to know."

"Is everything ok? Oh my God, they are there aren't they?" The phone was snatched back and a gruff voice snarled.

"We want the kids back, if you don't come back here right now, your friend will die. What do you say?"

"Okay, okay, we are on our way back. Don't touch my friend, she knows nothing about this." The phone went dead as the man on the end hung up. Karen had no intention of returning, if she did they would all die. She couldn't risk it. The two men also knew that Karen had no intention of returning.

"Where have they gone? Last time I'm asking you."

"I have told you, I don't know." Almost before Judy could finish her sentence, one of the men grabbed her arm and forced her onto her knees. As he held her arm out, a hammer crunched down onto the back of her hand. The pain was excruciating, burning through her hand, up her arm and into her brain. The pain made her vomit instantly and as she knelt there, her stomach heaving, the guy with the hammer said, "I told you that I would not ask again, you've had your chance." She was pulled outside and frog marched to the rear of the house where the hatch to the fosse septic tank sat twenty yards from the back door. She was struck again with the hammer, this time to the back of the head, causing her to black out and collapse onto the ground. She came too in the dark, both hands tied together, and realised that she was dangling above the stinking water in the cesspit. She looked up out of the hole at the sneering face of the man holding her.

"I told you that you should tell me bitch," he snarled as he yanked her up out of the hole.

"Thank you, thank you, I just don't know where they are," Judy sobbed with relief at being removed from the stinking hole.

"So you keep saying, but you are no use to me alive." He pulled out his knife and slit her throat wide open before dropping her back into the pit.

He turned back towards their car. "Let's go, we're wasting our time here."

As she sped along the motorway, her phone rang again and it flashed up the name David Brood, before she answered.

"Karen, your friend is dead. You had better keep running, keep hiding because I will find you and I will destroy you." The phone went silent and she was left with her own terrifying thoughts and grief for what she had inflicted on her friend.

# CHAPTER NINETEEN

Stephen, Tanya and Chris sat in the lounge whilst little Hector was fast asleep upstairs in his cot. Their whole world had collapsed around them, waves of tears engulfed Tanya but Stephen was in a different frame of mind. Search and destroy. The feeling of loss hurt intensely, but the burning desire to finish this was galvanising every sinew. Anxiety was eating Tanya alive as she stood and started pacing.

"How can we sit here and do nothing? These people are killing us, they have taken our children and Stephen you are doing nothing, just playing stupid games with criminals. It's all your fault you fucking bastard." She launched herself towards him and punched him hard in the chest, sobbing inconsolably. Stephen staggered back with the onslaught.

"Calm down Tanya," he yelled as she slapped his head twice more before he grabbed her arms.

"Get a fucking grip of yourself, I know how tough it is, they are my children as well. Falling to bits is going to help no one." They fell into each other's grasp, Chris placing his arms around them both, giving much needed comfort.

"Let's stay focused," he implored, "hurting each other doesn't get the twins back. We need to stay strong and as hard as it sounds, we must be focused. We have had enough tragedy in this family."

Stephen slumped onto the sofa, head tilted back staring at the ceiling, hoping to come up with a solution. Tanya still pacing, left the lounge and walked into the garden. Soft rain washed her face although she barely noticed. Chris joined her and tried to take her hand but she shrugged him off.

"All of this hurt has been caused by his bloody work. Why did he have to become a bloody hero and mess up our lives?"

"Tanya, it's not his fault, this all started with me, I created the monster Martin Heard, Stephen was trying to protect us all. If you need to apportion blame then it sits with me. But we are the good guys, you are losing track that we have done nothing wrong. They are the people to blame." She knew that Chris was right but it didn't matter. Her children were gone and nothing was been done to solve it, not even notifying the police. What a pathetic scenario. She kicked at a plastic flower pot sitting by the patio as she came to a decision.

"Okay Chris, we need to get control over this situation. Let's get inside and make a plan."

The three of them sat around the kitchen table, three hot drinks steaming away but untouched. Stephen was in full flow.

"What do we know for sure?" He ticked off a list on his fingers.

"Number one, the Broods have kidnapped our children but there is no ransom demand.

Number two, they were still alive and healthy in the last twenty-four hours as we saw them on camera.

Number three, the Broods want to corrupt me for an unknown reason, and therefore, if the children are hurt, their plan comes to nothing.

Finally, the fact that they are insisting on no police involvement means that they will want to conduct all negotiations with us, which means they will maintain contact. but time is critical. What have I missed?" He looked at Tanya and Chris, awaiting their input. Tanya looked at Stephen before leaning over and kissing him on the forehead.

"You are so right, we need to keep focused, keep in contact, but most importantly find out what they want from you in return for Ellie and Harry. However, this can't just be our secret, you need to speak to Terry, we need help. Phone him."

Terry's phone vibrated on the passenger seat of his car, he glanced down to see it was from Stephen. Pulling into a bus stop he took the call,

"I've been expecting a call from you Stephen, I guess you are going to tell me the whole story now?"

"Yeah, I think it's time Terry but not sure that you are going to like this one. Can you come over?"

"I'm half way there."

# CHAPTER TWENTY

Terry pulled into the driveway. It was just after midday and the car registered that it was just four degrees, proving that spring had not yet arrived. The door opened seconds before he could knock, and Tanya enveloped him in a hug. Terry kissed her cheek before releasing her and moving quickly through into the lounge where both Stephen and his father stood and shook Terry's hand. They sat and Terry listened to the story. Stephen spoke uninterrupted for a few minutes, absolutely focused and with the steely jaw of a man who wanted revenge.

Terry took notes, focusing on every detail, names, meeting places, discussions and demands. He stopped writing and gazed into the garden, deep in thought. A gray sky threatened drizzle and the muddy lawn displayed hours of pacing.

"I don't get it Stephen, I understand that you have disrupted their operation and cost them some cash, but what are they after? It doesn't add up." Tanya came in with coffee and handed him a mug.

"Thanks Tanya. I mean why try to discredit you? What's the benefit?" He took a sip and looked up again.

"What are the agreements for contact?" Stephen shrugged.

"They just phone or turn up, sometimes at the house or at work, they could be watching us right now."

"And the calls are nontraceable of course?"

"Yes, no numbers are left."

"Are the children old enough to know how to contact you?"

"They would struggle to find the house but they do have a number for the phone. It's sewn into Ellie's hair band. Name, address and contact details. Tanya always had it while at school, and continued the habit thank God."

"Does Ellie know it's there?" Terry continued firing questions as thoughts ran through his head.

"She might remember, I'm unsure mate to be honest," Stephen replied hopelessly.

"Okay," Terry looked at them all, "I need to make some calls, but there are no promises here. My friends may be able to help but they are busy around the world, the guys I would like to contact are either in Somalia or Yemen and they are under contract and up to their necks in trouble. I can only try."

Tanya's eyes pleaded with Terry, desperation on her face. He stood and gave her another hug.

"I will try, but in the meantime keep up the contact with them, no heroics and nothing stupid." Stephen and Chris nodded.

Terry climbed into his car, and pulled out into the lane driving deep in thought, so deep that he didn't notice the old silver Punto following him. The lane widened slightly as it passed a farm building, fields swept in all directions providing stunning views, not that they were appreciated at that time. It was almost dark, the clock in the car reading 16.30 and three degrees. Road works ahead jolted him back to his senses, they hadn't been there when he had driven passed earlier on and his tenses began tingling as his thought processes decided something wasn't right. A burly guy in an orange jacket flashed a stop sign and Terry considered driving through but saw the road was blocked. He checked the rearview mirror and noticed that he had another car behind him. Fuck it. He looked again in the mirror when he heard a car door bang, half expecting the guy behind to start an argument with the workers. The crash of his side window exploding under the force of the hammer shocked Terry and he instantly lurched away half covering the passenger seat. Both doors were ripped open and before he could react further, a flurry of blows tore into his head, face and body. There was nothing he could do as unseen hands dragged his bleeding body into the road. A well-placed boot crunched into his mouth and blood and shattered teeth were spat out to mix with the dirt and gravel beneath him. Terry curled up trying to protect himself but was dragged onto his feet and across the front of the car bonnet. From here, he saw his attackers, thick set men, early thirties and looking ready for action. They seemed professional and did not speak during the attack, not even during the thrill of the first blows. This was odd and proved this was no adrenaline filled threat, just cold-hearted violence.

Terry stared into their eyes, his thick bloody lips not allowing a word to come out as bubbles of blood and snot ran down his chin. The pain hadn't fully kicked in, but it held great promise. Two more heavy blows smashed into his ribs as he prayed for the attack to be over.

"You know who we are, just remember we can get you and your family whenever and wherever we want. Stay out of Byfield's fight."

With those words, Mr Orange jacket pulled out a battery-operated drill from a pocket, and switching it on, the rotating drill bit spun inches from Terry's face.

"This is a warning, some think of it as a calling card" he continued as the drill swung down towards his knee protruding from his now torn jeans.

"Your jogging days are over old man." The drill bit in and bore through bone, cartilage and nerves. The pain was so intense that Terry blacked out, woken again quickly by a hard blow to the head.

"We suggest you keep the fuck away." Another heavy blow smashed into Terry's nose shattering it. Collapsing onto the road he barely heard the cars pull away or smell the burning rubber from his own car as it burnt with a healthy glow in the dark. Rolling over and into a ditch brought a starburst of agony through his smashed body, and he lay passing in and out of consciousness in the freezing darkness.

"Can you hear me?"

Forcing open an eye, Terry could see the face of a man in a distinguishable firefighter's uniform. The cold puddles of ditch water had soaked into his clothing freezing him to the bone which at least went some way towards numbing the intense pain from his injuries.

“Don’t move mate, looks like you have had a serious accident. Paramedics are on the way,” Terry heard before darkness descended and he passed out again.

The white lights hurt Terry’s eyes as he forced them open. Nurses hurried around and one checked the monitors and made notes. She upped the dose on a drip attached to the back of his hand before glancing at his face and giving him a smile when she saw he was conscious.

“Don’t try to speak Mr Davies, we have had to do a bit of a repair job around your mouth and you will be very sore for a few days.”

It was the last thing he wanted to do, being in such pain. His head and ribs were thumping but the pain from his knee was like nothing on earth, blinding searing pain. He tried to look down but he couldn’t focus well enough to see what was going on down there.

“Your wife and friend Stephen have been here with you all morning but we’ve made them take a break. They’ll be back after lunch so relax and let the pain killers take effect and you might feel up to seeing them when they return."

He lay back and slept, the warm fully encompassing sleep that only large doses of heavy painkillers give you once they kick in. Waking again much later, he saw Jo sitting close to his bed and Stephen sat reading beside the window. Reaching out he stroked Jo’s arm. She jumped up and stood over him, kissing him gently on the forehead, afraid of causing him any more pain.

“Sweetheart, you’re back with us. Don’t try to talk, we have everything under control. The police want to speak with you at some point, they are outside the room keeping guard while they try to figure out what happened. Why would anyone want to do this?”

Terry shot a glance at Stephen, it was the sort of look that Stephen had seen before. Terry was saying nothing. He mumbled through broken lips, "Road rage, idiot cut me up and attacked me."

"Bastard, hope he gets caught." Jo kissed the back of his hand, "Just rest and focus on getting better darling."

# CHAPTER TWENTY-ONE

Terry pushed his wheelchair into the hospital bathroom. It had been a tough day and the complications related to the DIY on Terry's knee were causing a concern, the rest of the injuries were well managed and would recover but the knee, however, had extensive and irreversible damage. It was touch and go as to whether the leg would be saved and everyone was doing their best.

The police had bought into the road rage incident story and were investigating furiously, it had even made the day's local news.

There was a knock on the bathroom door. "Mr Davies, you have two visitors." Terry dried his hands and wheeled himself back to his room. Two suntanned men were sat on the plastic hospital chairs in silence.

"You ok guys?" Terry greeted them, "Looks as though that Yemen sunshine has done you some good so I hope you are ready for another war."

Kevin Brood's mobile vibrated silently in his prison cell, it was eight thirty in the evening and the buzz of the prison hid the fact that he was having a conversation on his illegal phone.

"Yes brother, unlike you to phone me, what's going on?"

There was a moment's hesitation before David replied "We have lost the shopping."

Kevin went silent for a moment, his brain buzzing about what two lost children really meant.

"What do you fucking mean, you have lost the shopping, it's not a set of fucking house keys. How do you lose the fucking shopping?"

"The girl grew a conscience, I don't know. All I know is that we don't know where she or where the shopping has gone to. We are looking."

"Your girl had better come back home if she values her life. Who else knows, how about the Byfields, are they aware?"

"No, not a clue but they're plotting against us Kevin, remember Terry Davies? He was there last night, we saw him, followed him and you know the rest. They clearly don't know."

"Phone Byfield now, use any excuse and tell him that we need to meet him tomorrow. Any bollocks, get on it and phone me back when you have done it. Tell him that if he doesn't co-operate, we will fuck his daughter." The phone went dead. Five minutes passed before the phone rang again.

"He has agreed to meet us at the Castle Pub in Bexhill, East Sussex tomorrow."

"Yeah, I know the place, we had a drink the year before I came in and we met the guys from Brighton there. So, he's in the dark about these events?"

"He knows nothing."

"Find them all. We don't know how long we have so keep on watching the targets, we will know where they are soon enough." He hung up and hid the phone, angry beyond words. He needed some blood, no violence no sleep. He thought, ten minutes before lock up so he'd better be quick.

Leaving his cell, he leaned over the landing railings looking for someone, anyone to seek revenge upon. Looking down at the pool tables he saw a group of young black London gangsters larking around and keeping the table to themselves. He walked down the two flights of stairs until he reached the ground floor, in prison terms known as the One's.

Walking over to the table he couldn't help but notice that the wing was paying attention to his actions, staff and prisoners alike. Kevin Brood never bothered to play games.

"Do you know me son?" he addressed one of the gang. The five lads looked at each other. They were all in their early twenties and were a bit of a deal at the moment. They controlled some minor drug sales and were extorting money from more vulnerable prisoners. Kevin knew all the scams and had allowed them to trade.

"Course we know you, we're not causing you any grief, walk away man," one of them answered before turning back to the table to continue with the game. Staff spoke on the radio as the growing tension could be tasted in the air. Some prisoners locked themselves into their cells and one officer left the wing for a toilet break. A number of prisoners leaned over the railings, knowing they were in for a show.

"You want me to walk away you muggy little cunt, you fucking want me to walk away?" He grabbed the black ball from the table and smashed it into the mouth of the first target he could reach. The man dropped onto the floor blood skating across the polished lino.

The others took a step back, a bad move, they should have taken their chance. With alarm bells ringing across the prison, Kevin grabbed the pool cue and smashed it over the table before crashing the next target firmly around the head. The man tried to run but Kevin was on his back and reaching around the side of his neck, he bit his ear off and spat it onto the floor.

As staff poured onto the wing with batons raised, putting his hands in the air Kevin Brood just stood, chest heaving as the staff crowded around him. Healthcare staff ran past and started picking up the pieces, in more ways than one. The Duty Governor walked onto the wing, demanding an explanation.

"The boy started it, I was minding my own business and he attacked me. Ask him and he will tell you."

"Get him down to the block until we know what is going on."

Kevin walked defiantly to the segregation, he knew that he wouldn't be there long. Sat on the hard segregation bed, Brood knew what to expect, health care to assess his suitability to be down there and then the Duty Governor to puff his chest out a bit. Brood had played this game before. The door opened, "Nurse to see you Brood."

A young black male nurse walked cautiously into the cell

watched by the staff.

"Do you have any injuries Mr Brood?"

"No."

"How are you feeling?"

"Not sure that I can cope with segregation, it makes me feel suicidal. When I was younger, I tried to hang myself in the seg. It's all too much for me, I need to be in the Health Care."

"Are you going to kill yourself?"

"I'm not sure that I can cope, I'm just telling you the truth."

"Okay, just wait on your bed for a second." The door was closed.

Within five seconds a member of staff was at the observation window watching him. This was all too fucking easy. The door opened again and in walked the Duty Governor. He introduced himself as though Brood should be impressed.

"Health Care won't sign you up for segregation as apparently you are a suicide risk. What a load of utter shit Brood."

"Your shout Governor, if you keep me down here and I do something, you lose your job. As I said, your shout."

"Don't play games Brood, you know the Health Care is full, it's always full. Do a night down here and I will have you back on the wing tomorrow."

"As I said, your shout. I am telling you that I will be dead by the morning if I stay here." The Governor shook his head.

"Can I speak with you without the officers listening please Governor? I want to talk in confidence." He looked around at his staff and nodded. "Okay, but no stupid games." The staff moved outside of the cell and Brood could hear them muttering about another stupid decision.

"Governor, It's Mr Barnes isn't it?"

"It is Brood."

"Good to meet you. Your two boys support Gillingham FC and drink in the Regent Pub... did you know they like a bit of the white powder? If I am down here for one more hour, I will ensure that their season tickets are never used again. You have an excuse to move me back so use it."

The blood left Colin Barnes' face. He turned and left, closing the door behind him. Five minutes later staff were taking Brood back to his cell. No charges were pressed and a full confession to starting the trouble was given by two of the victims. All CCTV evidence was unavailable as all cameras on the wing had been covered with paper. Police action was not requested and the establishment's hands were tied.

Brood sat back in his own cell. His blood lust satisfied and reputation intact, it was time for a good night's sleep.

# CHAPTER TWENTY-TWO

Karen pulled onto the M1. It was dark and a gentle stop start drizzle was frustrating the wipers, unsure whether to rush or idle across the windscreen. This was not a dilemma that Karen needed to answer, she knew that she had to go full pelt to stay ahead of the game. She glanced at the satnav, York was a million miles away and in this traffic and weather, about another five hours. The children were asleep in the back and the warm air was making her soporific too.

As she consumed the miles, she pondered how her life had come to this. She had been a bright school girl, with supportive parents who were very proud of her achievements. They were good honest people; her father had worked as a baggage handler at Stanstead airport since its opening and before this he had worked in a paper mill until made redundant at forty-five. He counted his blessings for Stanstead giving him a second chance.

Her mother had worked in the NHS as an administrative assistant and she had been proud to be part of this organisation until diagnosed with breast cancer in her late fifties. After being told that she was in remission, she realised that life was too short to worry about work so she took early retirement and enjoyed her spare time to the max. Learning new skills and hobbies, she wished that she had taken this step while in good health.

Karen had found school exhilarating, she loved the subjects and shone as a star pupil. She represented the school in athletics and netball and became Head Girl during her last year. She had longed for an exciting life which would offer her a career as well as the odd adrenaline rush and one day while walking through Colchester town centre with a group of friends, she noticed the

Army recruitment office. It was as though a giant arrow was pointing to where her life should head, and before she knew it, at the age of eighteen, she had joined up.
She had hoped to become an Officer, but during the training phase at Sandhurst she sustained a serious knee injury while falling from the twelve-foot wall during the assault course.

The Army stayed patient until the second operation on her left knee proved fruitless. On one warm August day, she was called into the office of the Commanding Officer and was discharged on medical grounds. Within the space of two hours she had gone from the best of the best to an unemployed woman sat on platform eleven at Reading train station, tears soaking her t-shirt and nobody giving her a second glance.

The train ride back to Essex was a long lonely journey, until one man paid any attention to her, a smartly dressed, good looking man who was returning to Colchester from London after a business meeting. He had sat and listened without judgment as she poured her heart out to him and her fears of no job and no future. He then mentioned that he had a contact who worked in a veterinary practice close to where she lived. If Karen was interested in giving it a go, he could make an appointment for her to speak to the head of the practice.

Karen had a love for animals, certainly needed a job and a contact like this could not be ignored. Her big fear was being stuck in an office doing the same monotonous tasks day in, day out and this offered an excellent alternative to that.

"I would really appreciate you doing that, thank you. That's amazing, this was the worst day of my life, then I met you, or rather you met me." she laughed, "and I don't even know your name?" He apologised and handed her his business card. She held it up reading it slowly.

"Mr David Brood, Financial Services." She looked back up at him. "Thank you so much David, you are a life saver."

Break lights ahead brought her back into the present. That chance meeting followed by expensive dinners and holidays had led to a solid relationship. She didn't agree with the business side of his life but could overlook it as she wasn't directly involved and she was very restricted with how much of it he discussed with her. In the last twenty-four hours, she had gone from loving him to running from him, a lover who wanted her dead.

Again, she snapped her mind back to the here and now. One of the children stirred but then lapsed back into sleep. She would have to explain everything to them in the morning, but just how would she kick that one off? *Sorry I am responsible for taking you away from Mummy and Daddy, driving you further away for two days and then refusing to let you speak to them. And oh yes, you remember the monsters who live under the bed? They are out from under the bed and want to kill me and steal you back again, then they will kill your daddy. Any questions?*

Karen pulled into the services and placed her debit card into the pump. She knew that this could be traced but she had given up caring about the police finding her, jail was an easy option.

The night air was chilly and the persistent drizzle reflected the situation. The bump of the pump stopping told Karen that the tank was full. She withdrew the nozzle, replaced the cap and looking around her as she stretched, the bright garage lights stung her tired eyes as she slid back into the smelly interior of the car. How two small kids could fart as much as these two was a mystery. Note to self, she thought with a tired smile, keep the window slightly open.

Pushing on northwards and half expecting to be stopped on route, the car began to eat up the miles. Town names she'd never heard of blurred into one and soon she was passing signs to places she had only seen on the football results. Doncaster, Leeds followed by the turn off for York. It was still some way away but leaving the motorway seemed a victory. Karen knew that her army training friend Janet Cole was waiting up for her. Karen had called her saying she was in a bit of a fix and asked for a bed for a few nights for her and two others she had with her. She said she would explain everything when she arrived and Janet had agreed to look after them all for a couple of weeks as she was currently on annual leave. She had shared a room with Karen at Sandhurst and they had become very close. She had shed a tear when she learnt that her best friend had been sacked, and did not hesitate to help out when Karen had called her out of the blue just a few hours previously.

Satnav ordered Karen to take a right followed by a sharp left. She was informed that she had reached her destination in the middle of a housing estate somewhere on the outskirts of the city. Peering through the rain she looked for number 38, which she found another few houses' down on the right before driving onto the short driveway. The blue front door opened and a pyjama clad woman yawned and beckoned them in.

"Give me a second sweetheart, I'll put my shoes on and help out," she called as she disappeared back inside. Janet came out and gave Karen a quick hug before grabbing a bag from the boot and glancing into the back of the car. "Wake those two up and I'll show you where you are all sleeping."

Karen and the very sleepy twins followed her through the door into a warm welcoming home and it wasn't long before the children were upstairs asleep again and Karen and Janet were on the sofa with a glass of wine. Turning towards her friend, Janet took a large gulp of wine before firing out the questions.

"So, what the hell is going on? Whose kids are they, why have you got them and who is after you?"

Karen started explaining and the pair never made it to bed until the early hours. Janet listened and asked questions to clarify points as the story unfolded and the seriousness of the situation became apparent.

"Janet, just one more thing and I am not sure how this will go down." Karen took another mouthful of wine before glancing back up at her friend.

"Go on."

"I think that the last person to help me was murdered horribly. I'm sorry."

Janet sprung up from the sofa spilling some of her wine as she did so. "Fucks sake Karen, now you tell me! I can give you a couple of days, but people will notice that you are here, everyone knows everyone's business around here. Sorry love but this is not good, people will be asking questions in no time. I thought that you were just having domestic problems, I'm out of my depth here. I have only just started as a Captain at Catterick and I can't be involved in illegal stuff, stuff like kidnapping kids and hiding from psychotic gangsters."

"Two days is great Janet, I understand. I feel like the grim reaper and I'm really sorry to have put you in any danger." Karen stood up and hugged her friend. Janet hugged her back.

"Don't worry, it will take a brave thug to get the better of me. Good luck to you though as I think you're going to need it." The two of them checked the house was secure before going to bed for what was left of the night.

The following morning Janet returned from buying a few bits for breakfast to see the driveway was empty and on the kitchen table a brief note.

*Sorry Janet, I have realized I am toxic. We will carry on running, stay safe. K x*

# CHAPTER TWENTY-THREE

With Terry out of action for the considerable future, Stephen had no choice other than to return to the prison without his trusty dep. The alarm rang at six and Stephen let out a sigh, he really wasn't ready to get back on the horse but he had no options at the moment. He would need to get in and try to seem normal, whatever normal was, it had been so long since anything seemed remotely normal. He showered and checked on Hector, he had taken a back seat for the last few days and both Tanya and Stephen felt more guilt over this. Poor little boy hadn't had the love he deserved while their whole focus had been, understandably, on finding the twins.

Terry's wife Jo and their son, Tom, had taken the burden of the responsibility for babysitting when needed and poor old Tom had become the big brother. For a child so young he had dealt with the last year so well.

For Tom to discover that he had been adopted and that his real father was a serial killer, and then to witness his death was hard on anyone. How could anyone expect him to bounce back, but he did and that was a testimony to Terry and Jo and the strength and love with which they surrounded him.

Stephen drove in wondering who would step into Terry's shoes. This job without a deputy governor would be very tricky, at the best of times, let alone when his mind was distracted with trying to find his missing children.

The Duty Governor from the weekend was photocopying reports just outside of Stephen's office.

"Hi boss, did you have a good break?"

"Not bad Brian, how was the weekend?" Stephen replied finding it hard to believe no one knew the inner torment he was facing, but at the same time knowing he had to keep it to himself.

"Busy. I was trying to phone Terry yesterday but he wasn't picking up. We had a strange new reception, I accepted him in but he's an odd one."

"Terry has had an accident and he's likely to be away for some time. What do you mean a strange one?"

"Poor Terry, didn't realize. That sounds bad, give him my best." Brian followed Stephen in to his office and pushed the door to.

"The new reception is a super grass. The police brought him over on Sunday morning. He's been in custody for a year but has just confessed to further offences. This time he is implicating big time criminals. We have been asked to keep him out of the general population until further notice and this has been agreed by the Deputy Director of Custody. I have put him out of the way in Health Care."

"Okay Brian, no need to report this at the morning briefing, let's keep it low key." Stephen knew there would be more to this story which he would no doubt discover before too long, but in the meantime, he set out on a tour of the prison to gauge the mood of the place in his absence.

It seemed okay, normal staff moans about staff shortfalls and health and safety, in fact it was almost comforting that the moans were so normal. At the end of his walk around he popped into Health Care to meet the mysterious new customer. A middle-aged man with long straggly hair sat at a chair by his table. The room smelt fresh and reminded Stephen that the Health Care was now a no-smoking unit. The man half turned and muttered a greeting towards him.

"Mind if I have a chat with you?" Stephen asked as he perched on the edge of the man's bed. The man looked at him and nodded. "Go ahead. I bet I know what you want to discuss."

"It's my prison, I am the Governor so it's a good idea if I know what is going on." Stephen replied with a smile.

"No problem, what do you want to know?"

"Who are you?" Stephen laughed as he asked. "I know your name, but I don't know anything about you."

"Okay, I will just keep it simple. My name is David Willard and this is the first time that I have ever been in trouble. I was a chemistry lecturer at Durham Uni. I was given an opportunity I couldn't refuse, make synthetic drugs for a crime gang or be shot. I made the drugs and got caught. I took the rap for everyone and got seven years. They left me to be hung out to dry, rotting in these places while they carried on living their lives in freedom. That really pissed me off so I gave information to the police in exchange for some form of early release, problem being, the gang found what I'd done and where I was, hence my move to you. I am due for release in six months."

"And then what?"

"I guess that they will find me and kill me."

"And who are they?"

"The Robinson's. Have you heard of them?"

Stephen pondered for a moment "The name sounds familiar. Let me speak to the powers that be and see what else I can find out."

Stephen walked away from the cell thinking that this was the last thing he wanted to deal with. These gangland bastards were everywhere and it reminded him that he had a meeting in Bexhill-On-Sea to attend tonight with another group of bastards.

Back in his office, he checked his on-line diary and booked himself out for the afternoon. Anyone checking would think that he was meeting the Health Care provider in Bristol, if only it were that simple.

The morning passed in a blur and before Stephen had blinked it was twelve o'clock. He felt exhausted and packed his things together for the drive home. Just as he reached his door, the red phone on his desk rang, reserved only for the select few who knew his direct line. For a second, Stephen debated whether to take the call or just leave. He took it.

"Hello Stephen." There was a pause, "Mark Blake speaking." Stephen sat down, it wasn't every day the CEO of the prison service phoned you directly.

"Morning Mr Blake, how can I help you?"

"Thought that I would give you a ring to find out how Mr Willard is? Sorry to drop him on you but it is vital that he is kept safe. Your prison was the only one in the area with an isolation cell in the Health Care that was free. I don't need to remind you of the importance of keeping this man safe. I'm sure?"

"No, we are up to this. Don't worry it will be fine. It's only six months, what can go wrong?" Stephen laughed. Mark Blake didn't.

"What indeed can go wrong? If it does however, you are finished in this job. Do I make myself clear?" Before Stephen could answer, the phone went dead. Mark Blake had a reputation for been a ruthless bastard. Odds on that his job would be gone as well. This must be a big deal and Mr Willard a bigger fish than he is letting on Stephen thought to himself. He felt uneasy, this wasn't as normal a case as he had first thought. He looked down the corridor to see if his Police Liaison was in. Unusually, he was and Stephen beckoned to him.

"Liam, can we have a quick chat?"

Liam Travers was a copper in his thirties who had been attached to the prison for nearly two years and liked Stephen and his strong leadership. He came into Stephen's office and Stephen sat at the coffee table just inside the door indicating Liam to do the same.

"What's the story with Mr Willard?"

"You know I can't tell you Stephen. It's confidential, even to you and more than my job's worth."

"Liam, this is important. Is there more I need to know to keep this man safe? I've just had Mark Blake on the phone making me all sorts of threats."

Liam stared at him intently for a few seconds before standing and leaving the office. He returned after a minute and placed a document on the table before walking out again and closing the door. It contained a bombshell.

The man Stephen had spoken to was not a lecturer at Durham Uni, nor was he a drug's manufacturer. He was in fact a member of MI5. He had uncovered a major arms smuggling organisation within the M.O.D. He wasn't serving any prison time and had not attended a court room in his life. He was being hidden to save his life before sending a number of prominent MP's to prison for a very long time. A number of organisations wanted him silenced, both criminal and Government. Prison was the only place the security services considered would be safe.

This indeed was a sensitive case and Stephen could expect a number of high-profile discussions over the coming days and weeks, just what he didn't need with his priorities lying in a different direction. He took the document back to Liam, no words were exchanged and the document disappeared back into a locked briefcase.

# CHAPTER TWENTY-FOUR

Stephen drove into Bexhill noticing it looked like a typical Victorian seaside town with charity shops and estate agents on every street. He signaled and turned into a car park next to the De La Warr pavilion and paid for two hours on his ticket. He then strode down the main shopping street before seeing a pub on the corner, The Devonshire. Not the one he was looking for, but he walked in and spoke to the bar man. The Castle was a five-minute walk away, and the guy had taken great delight in telling him of the sleezy reputation it had had before being taken over as yet another themed pub. Crossing the bridge and walking past a supermarket looking way beyond its best, Stephen saw the pub. Right in the middle of a town square and near the council office, it looked okay and fairly safe with plenty of people outside shopping and enjoying the afternoon spring sun. He entered the main bar to find the place empty. The young lady standing behind the bar took Stephen's order. There was no sign of anyone waiting for him.

"Are you Stephen Byfield sir?" she asked him as she put his drink down in front of him

"I am," he managed to utter as his heart skipped a beat.

"You have a private room booked sir, follow me please."

He followed her upstairs to where Stephen guessed the owners had once lived. At the top of the stairs the girl knocked on the first door they came to and then left. Stephen stood alone and waited a few moments before the door opened. A well-dressed man shook his hand.

"Welcome Stephen, my name is David Brood, please come in."

Stephen entered the room, which appeared to be an old function room, the sort that could take around fifty people with a bar in the corner and a wooden floor that had seen many a spilt pint. Another man sat alone at the back of the room.

He looked around wanting to believe he would see Harry and Ellie sitting in the corner, or appearing from behind the bar. It was immediately obvious that they were not there. He turned back to the man who had sat himself down at one of the tables in the room.

"Why am I here?"

"To keep your children alive I assume. Why do you think you are here?"

"Because you want something from me obviously. Where are my children?"

"Safe."

"Tell me what you want, how I can get them back."

"You owe us a million, and you're going to pay us back."

"You're crazy, I don't have a million." Stephen laughed and looked at him. 'I've asked you once, what do you want?"

David Brood nodded to the man sitting at the back of the room. He got up and coming forward placed a large bag onto the table where Brood unzipped it theatrically.

"Your favourite drug Mr Byfield, heroin, half a million pounds worth of the stuff and I want it in your prison."

"Fuck you. I am not doing it," Stephen spat at him.

"No problem, you have shown that you were prepared to do it in the past, do it again and you can have your kids back. Refuse and they are mine. Your son will watch his sister raped by multiple people who have shown an interest on the internet. Once she dies, as she will, your son will face the same fate. It doesn't float my boat but there are a lot of sick people out there." He glanced down at his open laptop, "Thirty-five sick people to be exact at a thousand pounds a go. I will make something back at least."

Stephen's fist hit the table and it shook as it vibrated on the wooden floor "Last time it was baby powder and I was played for a fool."

"This time it's heroin Mr Byfield. I know that you have had a liking for the stuff, I understand Martin Heard introduced you to the pleasure?"

"He made me take it, I didn't choose it then and I certainly won't choose it now."

"And now I'm making you take it." Brood nodded to the man at his side who took a wrap of the drug and a small pipe from the bag. "You will smoke this before you take it in, then you know it's for real this time."

"You can just go and fuck yourself, I am not doing it."

"Oh you can, and you will," Brood insisted. The large man held the pipe out, and before he registered what was happening, his knees buckled as Stephen jumped up and crashed a merciless punch onto the point of his chin. Leaping onto the man's collapsed body, he smashed five more blows into his face. Turning to Brood he said. "I am not taking that shit, understand?"

"Okay tiger, settle down." Brood looked on in disgust as the larger man staggered to his feet. "You useless idiot, get your stuff and piss off, leave me and Mr Byfield alone. And pick up that pipe before you fuck off for good."

Stephen sat back down, still panting from his exertions as the bag was pushed towards him.

"Now take this home and wait for our call. Remember what is at stake here."

Stephen leant forward towards Brood; "When I get the opportunity, I will tear you to bits."

"Charming Stephen, I will leave you with that. Wait for the call." With that he left the room. Stephen stayed in his chair looking at the bag, his life a complicated puzzle the pieces of which he was beginning to put in place. Leaving the pub, he noticed that night was falling and the temperature was dropping. He needed to get home and walking briskly along the road leading to the sea front, he tried to make sense of what was happening, the weight of the sports bag a constant reminder of the task set for him. A car honked at him as he tried to cross the road towards the car park and he saw to his disgust that it was Brood smiling and waving.

Finding his own car, he climbed into the driver's seat and phoned Tanya. He stared down at his hand and saw the cuts on his knuckles. They were starting to sting but it had been worthwhile. The ringing stopped and Tanya answered, her first words an immediate question. "Any news of the children?"

"They're still alive," Stephen was quick to reassure her, "But more than that I don't know. I'm just on my way home darling, I'm fine but I will tell you everything when I get back."

The drive seemed to take forever, and stopping at a service station for petrol and a quick coffee to keep himself awake, he pushed on, whilst in his head weighing up every option possible for getting his children back. The big question he kept asking himself was if it was time to involve the police, and what the consequences might be if he did so. Just as he convinced himself that this was the best option, the fear that it would put Harry and Ellie's lives at even more risk made him drop the idea again. Finally, with an exhausted sigh of relief, he pulled into his driveway and switched off the engine.

As the car door clunked shut Tanya opened the house door and walking inside Stephen dropped the hold-all and enveloped Tanya in a hug. Tanya looked up at him, holding his face in her hands.

"You look shattered darling, come and have some supper and tell me what happened."

Sitting at the kitchen table, a large plate of lasagna in front of him, Stephen retraced his footsteps through the afternoon, debating whether to mention taking the bag of drugs. There was no way he could keep something of that importance from her, he would have to tell her.

"They tried making me take heroin." He placed another mouthful of lasagna on his fork not wanting to look at her.

"Bastards! What happened?"

"They threatened the children unless I did what they told me. I had to fight one of the guys."

"You don't need forgiveness for that, you did what you had to do. I wish that you had killed them both. Let's talk more in the morning, you need sleep." Tanya got up, cleared his plate into the dishwasher and turning off the kitchen light, led him upstairs to bed.

Sleep was the last thing on his mind. Half a million pounds in heroin sat on his kitchen floor and a forthcoming appointment to deliver it was imminent. Stephen was still awake when his phone rang at 1.30am.

"Hi Stephen, David here. Glad that you got home safely. A couple of points for you. Firstly, the bag will be taken in on Friday, that means that you have to keep it safe for a few days. Secondly, we have an excellent video of you taking the bag from the pub, the editing is fantastic, you look as though you were having a ball. Shall I send a copy over?"

Stephen sighed wearily before replying "No, it's not needed, I am going to do this to get my kids back, then I want you out of my life."

"Good decision Stephen, I will phone you later with the details, sleep tight."

Stephen listened for a few moments to the dialing tone before replacing his phone on the bedside table "Bastards! Tanya, when this is done, we are moving on, new job, new house, new start."

Tanya, now fully awake following the call snuggled into the crook of Stephen's arm. "Let's get our children back sweetheart, then we will start again. Whatever that might mean."

# CHAPTER TWENTY-FIVE

The following morning, Stephen had no choice but to go into work as normal. As David Brood had informed him that the drug bag was not expected in the prison until Friday, he left it hidden on the bottom shelf in the pantry behind the spare jars Tanya kept for jam making, and tried to concentrate on the day ahead. He strolled towards the health care, having made an appointment to have a walk around with Diana Moss the head of the unit. In fact, he wanted the chance to talk to David Willard again. He liked Diana, she had performed well in her role of health care manager, standards had improved and an impressive system was in place that ensured all prisoners had good access to opticians, dentists and doctors. Even more impressive were the clinics she ran. The entire prison would be non-smoking in six months as her smoking cessation clinics had proved very successful with a fifty percent take up for patches and nicotine gum. She was still in her early thirty's and Stephen considered that she would have a bright future. He tried again to persuade her to join the prison service on an accelerated promotion scheme but she laughed.

"I have enough on my plate with this lot. Maybe next year."

He stood and left the office walking down stairs towards cell seventeen. He chatted with staff on the way informing them that he would be speaking to Mr Willard for a few minutes. As normal nobody cared where the Governor went but if he hadn't informed them, they would have made an issue of it. He opened the door and was surprised to see David sitting on his chair clean shaven and with a short haircut. He looked ten years younger.

"Looking very dapper Mr Willard, it seems that you have

found your feet very quickly."

"You have a good team of staff here Governor. They sorted me out in no time, I feel human again. Now what can I do for you?"

Stephen ploughed straight in. "Things don't add up Mr Willard, I have spoken to some of my colleagues from other prisons. They have never heard of you. Your entries on our system do not make any sense to me and Probation know nothing of you. It seems that you have some explaining to do."

"Didn't take long for that to fall to pieces did it?" David laughed. "Who else knows about my fake cover story?"

"Only me at the moment and I want it to stay that way." Willard glanced at the open door. "Can we go somewhere private please Governor? I have some talking to do." Diana walked past and looked in. "Everything okay in here?"

"All fine thanks, can I use your office for a quick meeting please?" Stephen asked. "Mr Willard and I have a few things to discuss."

"Sure. Lock up when you are done, I'm out until Friday."

Five minutes later the two of them were upstairs away from listening ears. Willard wasted no time in filling Stephen in on the real story behind his imprisonment. "Ok Governor, I am David Willard. That much is true, the rest is not. I have worked with the security services for the past seven years. I have worked extensively in African counties in the fight against IS and such. My life has largely been in the shadows collating information and debriefing real life James Bonds if you get the picture?" Stephen nodded, this was interesting stuff.

"A while ago, I discovered that British Servicemen had been involved in the sale of arms within North African countries. The news would have caused our government some difficulties as these weapons had been used in a mass shooting some months later where a number of Russian holiday makers were murdered. During these investigations a number of names were found on an unprotected laptop. Two front bench MP's complete with bank account details were implicated and this information was corroborated with information found in Libya earlier this year.

More worrying for you, Mr Byfield, is that on my return to the UK, I discovered information relating to three senior prison service managers. At this moment, we are unsure of their names but we will find out in time. They are deeply embedded sleepers within your organisation. This is all part of a plot by terror networks, either white supremacy groups or another organisation aiming to bring down the Government. These three people have been responsible for millions of pounds worth of drugs imported into prisons, and more worryingly they have set up training bases for radicalised white and Muslim men within high security prisons. These three men are responsible for up to ten attacks on UK and American soil.

They must and will be stopped, however I am the only person with the evidence. All names, dates, accounts numbers will be confirmed in days but in the meantime, all evidence is kept in my head. Everything else has been destroyed by rogue elements within our Government and Security services. They want me dead, but if I die, the evidence dies with me."

He stopped and stared at Stephen. "Bet you wished that you had never asked, you just need to keep me alive long enough for me to tell my tale."

"When is that?"

"I have a full debrief with my handlers in one week's time. They just have to debrief others involved firstly in order to put the pieces of the puzzle together. Then I will be out of your hair."

Stephen thought through what he had just heard "Not a word to anyone David, this must be kept absolutely silent."

"Not a word Governor, this is my life we're talking about. You shouldn't come down here to see me again, it will raise suspicion amongst your staff." David Willard was returned to his cell, while Stephen walked back to his office, a million things on his mind.

Back at his desk, he contemplated whether what he had just heard was true, at this stage he couldn't be sure. One thing he did know was that the police information would have been correct and why should Willard lie about the rest? So many questions went unanswered. Willard thought that his life was in danger, but by whom? It would seem that half of the prison senior management wanted him dead. For God's sake, it couldn't be true, surely. There was a knock on his office door, it was the Orderly Officer.

"Sorry to disturb you boss, the other Governors must be at lunch. I have a police production order for a prisoner that hasn't been signed. They are all sitting outside in the police van waiting to go but I don't have the authority to discharge him without a signature."

"No problems, let me look at the paperwork, is it an overnighter?"

"No, just for visiting some crime scenes and writing charges off, I think. The guy didn't want to go. We had to drag him into the van."

"Not good. Who is it?" Stephen glanced down the page. *David Willard.* He jumped to his feet heading for the door.

"Are they still outside?"

"Yes boss, just waiting for your sign off."

"Get him off the van now."

Stephen flew out of the office and across the yard into the sterile area where the van waited. He banged on the driver's window.

"Get that man out of your van now," he ordered. The driver pretended not to hear so he pulled the driver's door open.

"Get that man out of your van now. He is not leaving this prison."

The driver shrugged his shoulders and climbed out of the cab. "Whatever you say Governor. Hope that you know what you are doing, we had official orders to take him."

The back door was opened and a bleeding David Willard was helped out. Stephen spoke to the Orderly Officer. "Do not allow these men to leave and please call the police to verify they sent this van. This is a serious matter." He and Willard walked back towards the healthcare unit.

“Thanks Governor, I think that you believe me now. These people can get to me anywhere. Like I said just keep me alive.” He was shaking as he spoke, the adrenalin having kicked in as he contemplated his close escape. “I knew that when they turned up, they weren’t police, they just didn’t behave like coppers. As soon as I got in the van, they smashed me in the face, I would have been dead within five minutes of leaving here if you hadn’t stopped them. I expected this and still expect more. Please make sure that I have no social or legal visits, they are clearly desperate.”

As they arrived back at his cell, he shook Stephen’s hand, the bleeding nose was superficial but the abductor’s intentions had been deadly. Stephen grasped his hand firmly. “I’ll make sure nobody gets in here to see you without your permission. Can your handler see you before next week?”

“I have no way of contacting him, I know who he is of course, but they always contact us. It cuts down on what I need to know.”

He took something from his pocket and handed a prison envelope to Stephen.

“Put this in your safe, just in case I don’t make the week. If I do survive, I will take it back from you.”

When Stephen returned to his office, he looked at the sealed envelope wondering what was inside. He opened his safe and placed the letter on the top shelf. Hopefully he would be handing it back in seven day’s time. He’d just sat back in his chair when Liam the Police Liaison Officer came into his office.

“Stephen, the local Police know nothing of the production order. It was an organised hit, this is getting out of control. We have the van crew in custody but they’re keeping silent.”

“Yeah, so it seems, we’d better strap ourselves in for the next week Liam, this could get bumpy.” If only he knew the half of it, Stephen thought to himself. He pondered his present position, the facts relating to the past few days were a nightmare. His kids were under threat and were in the hands of a ruthless criminal gang who hated him, he had half a million pounds of drugs in his kitchen pantry which he was expected to smuggle into his own prison and he had half of the Government trying to murder one of his prisoners. On top of that the chances of him getting out of this alive were slim. It almost made the last year being chased by serial killer Martin Heard seem like a walk in the park.

The only person he could trust at the moment was lying in hospital as a result of trying to help him, but yet again, there was no way forward without him. He dialed Terry,

"Hi Terry, you up to a visit? We need a chat."

# CHAPTER TWENTY-SIX

Janet pulled her trainers on and stretched her muscles before going out for a run. She had one week left of her holiday and then it was back to the training unit. She needed to be fit, all instructors and staff were expected to be twice as fit as any recruit. She was three times as fit. Her mile and a half time for the basic fitness test that everyone had to pass was a nippy seven minutes and she had never been beaten by staff or recruits. Running always came easy to her.

Setting off through the estate, she quickly slipped into her pace, her headphones drowning out her other senses as she cruised through the first three miles before hitting the rising slopes leading to the moors. She loved this route as it was wild and un-spoilt and stormy, rainy days were a pleasure as no one else dared risk it. She had grown up in these parts and knew the area well, every climb, river and bridge were timing points and she was fifteen seconds ahead of schedule reaching the old viaduct. She was moving well and was gliding over the ground effortlessly.

The jogger coming in the other direction was the polar opposite, he had obviously pulled a muscle or had hurt himself in some other way and he was limping badly before stopping to sit on a grassy bank. She removed her ear phones. "You okay Bud?" He smiled, grimacing with pain, "No, I am in a shit state. I just turned my ankle over and I think it may be sprained. Do you have a phone I could borrow?"

She reached into her pocket and handed him the phone, "No problem, tell them you are at Archer's Viaduct, they will know where you are." He dialed the number and spoke, Janet only half hearing the conversation as she was trying to keep warm while waiting. This had messed up a good run and she would go out again later to make up for it. Peering over the city was always a good view, but time was passing so she turned to ask the man how he was. The punch to her face knocked her over and the serrated knife blade stung her throat as it rested firmly across it as she struggled to breath.

"Where is Karen? I know that she was with you, I have been into your house and found this." He produced the letter written from Karen. 'Where is she?"

"I don't know, she just left. I didn't know anything until she told me the trouble she was in and then I asked her to go."

"Fucking ask her to come back then," the jogger demanded, thrusting her phone at her. He had found the name Karen in her contacts and pressed call.

Karen answered on the second ring. "Hi sweetheart, sorry we split. I just didn't want you to become involved in my stuff."

The man dug the knife deeper into her neck, breaking the skin and making talking difficult as she tried to answer her friend. "Come back, it's okay, you'll be safe here. It would be great to discuss the old navy days."

"Navy? Are you okay Janet? They've got you, haven't they? Oh fuck, fuck, fuck, I am so sorry." The jogger grabbed the phone back. "Very clever you couple of bitches. I am on your arse girl, so keep running as I will find you." He cut the call and threw the phone on the ground. He looked down at Janet as she lay on the path with his knee and knife over her throat. He applied some weight and she struggled but couldn't keep the man's knee from her windpipe. He added more pressure watching her kick away the last breaths of her life. He never took his eyes from hers, he was enjoying the power that this gave him but he released the pressure just as the blackness of death formed around her. Janet gasped for breath.

"Normally, you would have been dead by now, but I don't think that today is your last day. Don't ask me why, maybe I like women in uniform. Either way it's your lucky day." The sound of a motorbike approaching caught the man's attention.

"That will be my taxi. Stay lucky, and give Karen our regards, I will be seeing her shortly."

Janet sat sobbing, her head ached from the blow to her face and the small cuts across her throat stung. She got to her feet looking for any signs that the man was still around. The distant noise of a departing motorbike gave her some comfort. She turned and jogged back home as quickly as her rasping throat would allow her. She entered the house and instantly saw that the back door had been forced open. Grabbing her tool box, she set to work to fix it telling herself that staying busy was the best way. She mended the door and cleaned the house, scrubbing the floors until they gleamed. She was still cleaning at midnight when she finally broke down. Sitting on the kitchen floor, leaning against the wall, she sobbed for what seemed a lifetime before the tears stopped. She stared around her before thinking bollocks to all this. She packed her bags and headed out to her car. She turned and looked at her home for the last time. It had been a good home for her, but it was time to move on. She gunned the engine and headed back towards the safety of her army base.

The following morning the house would be on the market, she couldn't give a damn about her possessions. The place had been violated by this monster and she wanted nothing further to do with it. The familiar feeling of walking towards her room in the Officers mess was a comfort, surrounded by security, friends, a fence and soldiers protecting the base. She showered and tried to scrub the memories away. Towelling her hair dry, she opened a can of coke from her little fridge. Lying back onto her small single bed she took her phone and dialed Karen. She answered straight away.

"Janice, thank god! How are you?"

"I am fine, he roughed me up a bit but he didn't want me. He is after you. He was on a motorbike and there were at least two of them."

"Yeah, that sounds about right. I have just pulled up for the night. I won't tell you where we are. When this is sorted can we meet up again. I am so sorry I put you through this."

"Just sort your stuff out, go to the police, do whatever you need to do or they will kill you Karen. They found me, heaven knows how, but they did within a few short hours. They are hot on your heels. Do not use your bank cards, it is a map that they can use to follow and find you."

"Oh shit, of course. I have just used it again thirty minutes ago. Bollocks, they will be in this area already."

"Stay inside and keep the doors locked. Keep running again when you have rested a bit and put some distance between you all."

"Will do. I will ring you again when it's safe."

With Janet's words of warning ringing in her ear, Karen looked through the net curtains of the Bed and Breakfast room she had booked for her and the twins for the night. She had thought that Scotland would be safe but tiredness had made her clumsy, she shouldn't have used her card in the petrol station. But although they would have an area to work on, it was a large area. For all they knew she could have been in Glasgow or Edinburgh. She would sit safe for now and bolt in the morning.

Looking at her watch she noticed that it was almost eleven thirty. They had enjoyed a fish and chip supper before the children had fallen asleep. They were trusting Karen at the moment as they seemed to know that they were heading home. She lay on top of the bed, scared to take her clothes off in case they needed to move quickly, listening for every noise outside of the house, every engine revving, each male voice in the street below the window.

Five miles away a silver MPV with tinted windows was parked up in a lay-by. The two men inside ate a Chinese takeaway out of the foil containers. They knew that they were close. The next mistake by her would be her last. Throwing the remains of the meal into a green roadside bin they sat looking at a local map. A circle was drawn around the village in which Karen was hiding. The jogger who had attacked Janet put his finger on the village.

"It's the only place that they can be, they filled up with fuel and drove in this direction. The main towns and cities would have been too far to get settled for the night. She must be around here." They cruised the streets looking at hotel car parks for any sign of her car that would give her away. Nothing. Street after street, driveway after driveway, car park by car park. Karen wasn't so tired that she had forgotten all security rules. The car was tucked away on a forest track, the half mile walk into the village had been a pain but they needed to be safe.

It was gone midnight when the men decided to return to the lay-by and wait for the morning, It was on the only road out of the village so there was no way she could leave without passing them.

Back in the room, Karen checked her online bank account. It showed a very healthy one hundred and twenty-five thousand pounds, most ironically put into the account by David Brood who wanted his girlfriend to have the means to buy herself what she wanted. Her car had been compromised and she needed one which would be invisible to the Broods. It was almost one o'clock but she couldn't sleep knowing they were so close on her tail. Checking cars for sale online she saw the perfect car, a black BMW, two years old and in good condition. Only twenty-five thousand miles on the clock and could be hers for twelve thousand pounds. The only problem was it was the middle of the night, but with desperate measures needed, she phoned the number.

When a sleepy voice answered, she was quick with her story. "Sorry to ring you at this time but my car has just died and I need to get to my parents down in Newcastle by tomorrow lunch. Any chance of seeing the car? I am so sorry that it's the middle of the night, but I am a bit desperate." The voice sounded a bit more awake at the thought of a quick sale.

"If you are so desperate that you want me out of bed at this time, it will cost another two hundred."

"No problem, that's the least I can do. I'm in Harthill village, where's the best place to meet you?"

"Okay you mad woman. I will be with a friend because this is all a bit weird. I'll meet you at the Tesco car park in Blackburn which is around ten minutes from you."

She quickly googled the directions and sneaked out of the door locking it behind her. She guessed that she could be back in forty minutes returning in a new car. She planned to give the Focus as part of the deal and hoped Avis didn't mind. It was an expensive BMW and they should appreciate the swap.

Soon after she had left, Ellie nudged Harry awake. "I think that Karen has just gone Harry, I just heard the door shut, go and have a look." Harry opened their bedroom door and walked into the small lounge area where Karen had been sleeping, Karen's sofa-bed was empty and the bathroom door was open. He ran back in to the bedroom. "She's gone Ellie, what shall we do?"

"Mummy and Daddy always told us to find a policeman if we were lost, or go to a shop and wait with the shop person. Shall we find a shop?"

"Maybe, I don't think that any policemen will be awake, it's dark and they will be in bed. But I remember some shops are open at night. We have passed lots with their lights on in the dark.

"Are we near any shops Harry? There are some near to our house. Do you think we are near there now?"

"I don't think so or Karen would have taken us to Mummy and Daddy." Ellie considered this for a moment before coming to a decision.

"Harry, I want to find Mummy and Daddy, let's go before she comes back." Harry, always the more cautious of the two wasn't so sure.

"She has been nice to us Ellie, I think she is trying to take us home."

"She is nicer than the other bad people," Ellie agreed, "they were scary. I don't want to see them again."

"Is she a good person or a bad person?" Harry wondered, very confused now.

"I don't know, I just want Mummy and Daddy." Ellie started crying a little. Harry remembered Daddy telling him he must look after his sister so made up his mind. "Let's go and find a shop, they will know what to do."

Getting dressed as quickly as they could, the two children talked about what they would do once they found a shop. They would ask the shop person to phone a policeman because they had been stolen. They walked back into the lounge area and Ellie saw the bathroom. "Harry, we need to wash our face and clean our teeth, or Mummy will be cross if we don't do that."

Hurriedly they washed and cleaned their teeth then fully ready to be seen in public, Ellie tried the door to the room. It was locked. They looked at each other in despair before Ellie remembered seeing Karen put a spare key in the drawer by the sofa bed. She ran over and found it, put the key in the lock and silently opened it. It was pitch black in the corridor and they clung to each other as they sneaked out and down the stairs. Opening the front door onto the street was easy as Karen had left it unlocked behind her so that she could get back in. As they stood there in the dark, there was no one around to ask where the shop was, and anyway, they would have been too scared to ask. Walking to the end of the street they found a small village square with a war memorial and an empty bus stop with a broken light that flashed intermittently. They didn't like this place at all. A taxi drove past them slowly before stopping. The driver wound down his window and asked

"Are you two okay?"

"Yes, we are just waiting for Mummy and Daddy, they will be here in a minute" Harry replied.

"Right you are, I will be back in two minutes and if you are still here, I will take you both home."

"They are looking for a shop," Ellie piped up.

"They will be looking for a long time, no shops around here are going to be open at this time." The taxi pulled off, the driver giving them another worried glance in his rearview mirror.

"Did you hear that Ellie?" Harry asked. "He said there are no shops open. Let's get back Ellie. I am scared." They held hands and ran back along the road, and sneaking back into the house and up the stairs, they saw that the room door was open,

They stopped, looking at each other. "She's back, we're for it now," Harry whispered.

Karen appeared at the door "Quick you two, get back in here. You gave me a fright, where have you been?"

"We were looking for you, we woke up and were scared. We want to go home." Ellie looked like tears were on their way back again. Karen shut and locked the door again.

"Sit down you two. Listen, I will get you home, I have told you that, you just need to trust me. The naughty people who stole you are still looking for you."

"But you are with the naughty people," Harry said puzzled.

"I was sweetheart, now I am with the good people. Just trust me."

"Will you really take us home?" Harry persisted.

"I will, but you need to sleep first. If Mummy and Daddy think that you are tired, I will get in trouble."

As the children settled back down to sleep, Karen thought about their next move. She had transferred the money for the car electronically but the guy needed to bring the log book over once the cash was safe in his bank. He had trusted her and liked the price he had negotiated. The Ford Focus on top was a great bonus, he would be able to change a few things and pass it off to a willing punter who didn't ask too many questions for a nearly new car at a knock down price.

The spring sunlight crept through the curtains at around seven o'clock. Karen woke the children up and bundled them into the car. They were both excited with the new purchase and enjoyed playing Karen's new game, sleeping lions, on the back seat. She pulled a hat firmly over her hair and drove out of the village. The occupants of the MPV in the lay-by didn't give her a second glance.

At eight thirty the car seller and his wife drove to Harthill with the log book. It was a great morning for him as he had just agreed to sell the Focus on for another four thousand. This early morning drive in it would be his first and last. Money was pouring in.

Radio One blared out as he passed the lay-by and pulling up at the junction where he checked the road for oncoming traffic. It was normally quiet but some idiots used it as a racetrack so you could never be sure. They both jumped with terror as the people carrier pulled alongside and two men got out, one pulling the driver's door of the Focus open whilst the other went around to the passenger's side.

"Get out of the fucking car. Who the fuck are you?"

"Who the fuck are you?" the driver had gathered his senses and was not going to be ordered around by a couple of thugs. "This isn't my car, so whoever you think I am, I am not." His wife was screaming like a B movie actor from the 1960's as her door was roughly yanked open and she was dragged out.

"Shut her up before I do it for you, where did you get the car?"

"Some woman sold it to me this morning, crazy woman with too much cash."

"What is she driving now?"

The driver didn't like the interrogation and liked the men even less.

"She bought my green Mini Cooper Sport, said she was heading North."

The men had heard enough "Get back in your car and fuck off Jock."

As the MPV pulled off leaving the man to deal with his hysterical wife, the passenger was speaking on the phone.

"Mr Brood, she has changed cars and is heading north."

"How do you know?"

"She sold the motor to a local, he told us all we needed to know, she's in a green Mini Cooper heading north."

There were a few second's silence. "Why would he offer up all that information free of charge? Don't believe a word of it. Wait where you are until I get back to you. On second thoughts boys, come back down and we will meet up in Birmingham, I have a feeling things are not as they seem."

# CHAPTER TWENTY-SEVEN

Stephen sat by the hospital bed. Terry sleeping and unaware that he was there suddenly opened his eyes, squinting to gain his focus for a second before recognizing his boss.

"Sorry Stephen, these meds knock me out. How are things and what news of the twins? It didn't sound very good on the phone earlier."

"Not the best few days mate." Stephen told the story almost in full but he couldn't bring himself to mention that he had agreed to bring in the drugs, the idea disgusted him to the core. Terry would hate the fact that Stephen had agreed and would report it. Stephen knew that there was a line with Terry and bent staff were way beyond the line.

"I have a team of guys out looking, they are doing well but have picked up on something that we can't figure out," Terry informed him as he struggled to hoist himself up into a sitting position. Stephen jumped up and helped position a pillow behind his head.

"What's that then?"

"They have had eyes on everyone, I mean everyone who seems to be working with or for the Broods."

"Yeah?"

"They've not had one sniff of the children."

"That sounds bad Terry." Stephen flopped back down into the hospital chair.

"I don't know, the guys found an old farm building way out in the sticks. The owners were terrified to talk but eventually said that the kids had been there. They were moved off in a horse box to the Irish Republic but we know the vehicle didn't arrive."

"So what does that mean?"

"Their plans have gone to shit somewhere along the line, I should know more in a day or so. We have a few people out looking, two of the guys have just picked up on a possible lead in Scotland.

Avis car hire had a car stolen from Holyhead, a woman and two kids hired it and failed to return it at the appointed time. The car has turned up near Glasgow, but don't get your hopes up yet, this may not be connected. Let's just wait and see what comes back from the guys."

"This is getting weird, but it makes a bit of sense. I have heard nothing from the children for a while. For the first couple of days they were sending me recordings or videos of them. Fuck it Terry, I am going to put it right onto the Broods. I am going to stop playing their games until I have some fresh contact with Harry and Ellie."

"Just wait a day or two Stephen and we should have a better idea of where they are and what they're doing with them." Terry looked at his friend in sympathy, he couldn't imagine the torment of not knowing where your children were or what was being done to them. He knew if it was his son Tom, he would be beside himself and wouldn't stop until he found him. Although he was stuck in hospital for the next few days, at least he had his contacts out there helping Stephen.

# CHAPTER TWENTY-EIGHT

Jon Thomlin and Daniel Reeve sat watching from the car. Both were early thirties and former Royal Marines now working wherever there was trouble and people needed protecting. The recent job in the Yemen had been a testing one. They were part of a small team protecting a high value British business man who needed to force through an arms deal with some guys he would not have normally met. When billions of British investment came down to a meeting in a bombed out building somewhere in the back of beyond you needed to be on your A game. These guys were always at the top of their game. Their athletic build and rugged good looks attracted plenty of attention from the ladies back at home and the recent suntans only added to the attraction. Cropped hair and expensive sunglasses, they would have looked quite at home in the South of France dodging in and out of casinos and clubs. Their relationship with Terry was forged through the Royal Marines. Terry had served with Jon's father in the Falkland War. He had the honour of being a Godparent to Jon and this had led to the forging of a solid friendship.

Today their target was very different to the bad guys that they had encountered in the military. Criminal gangs were a different breed, well organised, well-disciplined and with a tremendous motivation to succeed. The professional manner with which the Broods conducted operations and counter surveillance had surprised them both. It reminded them of operations within Northern Ireland where IRA targets were followed, and they figured that if they were rumbled, their fate would be the same as it would over there, torture followed by death.

There had been a lot of movement in and out of the Orpington sports club, no major players were seen but the traffic flow through the door had been frantic. It was time to move on, they had been sitting watching for an hour, just enough time to avoid suspicion. They headed for the KFC drive through and sat in the car park munching through a bargain bucket whilst considering the available options before they set out for the reconnaissance trip of the Brood's residences. Dan made a quick call to a friend working in the Met Police.

"Hi Jimmy, anything from either of the Broods that we need to know about?"

"All silent bud, I will contact you if I hear any noise."

"No probs, we are out tonight on an OP, just thought I would let you know mate." Hanging up he turned to Jon. "You ready then wanker?" They pulled out into the traffic and headed back to the hotel to get ready.

Checking kit and running through all contingencies was normal to them. How to get in, how to get out, what happened if it all went to shit, were usual deliberations. They knew that when on the mission, they didn't need to be thinking about what to do. they just needed to do it and do it right. Practicing until it was second nature had saved lives many times in the past and was drilled into them

David Brood's house sat within a couple of acres of woodland, ideal for snooping around and watching without been spotted. Very pretty it was worth two or three million in that part of the country.

The intelligence that they had, indicated that he didn't have a dog which was a surprise bonus but he did have a decent security system inside the house. An earlier recce had not seen evidence of external patrols or detection equipment in the grounds. Maybe the Broods felt that they were untouchable. Driving past the gates it appeared that there were lights on in the main house. It was slightly before ten thirty and they planned to be in position by eleven pm. Brood was a night owl and it was highly likely that business would be done at night. They parked up a couple of hundred yards from the walled garden, the car nicely hidden in plain sight in the middle of a pub car park. It was always busy and the locals used it to park off the road. Grabbing the sports-bag of kit from the back seat, they slipped off into the dark. Soon they were off the beaten track walking through a wooded area and keeping to a small path they moved quickly and quietly. If they were bumped by the locals, they would have turned into a gay couple looking for somewhere secluded, people tended not to hang around and ask questions in those situations. The gray corner of the stone wall came into view and they slipped into the bushes beneath it waiting and watching. If it appeared that they had been followed they would bug out and go back to the hotel to reconsider their plan. Ten minutes passed, and with no signs of anyone around they moved on. The wall was an easy climb, six feet high and constructed of old stone which made climbing it as easy as climbing a ladder. Jon went over first taking the bag with him. He dropped onto the other side and crouched in silence, listening. Again nothing, so Dan followed him over and they moved quickly into the cover of a deep bush. Burying themselves in, they had a direct view of the front door and a number of the windows on the front of the house. Again, they lay silently getting accustomed to the area and noises, their eyes gaining the night vision needed.

Through the window to the left of the front door, David Brood could be seen sitting at what appeared to be an office desk. He took a number of phone calls before something seemed to disturb him, and he jumped up and paced angrily across the room talking animatedly into the phone. Dan unzipped the backpack and took out a small package. "Let's see what this guy is so upset about."

He placed the listening device into his jacket pocket and slowly left the hide. Crawling slowly forward he inched towards the window. A grinding sound stopped him in his tracks as the main gate to the driveway opened up. The car headlights sweeping up the driveway and across the lawn threatened to illuminate him as he hugged the wet grass. The car door opened along with the front door and David Brood's voice floated across the spring night air.

"Does that dog of yours need a pee before we start?" Dan's muscles tensed and prepared to explode and hurtle him towards the wall as a cold sweat dripped down from his forehead. Jon, under cover of the bush, was observing every detail second guessing Dan's thoughts. They had planned for just this sort of obstacle.

"No thanks David, he's fine, I'll leave him in the car. I know you're not keen on the hairs around the house."

The front door closed. In a split second, Dan had moved forward and placed the device into position under the window before returning to the OP under the bush. He gave Jon a knowing smile and they settled back down to listen in. They had sat in a number of OPs such as this and they didn't talk unless it was absolutely vital. Sign language was the normal routine for communication and anyway, this one should be easy, no need for food, sleep or crapping into a plastic bag, just simple observation and then back to the hotel to put the information together. The wet grass soaked into their clothing and even in the cool temperature, the insects bit lumps out of their ears, so all in all, it was a normal night in the office.

Two hours later the meeting between the two men finished, it was just after three in the morning and a chilly two degrees. Brood and his accomplice shook hands at the front door, it seemed the meeting had gone well as both men looked in good spirits. Dan and Jon slipped back over the wall before the men had reached the front door. As they walked back to the car park, they could hear the sound of barking coming from the garden. The dog, let out now for his pee had found the OP. The guys however had left no trace of being there and Brood would have no idea.

It was only when they were back in the car that they spoke, again. Jon turned the engine on and put the heating on full as Dan relaxed back into his seat. "Thought that we were in a bit of trouble there Jon mon ami." He let out a long laugh.

"Me too mate, let's get back and have a listen to what has been going on in the Brood's world."

Terry's phone buzzed on silent mode vibrating across the top of the hospital bedside cabinet. He reached over with a wince of pain and glanced at the brightly lit face, it was seven in the morning and Jon's name was across the screen. He pressed the answer button.

"Yes mate, how did it go?"

"They haven't got a clue where the kids are Terry, they are trying to find Brood's former girlfriend Karen. She has taken the kids and gone into hiding. It appears she developed a conscience on the way to Ireland and abducted them from their abductors. They have two teams of two out looking for her but she gave them the slip in Scotland. They think that she may now be heading back south."

"I thought so, anything else?"

"She is dead when they find her without a doubt, and they will in time unless we stop them. Terry, they also talked about your friend Stephen."

"Go on."

"He has half a mill of heroin in his house which is due to go into your prison at the end of the week."

"Shut the fuck up! He wouldn't do that."

"Sounds like he had no choice Terry, but now the kids are on the trot the rules change. We're going to go back and have a closer look, see if we can find any clues."

"You shouldn't do that mate, it could be a big risk."

"Don't worry about us, he will have no idea that we have been there in the first place, it will be fine. We need to find those kids."

"Okay thanks lads I owe you. We also need to find this Karen before they do. We'll speak later." Terry rang off before immediately redialing. Wasting no time on pleasantries, he spoke

"Stephen, come over to speak with me asap, I have news."

The drive to the hospital was a blur, and finding the first available parking space Stephen walked briskly through the almost empty corridors dodging trolleys of dirty bedding and breakfast trays. On entering the room, he saw that Terry was propped up against a number of pillows with an odd look on his face. Stephen couldn't work out if this were good or bad.

"What's happening Terry?"

Terry took a deep breath, "Firstly, the Broods do not have the children, they are on the run with the ex-girlfriend of David Brood. We are trying to find them before the Broods do so it's a race." He looked at Stephen. "I think, or hope that this gives us the chance that we have hoped for Stephen, without the kids, their bargaining power goes down."

"Bloody hell, can't get my head around that." Stephen sat on the edge of the bed. Terry's face then flashed with anger.

"Second thing, why the fuck didn't you tell me about the drugs you fucking idiot. I thought that this thing was based on trust?"

Stephen's head spun, he could feel his face growing red and flushed and not knowing what to say he just dropped his gaze to the floor.

"I just didn't know what to say to you Terry, things are not what they seem. I just want this thing over with and when they were given to me, I felt I had no choice but to take them."

"We all want this over with and I know you're under huge pressure but what the fuck were you thinking? Are they still in your house?"

"Pantry."

"Someone will be over today, give them the stuff." Stephen nodded but Terry continued.

"I'm tired and very pissed off with the whole situation, I need time to think. That's a trust thing mate, you didn't trust me, and now I'm not sure where we stand. You have stepped right over the line. Bringing drugs into the prison, it goes against everything we hold dear. Fucks sake, you were willing to do that and I can't believe it." He fell back against his pillows and closed his eyes. "Go home and wait for me to contact you when I have more news." Stephen was not going anywhere until he had explained himself.

"I didn't tell you because there is no way in hell I am taking anything into my prison. I would rather die. I'm sorry that you thought I would."

"I just need a bit of thinking time, sorry I jumped the gun. I should have known better." Terry put his hand on Stephen's shoulder. "Let's get the kids back as our first priority. My guys will be with you within the next couple of hours."

Stephen drove home feeling a lot more positive. The Broods were in turmoil and he had another half a million pounds of their money which he had no intention of handing over. Furthermore, the children were out of their grasp for the moment.

He arrived home and wasted no time in telling Tanya the latest developments. They sat in the kitchen while Stephen described every event from the conversation with Terry. She was euphoric that the children were out of the hands of the Broods and so relieved that the bag full of hate hidden in the pantry would soon be gone.

True to Terry's word, after what only seemed to be a few minutes the doorbell rang. Before answering Stephen fetched the bag of drugs from the pantry and took it with him to the front door. He opened the door to find David Willard standing on the doorstep.

"What the hell are you doing at my house, and why are you out of prison?" he asked in disbelief. Yesterday he had the price of his life on his head and today he was larger than life outside Stephen's home.

"My handler came good and my statement along with all evidence has been logged so I am out and back at work albeit out of public view. You've been good to me Stephen and when a friend of a friend told me to contact Terry in hospital, I did. He understands that I am MI5 and ready to help but he knows nothing else. If we all work together, I think we have a fighting chance of getting your children back and dealing with the Broods once and for all. I will just need your help when all this is done, as we will have some of your managers to sort out."

Stephen stared at him, not quite believing that yesterday he felt he was dealing with every bit of this hideous situation on his own and today, he had the almighty power of one of the largest government agencies on his side.

"I am grateful, a bit freaked but very grateful. What resources do you have?"

"Everything that you could have hoped for and more," David promised.

"Just get my children home safely please, it is all I ask at the moment."

"Listen Stephen, we will find your children, count on us. I will also make sure that this is analysed," here he pointed to the bag of heroin, "and used to bring the bastards down." He disappeared as quickly as he came, and Tanya walking into the hall way to see what was keeping Stephen so long asked "Who was that darling?"

Stephen closed the door. "Not sure who he was really, the bag has gone though so one less thing to worry about. As I just said to you, darling, the tide is turning in our favour."

# CHAPTER TWENTY-NINE

Karen's phone rang, she saw it was a call from her father and she let it ring off before turning into the services on the M1. She needed fuel and some food for the children but this time they would be coming with her. She quickly phoned her father back.

"Hi Dad, are you ok?"

"We are fine Karen but there are an awful lot of unpleasant men looking for you. If you're in some sort of trouble, can you come home?

"I'd love to Dad, but I just need to lie low for a bit till I've sorted a few things out. I don't want to bring any trouble to you and Mum."

"I think that I might have a solution then. We have friends, the Whitfords, who needs a house sitter for a couple of months in SW France. A guy I worked with at Stansted has his own private licence and might be up for flying you over. Just thought it might be a useful break for you, do you want me to ask him? I think he lives Oxford way now but I can find out."

Karen thought briefly, this might be the ideal opportunity to get away from those chasing her while she thought about how she was going to get out of this situation alive.

"Dad you are a legend, I think that's a great idea but it needs to be soon."

"Give me a few minutes and I'll call you straight back."

It wasn't long before Karen's phone rang again and her father confirmed the plans.

"Oxford City airport at Kidlington tomorrow morning. Leaves at 0930. He knows some guys who can get around the passport thing and he will fly you to the local airstrip where the

Whitfords will meet you. The least you know the better at this stage."

"I love you dad."

"You too darling. Meet my friend outside the pub in a village called Woodstock, it's near Blenheim Palace. His name is Ed, he will be in the car park at 0800. Good luck sweetheart, just keep in touch and let us know you're okay." The phone went dead, Karen stared at the key pad longing to be back at home.

"Karen, I need the toilet." She shook herself back into the real world to see Ellie wriggling around on the back seat.

"Okay, let's go in, use the toilets and get some food from here. I want to tell you what we are doing next."

The children sat in the back seat eating nuggets and chips. They never took their eyes from Karen as she discussed the plane ride and the house in France.

"It is just for a few days, then the bad people will have gone and you will be safely back at home with Mummy and Daddy."

"Do you promise Karen?" Ellie wanted more reassurance.

"On my life." That was more than enough for Harry,
"Ellie, a ride in a plane. Cool!"

# CHAPTER THIRTY

The sports bar in Orpington was buzzing, West Ham was on the TV again and the match was going well. A local derby with Spurs always upped the atmosphere. David Brood walked through the bar and past the doormen into the casino. He was still pissed at Karen getting the better of them and was looking for someone to bear the brunt of his anger. Four roulette wheels were spinning with a good group of locals and Chinese guys gambling away. The poker table was in operation with a high stakes game in progress and strong cocktails were on offer to the punters to keep them happy while thousands of pounds were at stake.

The blackjack dealer gave cards to the two Indian men sat at the table, both leering at her lowcut top and forgetting that they had just lost a thousand pounds each. A number of younger lads sat at the bar watching as the boss surveyed the room. They all wanted to be in the inner circle but they needed the invite first and these were hard to come by.

David had an eye for detail, he liked the wheels to spin every minute if possible and he had arranged for the poker tables to be in a VIP area separated from the rest of the room with a floor to ceiling window. Players felt special and lost money at alarming rates. He checked behind the bar chatting to the bar manager, his eyes running over the stock. The totals from the previous evening were given to him as David insisted on covering every detail.

"Good work, up from last weekend. What are they drinking at the moment?"

"We've started shifting a lot of the Russian vodka, the youngsters are loving it."

"Excellent, make sure that we have plenty in. Who serves at the tables?"

"A new girl, Polish, she also cleans the whole club, bar to toilets."

"Send her to my office please."

"Yes sir."

David walked through the room and into his office which doubled up as the board room for family business. There was a knock at the door. "Enter," he instructed as he sat down behind his large oak desk. A young girl, maybe only eighteen or nineteen years old walked in and stood in front of his desk.

"Yes sir, you wanted to see me?"

David was impressed with her English which only had a slight accent to it. "I have just inspected the club, I understand that you are responsible for the table service and cleaning?"

"Yes, I am sir."

"The club is in immaculate condition and I have never seen it so clean." The girl nodded as if there should be a 'but' coming. She didn't have long to wait.

"I like loyal people around me. Are you loyal?"

She nodded, a tight feeling coming across her chest as she realised where this was going. He had discovered that she was stealing from drunk punters while serving tables.

"You do realise that I know and see everything that goes on in here? I know every scam because I have seen them all before."

Again, she nodded, hardly able to breathe.

"I know that you have stolen a lot of money during your short time here, I have seen the CCTV. You are good, I will give you that. It's just not your money to steal darling."

A tear came down her cheek, she knew the trouble that she was in, she also understood his reputation for violence.

"No good crying sweetheart, especially as I'm not after you. I know that bar manager of mine has his fat fingers in the till hasn't he?"

"Yes sir."

"How is he stealing from me?"

“He steals bottles of vodka and sells them on, the stuff sold to the younger punters is watered down. He told me that he makes around five hundred pounds every week. I am sorry I took money.”

He took an envelope from his jacket pocket and passed it to her.

“Like I said I value loyalty, there is two thousand pounds in that envelope, it’s for you as I think you need it. Just keep your mouth shut. When you get back to the bar tell the bar manager that I want to see him in half an hour, tell him nothing else. Do you understand?” She nodded, fumbling with the envelope not really knowing what to say. She elected to say nothing. Nodding again she left the office and went to the staff room to hide her three pieces of silver.

David took the rear door from his office which led into a large car park. He made a call while reflecting on the people he surrounded himself with, and how it was a full-time job ensuring they were all with him and not against him. Maybe one day he would hand the family business over and settle for a life of normal living. Just not today, that was going to be far from normal.

He returned to his office and settled back into his chair and awaited the knock which came a few minutes later “Enter.” Gerald, the bar manager stood in the doorway

“You wanted to see me Mr Brood?”

“Yes Gerald, go and fetch the last three months inventory for the bar along with the sales figures, I need to audit them.”

“Sure.” He turned and left, his heart thumping, hoping that his seedy scam would remain uncovered. When he returned David Brood was sitting with another man, older and looking very serious. Thick black glasses perched on the top of his nose and a discreet hearing aid sat in his left ear.

“Gerald, this is a great friend of mine, he has looked after our family affairs for a number of years. Take a seat while he looks through the books.”

He sat, his heart pounding, knowing this was not going to end well. He glanced up at the photos which adorned the walls,

David Brood seems to have met a large number of both famous and infamous people and had photos taken on each occasion. It resembled a trophy hunter's wall, just as classless and seedy, and somewhat out of place for David Brood. He remembered seeing shots of the Kray twins in similar circumstances, maybe it was just a gangster thing Gerald thought as the older guy thumbed through the accounts cross checking each figure. After a long thirty minutes he stopped and looking at Gerald, he spoke.

"I could keep checking for another week but I don't really need to though. You are a thief Gerald, and whether you have stolen five hundred or five thousand pounds is not important, the fact is that you are stealing from this business." He turned to David Brood.

"There is absolutely no doubt, you have been fleeced for a long time."

David nodded "Thank you for confirming my suspicions. If you could leave us now and on your way out, ask my two colleges to come in, it would be appreciated. Give my regards to your wife."

The accountant shook David's hand and left, not bothering to look at the now sobbing bar manager.

"Please Mr Brood, I will pay you back, I needed money. I was always going to pay you back." The door opened and a shadow covered Gerald. Brood ignored his pleas and spoke to the men.

"Help him out into the van gentlemen, I will join you in a second." A crunching punch knocked Gerald off the seat as he continued to sob. Dragged to his feet and pulled by his hair towards the door, an inpatient gorilla of a man punched him so hard he collapsed unconscious and was carried to the awaiting van before being thrown unceremoniously into the back.

David walked outside into the car park. He placed staff members at the car park entrance with orders that no one should pass them and under no circumstances was he to be disturbed. Walking towards the rear of the club, he opened the rear shutter of the Luton van to see the now conscious Gerald.

"Right, you thieving little cunt," he addressed him as he climbed in. Regaining consciousness in the back of a van wallpapered and carpeted with thick plastic was a scary enough prospect in itself. Finding yourself gagged and tied to a chair was another level of fear. Seeing David Brood climbing into a van to join his two thugs was premier league fear.

"When you came to me for a job Gerald, I told you that I value loyalty above all things. I can accept mistakes if they are honest, I can accept most things, if they are honest. You my friend are not an honest person. What did you think would happen to you when I caught you stealing from us?" He nodded to the larger man. "Take the tape from his mouth, I want to hear him speak." The tape was ripped off.

"Are you aware of the consequences of stealing from me Gerald?" Gerald nodded.

"Good, good. What are the consequences Gerald?" The tone of the voice was chilling.

"You will hurt me Mr Brood."

"Good boy, I will hurt you, correct answer." Reaching into his inside jacket pocket he produced a meat cleaver.

"Are you aware of what happens to people in the middle east who are caught stealing?" He smiled, "Bit of a rhetorical question that one Gerald. That's a question that doesn't require an answer which is just as well." He nodded again at the big man, who grabbed Gerald around the neck, forcing open his mouth and dragging out his tongue.

"A change of tools I think for this little job," Brood muttered, reaching into his side pocket and producing a beautifully engraved cut throat razor.

"My favourite little friend here, has a long and distinguished history."
He flashed it in front of Gerald's eyes before placing it under his nose.

"Can you smell the quality of the embossed oak handle?" he asked before sharply slicing down and cutting into the exposed tongue. The muscle came free in his hand before he dropped it with distaste.

"Funny things aren't they, tongues. Get you in so much trouble yet look how small they are." He continued to stare at the floor as he spoke.

"You won't lie to me again, and now I'll make sure you won't steal from me again." He set to work with the cleaver, carefully chopping at each finger in turn before instructing his helper "I want his toes please." Barely conscious Gerald became aware of his shoes and socks been torn off, before the intense pain began again and darkness once again became his friend.

The splash of the water brought him back to his senses where he found the pain had gone. David smiled at him.

"We have given you something to ease the pain old friend as we want you to enjoy the ride."

The van pulled away, as David Brood stayed in the back of the van watching him bleeding in an opiate haze. The van bumped out of the car park and headed into oblivion for the unfortunate Gerald.

David continued talking to the subconscious man.

"You know I am not gay Gerald but I have a group of customers who have particular needs. In your case I have two oddballs who enjoy violent male rape and, guess what? They like human flesh. Odd fucking bastards. Anyway, to cut a long story short, you are their evening entertainment and dinner. On top of that they have paid me an awful lot of money for your company, so a win-win situation as I see it. Oh, with one exception, you, you lose."

The van stopped and the shutters opened.

"All yours boys," Brood greeted them as he jumped out.

Gerald could feel himself being dragged out of the van and thrown into the boot of a car before it disappeared off into the distance.

David Brood jumped into the front seat of the van while the two hired thugs cleaned up the plastic.

"Hurry up lads, I have worked up a real hunger, let's get back home in time for dinner."

The van pulled up back at the club. They had been gone for around an hour and the West Ham game was coming to a sad ending, another victory for the old enemy Spurs at two goals to one.

Walking back into the casino, the staff stared at Brood in terror, knowing something bad had happened to their colleague.

"Okay, I need a new bar manager," Brood greeted them. "Gerald has decided to leave the position, you will not be seeing him again any time soon. Any one fancy the job?" He looked around at the staff on duty.

"Me sir, I will do it," the young Polish girl put her hand up.

"You have got some courage lady, you think that you can do it?" Brood asked her.

"Sure, why not?"

"Rip me off and pay the consequences," he warned her.

She looked him in the eye, "No problem, when do I start?"

"Come to my office now and we'll discuss terms." She followed him into the office and the door closed, he turned the key and checked the door was locked. He was still turned on from the thrill of the afternoon and it appeared she was handing herself to him on a plate.

"I like a girl with a bit of spirit."

"I like a guy with balls." She shrugged her shoulders and laughed.

"Come here you dirty Polish bitch." He grabbed her and pulled her black T Shirt over her head exposing her white lacy bra. She giggled and kicked her shoes off quickly before pulling down her short skirt. He undid her bra exposing firm breasts and hard nipples, she undid his trousers and rubbed his erect penis. Pushing her back onto the desk he opened her legs and licked her shaven pussy. She moaned and leant backwards, he stood and pulled his trousers down exposing his large hard penis. He pushed it home and fucked her hard on the desk until he came inside her. He stood back up rearranging his clothing, "As I said, I like loyalty, keep your mouth shut and you will be fine."

"Yes, Mr Brood, will you be interviewing me again?"

"Whenever I need to interview you, I will call."

She dressed quickly and heading for the door, looked back over her shoulder, "just give me a shout, I have some excellent interview techniques to show you." She left the office and went straight behind the bar checking the stock, as if nothing had happened.

# CHAPTER THIRTY-ONE

Kevin Brood sat waiting for the staff to collect him before his move back to an open establishment, probably the quickest about turn in history. Since his discussion with the Duty Governor all sorts of good things had happened, a rise to the best behaviour grade of Enhanced, his security level reviewed as a Category D prisoner and an agreed move to HMP Statford Hill, one of the easiest places to do his time. He could be home in the next year if he played the game well. His cell door opened.

"Ahhh Governor Barnes, have you come to say goodbye and wish me well?"

"No, I'm just here to tell you that we are through, I have done my part of the deal and I owe you nothing."

"I fucking tell you when we are through Governor. You have taken thirty-five thousand for services provided. That is an awful lot of money Colin. Now fuck off and wait for me to call you again. Any bollocks and we grass you up. Simple." The governor turned a nasty shade of puce.

"I hope you rot you bastard."

"Fuck off Colin, hope you enjoyed the little holiday in Rome that I paid for. Give my love to the family, especially that lovely blond wife of yours." The door slammed shut and Kevin laughed. He had given the Governor's contact details to the next person who would use him. There was no escape for a bent screw. He picked up his phone, this would be the last call he could make until he reached the new prison. After this he would sell the phone off before getting to reception for a search. No point in taking silly chances.

"Hi brother, just thought I would give you a quick ring before

I move. How are things going into the search for that bitch of yours?"
David was quick to dispute this fact.

"I can assure you she is no longer any bitch of mine. We have had some joy, she used her card again just outside Wakefield and she is heading South. Not sure of the car she is driving at the moment, we have people watching. If she was at Wakefield at lunchtime there is a chance she will stop for food and a hotel so I am guessing she may stop around Watford. We have the guys out looking."

"Okay David, let me know the minute you get the brats back, we need Byfield back under our control."
He placed the phone into a pillow case along with some other things that he wouldn't get past the reception staff. Tying it to a long line of ripped sheets he swung it out of his window, shouting as he did so to the cell below his.

"Oy, number 27!"

"What you want bruv?"

"Look out of your window." Two seconds later the parcel was retrieved.

"Cool Bro, what can I do for you?"

"It's all good, enjoy." Kevin Brood's door was opened and the newly confirmed category D good boy was led to reception where the duty officer signed him out.

"We have a taxi arranged Brood, you will go on license. Don't let us see you back here." Climbing into the car Kevin looked back at the prison gates as he left the long driveway.

"How long until we get there driver?"

"Two and a half, maybe three hours depending on the traffic."

"How about four hours and I see my wife on the way and give you a couple of hundred quid?"

"How about you shut the fuck up and go to sleep?"
In the real world the driver would now be a pool of blood, in this world Kevin laughed. He liked people with integrity. What a strange world he moved in.

The driver woke Kevin up, "We are there mate, HMP bloody

Butlins."

"Cheers driver, I would give you a tip but you didn't earn it, see ya." He jumped out of the cab and took his bags from the boot. Walking towards the main gate he knew that his reputation would precede him so he would play the polite, innocent, oh how jail has changed me routine. People liked that. The screws at these open prisons also liked to think that they were the ones in charge. Most of them had worked somewhere else a hundred years ago, but the majority of them were shit scared about going into a real prison. Sitting here waiting for retirement seemed a safe option. Ringing on the bell he announced his arrival to the officer who came to the door.

"Afternoon Officer, Kevin Brood on transfer." He took a second look at the man. "I know you boss, you banged me up years ago. You were the fairest person I have ever met in prison, what a small world!" And so the act began.

Kevin knew one other officer from this prison, he was a crooked PE officer who he had met over twenty years ago. Why it was always the gym staff who wanted to make extra cash bemused him.

He headed straight for the gym where sure enough, his old friend was on duty.

"Mr O'Dell what a nice surprise!" He looked around and saw that nobody else was around before continuing.

"Do you remember when you used to bring me weed into the prison? You even smoked it with me on that outward-bound course. You still game?"

"Well, Mr Brood, fancy seeing you again, glad to resume our business agreement. What are you looking for? Better be quick, I am part time and looking to retire. I have heard this place could shut in the next couple of years and when it does, I am off. Fuck those bigger jails, I don't want that shit at my age."

"Good for you, stay away from those places, they're full of dangerous people" Kevin laughed. "I need a phone and in time I will need a job outside, can you help?"

"No problem. I need an orderly in the gym, up for the job?"

"Just like old times Chris. I will do the induction, find my way around and start in a couple of weeks to avoid suspicion, how does that sound?"

"Good mate, see you tomorrow with the phone, it will be seven fifty, cash. Then we will keep apart until the job comes up." Kevin walked back out of the gym and found his room, ensuite, nice view and non-smoking, all looked perfect. One of his people on the outside would arrange for the seven hundred and fifty pounds to be delivered into him directly he had the phone to call them. He walked down the corridor, another fifteen people shared the building and within two minutes everyone knew he had arrived. The new king was in town.

Sitting on the single bed later that afternoon, Kevin flicked through the tv channels, his mind planning how he could get this small problem back on track. The children disappearing had thrown a large spanner in the works. A lot of time and money had been invested into this project and should Byfield be able to walk away unscathed, the Brood dynasty could be over. For a start, they would all be banged up. Once any investigations began the whole house of cards could tumble, a large arm's deal with North African friends was already on hold due to David's inability to manage the situation. It felt as though two small kids could bring them all down. He needed to get out and take control, even a five-day license out of prison could help salvage things but he had only been in open conditions for one day so no way would he qualify for time out yet. Kevin knew the system, the only way he could get home would be through greasing some palms, which was difficult when he hadn't had time to do the groundwork.

He would need to call in another favour from Chris O'Dell. He pulled his trainers on and strode off into the spring sunshine. Arriving at the gym he found Chris taking a class for circuit training, leading the sweating group over a blue padded gym mat pushing out another twenty press ups. He looked at Kevin, "Give me five minutes mate, last lap. Grab a mop and start cleaning, you are on trial for the job."

"What about the two-week induction?"

"Your choice, take it or leave it."

Kevin strode down the gym and found the cleaning cupboard. He grabbed the mop and an old steel mop bucket, filling it with hot water and cheap detergent. He had been through this routine a million times. Sweeping through the gym as people were finishing, he cleared mats and weight bars away. Some prisoners looked at him, he could see they wanted to ask the question as to why he had got the job so quickly. He had been around long enough to know he had to deal with this quickly. Strolling into the shower he quickly spotted two of the prisoners who had given him a bad look.

"Have you two wankers got a problem with me? If you have let's have it out." Silence descended and other prisoners stepped out of the showers to watch. Kevin had the smell of victory is his nostrils, he could see they had no stomach for a fight. He grabbed them both by the arms and they followed him like children. Taking them into the middle of the changing area he turned the situation into a boxing arena, people watching from all sides.

"I will do you both together or separately, how do you want it?" One of the guys was quick to back down.

"We don't, I don't have a problem with you, I don't even know you."

"You soon will. Look at me like that again and I will take you to pieces, you understand?"

"Yes, no issues, can I go please?" Kevin nodded and turned to the other man. No need to say anymore, he was backing away towards the showers. Kevin turned 360 degrees, "Anyone else have an issue with my job?" One older, wiser prisoner answered. "No Mr Brood, no issues."

"I will get back on with my work then, good afternoon gentlemen." He strode back into the gym and picked up his mop. He finished brushing and mopping the gym area before taking a cup of tea into the Office.

"There you go Mr O'Dell, have I passed my trial?"

"Yes Kev, you have the job. Look in the top drawer, it's your first request." Kevin opened the drawer and saw the phone.

"Seven fifty for that? Your prices have shot up Chris. The first phone you got me cost fifty quid."

"Supply and demand. You are my only customer, and if I am taking risks you pay the price."

Kevin nodded at him. "Fair enough, but I have another five grand to spend and I want five days out on license." Chris puffed out his cheeks, "That's a big ask, you have only been here two minutes. Did you know anyone at your last jail who did you a favour or two?"

"Why?"

"If you came here with a promise of five days license from your last nick, the boss may just go with it."

"Brilliant, I do have someone who still owes me, can you give him a ring for me? He is a grubby governor but could come good. He is in the Offender Management Unit. Colin Barnes."

"Never heard of him, how deep is he in?"

"Thirty-five grand."

"Easy, leave it with me, come back down here for the evening session, and bring your kit you lazy bastard."

Kevin returned to his room, news of the events in the gym had spread and one guy came to his room. He knocked on the door before entering. Kevin looked up and sized up the threat. There was none, the body language was passive and he seemed a decent man.

"What can I do for you?"

"Mr Brood, there is no need to be worried about anyone in this building, we just get on with our stuff and want to get home."

"Fantastic, same here, can I get you a brew?"

The two sat and chatted for an hour, they had both been around the block and Kevin had heard of this man before. Fifteen years ago, he had spent a lot of time in segregation units around the country. Kev had heard of his reputation and how God had changed his life. He had an interesting history and Kevin was captivated by him.

"I know all about you mate and it's a pleasure to meet you." He stood up, "Let's have lunch and you can tell me some more about your changed life."

Later that afternoon, Kevin wandered down to the gym where he found the gym instructor in his office.

"Bloody hell Chris, I've just spent a few hours with Tony Jones, he has changed."

"Not half, nice bloke though," the gym instructor agreed. You ready for a work out?"

"I'm ready for some home leave?"

Chris bent down to the top drawer of his desk and produced a document.

"This is authority for your Home Leave, your mate Colin came through. It's not official of course, but the boss may support your application. I have had a chat with him and said that you had been promised. He wants you to put in an application."

"I'll bang it in this evening, I need to get out quickly. Cheers Chris, I owe you." Chris laughed "Yes you do, now get your kit on."

The following morning a very sore Kevin Brood noticed the governor walking across the road towards the office and jogged over to intercept him.

"Morning boss, can I have two seconds with you?"

"Of course you can Mr Brood, I guess it is about your time out of the establishment?"

"Yes boss, I had it provisionally approved at the last place, I have the document here." Kevin produced the form and gave it to the Governor.

"I had some appointments booked with the bank and probation already so I was hoping for tomorrow. Any chance?"

"Big ask Kevin, let me look at the appointments you have made. So long as you are fully occupied for the five days, I may go for it. Give me a couple of hours to look over the paperwork."

"Thanks boss, I appreciate your help. This has to be my last time inside, I have had enough. Just need to sort everything out before I hit the streets again." They parted ways, Kevin feeling positive about his reformed character performance. Sitting eating a sandwich at the table in the canteen area for lunch, Kevin was surprised to see the Governor walking towards him.

"Afternoon Kevin, I have just spoken with Mr Barnes and he has confirmed that they were happy for your Release on Temporary Licence." Kevin nodded, waiting for the next part of the message.

"You can go home tomorrow morning and return on Monday afternoon, how does that sound?"

"Music to my ears boss, thank you so much. This will really help me get my life back on track." As the governor walked off, Kevin quickly finished his sandwich before hurrying back to his room. Grabbing the illicit mobile, he phoned David immediately.

"Get a meeting booked for tomorrow evening at seven, I'm home for a bit." Kevin knocked on Tony's door, "Tony look after my gear for a bit, I have been given a license for a few days. Can I stick my phone in your room buddy? No problems if it's too much."

"Don't be daft mate, drop it in and I will take care of it. Kevin, don't mess up mate, you are nearly out."

"Trust me Tony, it will be fine. See you soon."

The meeting room in the sports club was buzzing. Present at the meeting were David Brood, Sandra Brooks, the Operational Field Manager, Susan Turner, Business Manager and Keith Harding. The latter had been a longtime member of the Parachute Regiment, served nine years within the SAS and was a gun for hire. He had distinguished himself while working within Libya during the uprising. He had also seen action within a number of African countries and more recently Iraq with a private security company. Sandra had head hunted him for the organisation. He ran the hunt teams finding and eliminating targets. The door opened and Kevin Brood entered like the homecoming hero. This type of egotism had always annoyed David but he tolerated it for the moment. Kevin took his seat next to David and nursed a large ice-cold glass of coke, this was time for a clear head and alcohol was banned at all his meetings. Kevin spoke and the room hushed.

"We're here to brief the team in regard to our present position. I want to know about Byfield, the whereabouts of the kids and the arms deal with the Africans. Who is going first?" Sandra began, she produced a number of sheets of information and passed them around.

"Firstly, Stephen Byfield has to date been very compliant with our requests. He has in his possession five hundred thousand pounds of heroin which he has agreed to take into his prison for distribution. He must believe that the children are still with us or our bargaining tool is lost. That brings me to my second point, the children have been taken by Karen Matthews from Holyhead ferry terminal. She rented a Ford Focus from Avis and bolted. We have traced her to Cheltenham where we eliminated her friend, and then through to York and Scotland. At present she is in an unknown car heading South and we believe that she is heading to the South East of England. I will let Mr Harding give you more details on those developments." Kevin interjected.

"So we have lost the brats and therefore risk losing our hold over Byfield? What use are you?" Sandra stuttered, trying to come up with some justification.

"Don't fucking sit there stuttering you stupid cow, do your fucking job. Last chance, do I make myself clear?"

"Yes Mr Brood." She closed her file and sat down. Keith Harding stood and spoke. He looked an imposing figure but this didn't cut the ice with Kevin, he had dealt with lots of imposing figures.

"We have two search teams out at the moment, we have questioned friends and family and have taken care of one of her friends in Cheltenham. We will keep the pressure on. We have arrangements in place for her parents who are actively supporting her at the moment. She is, as Sandra said, heading south. I have had a team waiting at Watford Gap where I believed she would have had to stop but this was fruitless. We have a trace on her phone and Bank Cards. She has been in touch with her father and she may be heading to the Essex area but we can't confirm that at the moment. I have a team watching her parent's address.

We run the risk of being compromised by Byfield, as has been said already, but we have taken out his main supporter Terry Davies. He is presently in hospital awaiting an amputation of his leg. We understand that he has a small team around him that are also searching for Karen Matthews. We also have some evidence that David has been the target of some surveillance. Our fear is that if they find out we do not have the children Byfield will obviously not cooperate."

David looked up, "That makes some sense, I had the feeling that someone had been in the grounds the other night. A friend's dog went crazy around the bushes, that could explain why."

Kevin spoke, "Susan, give me some good news please, this is sounding dire."

"It's not great Kevin, we need the kids, simple as that. However, on the other matter, I still have confidence that the deal with the Africans can come off. We have a lot of automatic weapons and ammo stored away and a deal has been reached with wealthy buyers. The complication in this deal revolves around the killing of the Russian tourists. The same batch of guns were used so everyone has slowed down a tad. I believe that this will happen within the next six months and will offer us a profit in the range of fifteen million pounds. A significant amount. We have control over three senior prison service managers and have a continuous supply chain of class A drugs entering High Security prisons. We have contacts building with the group English Blood who some may say are white supremacists. We are also cultivating Muslim prisoners but I will not elaborate upon that plan at this time."

"And what do we plan to do with Byfield?"

"He will be killed once he has fulfilled his purpose, we have that already organized." Again, Kevin spoke, he looked slightly anxious as he scanned the information.

“So, we need the kids, if we get them, we are back in the business of getting Byfield discredited, a goal of ours for a long time now. The arms deal will be the making of us and it must happen. People went to a great deal of trouble to get us those weapons and brave people lost their lives in that operation. I will not tolerate this failing, do I make myself clear?”
Everyone nodded.

“Keith, Sandra, sort your shit out. If you don’t find the kids you will be replaced, understand?” It was a clear threat and a question not needing an answer.

“I suggest you redouble your efforts, whatever you need you can have, just ask. Go and get to it.” The look he gave suggested the meeting was over, and the two left with no doubt in their mind that they had better come up with the goods or they would be made permanently redundant. Kevin then turned to Susan. “Can we minimise the risk should this all go wrong?” Susan needed no time to think about this and was quick to let Kevin hear her thoughts.

“We should clean up anything that will be found by the security services or serious crime organisations. We can hold anything that may be of use to a prosecutor either electronic or hard copy in a safe area. I have negotiated a number of safe deposit areas around London where they will not be found. Do you want to issue this as an order? If so, I will facilitate the deposits.”

“Great plan,” Kevin agreed, “thank God someone is on the ball around here. Let’s get that done ASAP, I will order that this all comes to you this week. Is that ok with you David?” David nodded his agreement. “Makes sense. If we are going to get picked up, I would rather do a small amount of time for simple stuff than spend serious time away. Let’s get it done.”

# CHAPTER THIRTY-TWO

Today was the day that Terry would be discharged from hospital, he had by all accounts proved to be one of the most miserable patients that they had on the ward. What they didn't know was that Terry was trying to plan a rescue mission while worrying about saving his leg. The operation was scheduled for later in the month and there was little else they could do until this had happened so on the insistence of Terry himself, he was allowed home. Although his running days were over, the hospital had saved his leg and with some good quality physio, he might just get away with a slight limp. There would just be some reconstruction needed later. This was no real consolation to him, he wanted revenge on the men who had hurt him so mercilessly and he wanted the Brood family smashed. But above everything, he wanted the children to be found.

Jo and Stephen drove to the hospital together to pick up Terry. They chatted on the way but Stephen could tell that there was an undercurrent. It didn't take a psychotherapist to work out that she blamed him for all that had happened during the past year, her being taken hostage by a mad man and now her husband so badly hurt that he may never be the same again. If it was any consolation to Jo, he blamed himself too, nobody had wanted this to happen. Arriving at the hospital they eventually found a car park space after circling the place five times.

"Five quid to stop for one hour, what a bloody rip off." As soon as the words left his lips, he knew that it was a bad thing to say as Jo spun around and ripped into him.

"You are moaning about a bloody fiver, how about Terry? He is a cripple because he stood up for you. A bloody fiver!" Stephen knew that she had more to add but somehow, she managed to control her temper and they walked in an uncomfortable silence into the hospital. The lift up to floor C was a frosty affair but thankfully they quickly reached the ward. Terry was sitting waiting for them, the wheelchair replaced with a pair of crutches which was a positive sight. A nurse approached them and smiled at Jo.

"Hi Mrs Davies, we just need to sort out the medication and his follow up surgery, hopefully we will be done in around an hour. We will have some very strict rules and exercises that Terry must follow at home though."

Jo looked at Terry and smiled. "Are you listening to this? You have to do as you're told."

Terry smiled back at her. "I just want to get home darling, I am sick of this place, it's worse than being at work." Here he glanced at Stephen. Jo followed the nurse towards the pharmacy to collect the mountain of tablets needed and Terry took his opportunity to speak to Stephen.

"I have arranged a meeting with the guys who are helping, we have five of my boys plus the guy that you met in the prison. He is still in hiding but we can still contact him by phone for the majority of the time. He has unfinished business apparently so we only have him for a couple of weeks before he is posted elsewhere. He has access to lots of resources so is worth including in our plans." Stephen nodded in agreement. "When are we meeting?"

"Lunch time tomorrow, Jo is out for the day, so I thought we could use the meeting room in the Queens hotel in Bristol. I have booked it for two hours, can you pick me up for it?"

"Course I can, any progress?"

"Yes lots, we still haven't found Harry and Ellie but we are close."

"Can I tell Tanya and Dad anything?"

"Not yet, let's have the meeting first and hopefully we'll have something concrete to tell them."

Jo returned with a large plastic bag filled with boxes of tablets.

"Everything is sorted, I have your appointments, home exercise this week and then back into the hospital later this month. Let's get you home darling."

They made their way back down to the car with Stephen feeling a little unsure as to the level of help he should offer. Jo was taking full control of everything and he felt a little shunned at first but on the drive home he reflected that this was just a normal reaction. It was difficult but he felt that he had to say something.

"Jo, I know that me being here is difficult, and that Terry was put in harm's way helping me, but I am not the bad guy. I am suffering too, my bloody kids are out there somewhere and we have no idea where. You can hate me for eternity but I am not the cause of these problems. The Brood family hurt Terry, not me." Terry, sitting in the front seat next to Stephen answered.

"She knows Stephen, we have spoken about it. Just let things settle a bit, we are all still friends." Stephen glanced at Jo in the rearview mirror and she nodded, he felt her hand on his shoulder and the warmth swept through his body. He wondered if she knew that Terry would be involved in meeting up for a council of war in a day's time and would she still be so forgiving if she found out?

# CHAPTER THIRTY-THREE

Karen pulled in to the caravan park in Banbury, she had taken no chances with the booking arrangements and her father had taken care of the payment and all the added extras the children would need. The park was busy with visitors and would provide a great distraction for the children until tomorrow when they were in for a busy day. The flight was arranged and all they needed to do was stay safe in the UK for another eighteen hours or so. This was the sort of place the Broods would never consider as an option, sometimes hiding in plain sight was the best way. Karen needed the children to understand that they could trust her and if they were to all survive together for a couple of weeks in France then they needed to feel comfortable with her. She had to make it clear to them that everything she did was in aid of her getting them back to their parents safely.

Harry and Ellie loved the new location, swimming, games, arcades and a show in the evening. Karen made sure that they enjoyed the day, and she checked the schedule for the evening show. If it was a magician she would skip it. The kids would have a melt down and may well draw attention to them all. Luckily it was a remake of the musical Grease, great fun and cheesy but they all arrived back at the caravan exhausted but happy. She snuggled them into their bunk beds, glad to see that fear was no longer spread across their faces.

"Right sleep time you two, you have a belly full of fish and chips and coke, let's all get some rest as we have a busy day tomorrow." Harry bent over the side of his bunk to look at his sister.

"We are going on an airplane Ellie, wonder if we are going to

Spain?" Karen smiled at him.

"Don't think that we will make Spain, but we may get close. Now, lights off, time for sleep." As the twins fell asleep, Karen sat on the bench seat that would shortly become her bed, and looked around her. There was something comforting about the smell of a caravan, it felt so safe, so cosy and she wished that she was here on holiday with the children rather than hiding from a gang intent on killing her and doing God knows what with the kids. Not for the first time, she pondered how she had got herself in this situation, and more to the point, how she would get them all out of it safely.

The sudden noise brought her abruptly awake and looking at her watch she realized the alarm was going off. It was 06.30, and she would need to get ready as the meeting time was 08.00 and was about thirty minutes away. She didn't want to be waiting at the pub for long, it would be too obvious and she might be caught on CCTV. She also needed to hide the car, not easy when she didn't know the area. She would have to suss it out when she got there, maybe she could leave it in the pub car park or maybe the airport had good parking. She needed to work this one out as the longer it took David and his henchmen to realise she had left the country, the better. Waking the children, she made them a quick cold breakfast while they struggled into their clothes. They were chilly, still tired and needed chivying along if they were going to make the rendezvous.

Locking up the caravan Karen was a little sad to see the back of the camp, it was the safest she had felt for days and pulling onto the M40 it felt as though she was back into the same routine of continuously looking in the rearview mirror. The junction for the A34 came quickly and Karen turned off heading towards Kidlington. It was a simple drive and she soon saw the signs for Woodstock. The road took them past Oxford airport which she could see was a small operation and she could see how they could slip out of the country without too much drama. Checking her watch, she saw that they had two minutes to spare as they found the pub and drove into the carpark. A man got out of his car and approached them. She wound down her window but remained in the car.

"Hi, I take it that you are Karen?" She nodded.

"Follow me, you can park in my space at the airport. The car will be safe there and we can take off within an hour, if you are ready?" The children clapped and cheered in the backseat of the car, and she smiled. "I think we are ready. I am so grateful."

"Your father has explained some of the story, I am sure that you don't mind if I don't introduce myself. I would hate to meet your friends." He looked at the children, "Poor little buggers," he whispered. "Let's get you all safe."

The convoy swept into the airport, and jumping out of his car, he again approached her. "Wait in the car, I will be back just before takeoff. Don't panic, everything is okay, I just need to make some final checks."

Karen wound the window up and locked the car doors. "Nice and quiet now you two, we'll be on the plane soon."

After only ten minutes he reappeared waving at them to join him. Locking up the car they walked towards the portacabin where he was standing.

"Come on inside and I will brief you about the trip." The room was very basic with some hard, plastic chairs, a coffee machine and a number of committee notices hanging limply from an old notice board.

"Okay, we take off in ten minutes, all the checks have been done on the plane and we are ready to go. It is an eight-seater so plenty of space and we also have enough fuel for the trip so we don't need to stop. Use the toilet now as there isn't one on the plane. We are flying to a small airstrip in South West France called La Reole. A car will meet you on the airstrip and you will be taken to the house. You will not see me again after the landing. You do not need to worry about passports, it's all been taken care of." He handed Karen a large envelope.

"This is from your father, it is enough money to last until we can get you all back safely. He doesn't want you using your card and risk being followed. Right, follow me and let's get going."

The children climbed onto the plane and into their seats and watched in wonder as the seat belts were applied. The noise of the propellers made talking impossible so they were all given a headset to communicate which caused great hilarity between the twins as they passed numerous messages of no importance between themselves. The engines roared and the plane rose into the sky. As the fields of Oxfordshire disappeared beneath them, Karen felt a release of the pressure within her. The hunters were left behind - at one point the Broods were within five minutes of catching them all and now they had a sea and six hundred miles between them. She just had to trust that the police and the twins' parents, or whoever was involved, could sort out the mess left behind.

Stansted was buzzing with the number of people getting away for a Spring break. Simon Matthews was taking a well-earned break from shifting the tons of luggage that came towards them on the conveyor belts like a mudslide. The tea room door opened and Simon could see that a security guard was talking to two smartly dressed men just outside in the corridor. Eventually the guard stuck his head through the door.

“Simon, there are two guys here who say that they want to chat to you about your daughter. Security have let them through this far, do you want to talk to them?” His heart dropped and a churning feeling in his stomach made him want to retch.

“Only if you come in as well mate, I don’t know who these people are.”

“No problems, I have five minutes,” and he brought the men into the room. Simon couldn’t read their body language, they looked like trouble but didn’t offer the feeling of violence. They seemed controlled and professional. One of them addressed him.

“Mr Matthews, we would like to talk in private if possible, the things that we would like to discuss are of a sensitive nature. I am sure that you understand?” The man talking looked at

Simon and then at the security guard before he got the right response. Simon looked at the guard,

"Thanks mate, I can deal with this, it will be okay."

"If you're happy, no problem." He left closing the door behind him. The same man continued to address Simon.

"Simon, we are here as we need to find Karen and the children before other people do. Have you heard of a gang called the Broods?" Simon nodded, "They have been to the house, I couldn't tell them anything and they said that they would be back."

"Okay, well we need to find Karen before the Broods do, they will kill her and probably the children too."

"I know they will." Simon looked from one to the other of the men, "Who are you anyway?"

"We can't tell you exactly but rest assured we are here to help your daughter. We are employed to find people, that's why we are speaking to you. Where is Karen?" The man held Simon's stare for five seconds of silence before he made his decision.

"France, they have flown out to South West France, a small town called Monsegur. Can you help them?"

"It's what we do, when did they go?"

"This morning, they will be there now. Please bring them home safely." The men stood and shook Simon's hand. "You have done the right thing, don't talk to anyone else though, lives are at stake."

"Sure, thank you for helping us, and for helping to get those children back to their parents." He sat with the coffee still steaming in front of him, unsure of what was going on or where it would lead. At least he had got some help in sorting this mess out for his daughter.

The car park at Stanstead was chilly, a weak sun offering more than it could deliver. The two men climbed into their car.

"Good work mate that saved us a lot of time, let's phone it in and book our tunnel tickets." The phone rang three times before it was answered. "David Brood, what have you got for me?"

"Hi boss, we know where they are hiding, get the passports

ready."

Simon drove home at the end of the long day, his body and mind aching as he opened the front door. Walking into the kitchen, he opened the fridge and pulled out a beer as he greeted his wife.

"Hello darling, how's your day been? The Airport has been heaving all day but more importantly, I had a strange meeting this morning with a couple of guys looking for Karen."

Sara, who was busy peeling potatoes for their supper stopped what she was doing. "Snap, oh my God, what did you say?"'

"It's okay, they were on our side, I trusted them. I told them where she had gone so they can help bring them all home safely."

Sara put the knife down and came to stand by the table where Simon had taken a seat.

"What do you mean, you trusted them?" she asked.

"They were very professional looking, you know, business suits, like they worked for a government agency or something. Why, who came to see you?"

"Two friends of Stephen Byfield, the children's father. They had military identification, what did your guys have?"

Simon's face paled as he realized what he had done.

"Oh dear Christ, I didn't check." A lump came into his throat and a confused spinning feeling came over his head. He knew he had screwed up and it would come down to a straight race into who could find Karen first. He picked up his phone and dialed. When it went to answer phone, Simon wasted no time in leaving a message "Karen it's Dad. I have screwed up, the Broods are on their way to France. I am so sorry darling, trust nobody."

As he disconnected, Sara looked at him. She knew that nothing she said could make him feel any worse than he did already. He had idolized Karen from the day she was born and knowing he had now put her life in imminent danger would be killing him. Simon stared at his beer bottle, unable to meet his wife's eyes. Trust nobody, the words echoed around his head, Trust nobody, not even me, especially not me. He now just had to hope the right people got to his daughter first.

# CHAPTER THIRTY-FOUR

The plane touched down on the small airstrip in La Reole, South West France. The pilot taxied over to the side of the runway and behind a large hanger where he cut the engines. The silence was immediate and very welcome. He pulled off his head set before unbuckling his seat belt and heading to open the cabin door.

"Just wait here for a minute, I need to make sure everything is in place for a safe exit," he instructed as he climbed out and headed for the hanger. Karen helped the twins unbuckle themselves.

"Okay you two, we need to make sure those nasty men have gone before we go back to Mummy and Daddy so we are having a little holiday here first." Looking in to their little faces, full of trust, the weight of her responsibility towards them weighed heavily on her and she was growing fonder of them by the day. Ellie looked a state, her hair was windswept and most had escaped from the hairband. Karen pulled her little hairband off and brushed her hair while they waited.

"Let's make you look like a princess sweetheart," she smiled at her as Ellie held the hairband and twisted it inside out in her hands. Writing on the band caught Karen's attention.

"What's that written in your hairband Ellie?" She squinted trying to read the small writing. Ellie glanced down at her hands.

"Oh!" she replied, "Mummy writes our phone number in my hair band in case I get lost."

"So that is Mummy and Daddy's number?"

"Yes, course it is silly."

"Let me see darling." Ellie passed the hair band to Karen and she studied the number.

"Your mummy is a clever lady Ellie, I like her."

The children didn't answer, they were too busy watching the pilot returning. He bounded up the steps and poked his head through the cabin door.

"Okay you lot, grab your bags, we have a car waiting. Be quick, I have to get out of here quickly. And Karen, good luck."

Karen nodded and looked at the smart 4x4 Duster sitting in the small car park. The doors were open and a couple in their fifties were standing and watching them exit the plane. They half walked and half jogged to the car before quickly getting into the back seat. Once they were all inside, the man turned in his seat so he could see Karen.

"Introductions in a bit Karen, let's get on the road first." They swept out onto a deserted road and headed towards the town on the hill in front of them.

The lady turned to Karen, she had a kind smile, short blonde hair and a slim figure.

"My name is Jane, this is Ted. We are really pleased to meet you. We have spoken to your father so we are fully in the picture and are glad we can help. We are leaving tomorrow so have plenty of time to show you around and how everything works." She looked at the twins, sitting silently, looking at her with solemn eyes. "Hello you two, I think you're going to enjoy it here, we have lots of fun things for you to do." She was pleased to see a small smile on their faces.

Karen smiled back at her. "Thanks so much, I am just so relieved that we are out here. Hopefully this mess will be sorted out quickly and I can get these two home. When are you back?"

"Officially we are away for six weeks, although we can be back a little sooner if necessary. We've tagged a spa break in France on to the end of our trip before coming back home. If we need to cancel this, it's no problem." Ten minutes later they turned off the main road, another fifty metres and they were outside tall, black electronic gates which swung open as Ted pushed the remote control. Karen looked at the large house in front of her before exclaiming, "Oh my gosh Jane, this looks fantastic." A collective wow came from both children sitting beside her. They jumped out of the car as Ted parked up in front of the house. Jane headed off to the side of the house calling "Come on then, I'll show you around outside before we go in, I know the children will love it."

Walking around the side of the house they could see acres of garden laid out before them complete with a beautiful lake with a little rowing boat moored up. Four stables stood empty, a testament to the previous owners love of horses but now occupied by half a dozen clucking hens. A small golf course weaved its way around the garden and a swimming pool sparkled to the rear of the house. The room which adjoined it was full of games, pool table, table tennis, darts and a fully stocked bar. Everything that they could ever need was here. The children stared at it all in wonder and giggled as they tried to hit a table tennis ball at each other, their heads not far above the edge of the table.

"Look at this you two." Jane nodded towards boxes filled with Lego, Brio, Playmobile, toys that every child loved to play with, Harry and Ellie being no exception. Leaving the children engrossed with the toys, Jane finished showing Karen around. Standing beside the house was a large garage with holiday accommodation above it.

"We've closed this while we are away," Jane explained, "so no one has booked and you will have the place to yourselves Karen."

As they returned to the front of the house, Jane went back to the games room to find the children whilst Ted picked up the bags. "Let me show you the basics inside Karen, it is all very straight forward." They did the grand tour and Karen was given written instructions for working everything from the boiler to the swimming pool pump. They finished up in the cavernous lounge which had numerous doors leading from it along with a small brick staircase leading downwards. Ted stopped here and looked at Karen, a serious look on his face.

"Now Karen, this may be an important bit for you, although I sincerely hope not."

"Sounds intriguing Ted, tell me more." She liked these two people, it was just a pity that they were involved in this big mess of hers. Ted continued, "Don't ask me why but the previous owner put in a very secure basement room and the only way in is down these stairs." He pointed to the small brick staircase. "After you." She went down and entered the large basement room. Ted followed. They could faintly hear the children playing with Jane in the games room which backed on to the basement room.

"If things do go wrong come down here with the children. Look at the door," he instructed. It appeared to be solid metal. "Close the door and pull this lever," he demonstrated. "Now you do it." Karen pushed the door shut and was surprised at how easy the door locked. "That was simple."

"Yep, and nobody will get through. You will be safe in here until help arrives, understand what I am saying?" Karen nodded, the feeling of unease again returning to her stomach.

"Yes Ted. Let's just hope that I don't need it." They walked back into the large lounge, a converted barn with the ceiling towering twenty-five feet above them. Karen looked round for a socket to plug her mobile in to recharge, it had run out of battery whilst they were on the plane over. Ted showed her one next to the sofa and then pointed to a phone by the door.

"There's the house phone, it might be better for you to use that if you need to make any calls as there will not be any trace on it as no one knows you are here. Make yourself at home, read through the handover notes I've left as we'll be leaving early tomorrow morning so if you have any questions, you need to ask them tonight." Jane came in the front door with the two children each clutching a Lego model they had constructed in the games room.

"There are squash and biscuits in the kitchen, we are just popping out for an hour, so make yourselves at home in the meantime." She and Ted climbed in the car and the gates swung shut behind them leaving the three of them together alone.

"Harry, Ellie shall we phone your mummy and daddy?" Karen's heart thumped as she spoke, "shall we tell them that you are nice and safe?"

"Yes! Yes! Yes!" they shouted in unison. Karen's hands trembled as she dialed the number from the hairband. The phone was answered after four rings.

"Hello Stephen Byfield speaking."

"Hi Stephen, my name is Karen Matthews, I have your children with me, they are safe and well. I just want to get them home to you." She started to sob as she handed the phone to the children. Tears and laughter rang out before Ellie handed the phone back to Karen. "Daddy wants to talk to you." Karen took the phone, choking back her tears.

"Hi Stephen, I am sorry that I have given you nine days of hell, I promise that I have taken care of them."

"Yes, I know Karen and I am very grateful." Karen could hear the emotion in his voice having talked to his children for the first time in over a week. He continued, "We have some people in the area who are going to bring you home safely. Don't be scared but you need to know that the Broods are looking too. Don't take any chances. Where are you exactly?"

"I am not sure to be honest, we are in between the towns of Monsegur and La Reole, it's a large house set back from the main road. We have just got here, and at the moment we are safe."

"Okay, phone me when you know the location and I will get the men out looking for you. We will get you all home safely."

"Stephen, the Broods, what are they going to do with me?" Karen gave another sob into the phone.

"Nothing," Stephen reassured her, "they won't find you."

Once Stephen had got Tanya to speak to the twins, they ended the call and an uneasy feeling swept over Karen. She once again visited the panic room, and checked and double checked the mechanism on the door.

Ted and Jane returned into the driveway and an anxious Karen looked through the glass front door to see who it was before relaxing with relief. Hearing that the Broods might also know where she was had heightened her sense of fear and anxiety. How had they possibly found out that they were in France? They seemed to be able to track her where ever she was but she was sure no one would be able to find them here in the middle of the French countryside.

“Hi Karen,” boomed Ted as Jane gathered up the twins and took them around to the pool. “Is the place still in one piece or have those terrors trashed our home already?”

Karen laughed, she didn’t have the heart or the inclination to tell him that it was potentially going to be a battle ground any time from now. There was a large splash outside followed by a shriek of laughter. Karen and Ted followed the noise.

“You little rascals,” said a very wet Jane. She was dressed in her swimwear and was climbing out of the pool.

“I was just leaning over the side of the pool wiggling my big butt and one of these two shoved me in.” She winked at Karen. “I think that I have to inspect the other side of the pool now, I’m sure I saw some stones on the bottom.” Leaning over she pretended not to notice the twins charge behind her pushing her straight back in.

Amidst the howls of laughter, Karen shivered. “Rather you than me Jane, looks a bit chilly.”

“Sixteen degrees at the moment, just a bit nippy,” she laughed. "It’s fine when you get in.”

“I’ll give it a miss. Ellie, Harry take your shorts off and jump in, tell me if it’s okay.” They didn’t waste a second and arm bands on jumped into the shallow end. They played without a care in the world for fifteen minutes before starting to shiver. Karen dried them both before wrapping them in big fluffy towels.

“I will just get you some dry clothes, don’t jump back in while I’m gone.” Before she reached the side of the house, she heard the sound of two splashes followed by Jane roaring with laughter.

“That wasn’t fair," shouted Harry. "I wasn’t looking.”

“Nor was I Aunty Jane,” shrieked Ellie, "Karen will be cross with us now for getting wet again.” Karen smiled to herself, it was so lovely to hear them having fun after the traumas they had suffered.

When she returned with the dry clothes, she spoke to Ted. "Ted, where exactly are we? I need to give the children's father our address as he has some friends who are looking for us and who will take us home when it's safe."

"It's all in the pack Karen. I have given detailed instructions given this eventuality. Have a read." She went back inside and picked up the pack. She thought that Ted was been a bit of a jobs worth by continuously telling her to read the pack but as she read it, she realized it was all there including specific instructions to locate the house. She pondered on this. If she phoned Stephen tonight it would be all over, but what would become of her? If she considered it for another day would the Broods find her first? She definitely needed a plan B. She picked up the phone again and called Stephen. He answered immediately.

"Hi Stephen, the kids are fine and playing in the pool, I have the address for you."

"Brilliant Karen, where are you?"

"I need a favour firstly. When I have handed the children over, I will become very vulnerable, both to the Broods who I don't ever want to see again, but also to the police. I need some reassurance that if I give evidence against them, I will be immune to prosecution. Can you do that?" Stephen thought for a few moments before replying.

"I can try. Come on though, this has been horrific for us too and I need the children back Karen."

"And I need my life Stephen. I haven't asked for much and I have risked my life getting them away from the Broods. If you do this for me, I will give you the address. Trust me, you won't find us otherwise, I have become very proficient in hiding."

"Bloody hell Karen! Okay, give me some time to see what I can do. Can I phone you back when I get an answer?"

"Please Stephen, I am not that simple, I will phone you in a day or two at most, we are safe here at the moment. I don't want to make too many calls as it makes it easier for anyone to trace."

Stephen knew she had the upper hand at the moment, just when he was so close to getting the children home. He had to remember that it was thanks to her the Broods no longer had them and he was no longer under their control.

"Don't take any bloody risks Karen, I will do my best to get you an answer." She hung up. This was the first time in a long time that she was calling the shots and it felt good to be in control of something at last.

They all sat in the dining room, it was seven in the evening and the British TV channel broadcast the news silently in the corner. Jane had prepared a large all in one chicken meal. Roast chicken thighs cooked in a pot with roast potatoes and veg. The homemade chicken gravy poured over it was to die for. Ted leaned back in his chair, his stomach full.

"Okay Karen, we will be going up to pack the rest of our things and get some sleep in around an hour. If there are any questions you need to ask me now." Ted was looking very calm for a man about to leave his home in the hands of a stranger.

"No, its fine, I have been through a couple of things with Jane. It all looks good. Thanks so much for everything and have a brilliant holiday. I will make sure that everything is still in one piece when you get home." She felt herself crossing her fingers as she said these last words.

# CHAPTER THIRTY-FIVE

David Brood paced the lounge; he held the phone in his hand as he worked on a plan. She is in France, in a town called Monsegur, two children in tow, how difficult can this be? He dialed the phone, "Kevin, can you come over brother, we have found where they are hiding."

Half an hour later Keven rang the intercom, "Let me in then David, I only have another couple of days out at large so let's not waste time." The gate swung open and he cruised up towards the house. David was standing at the top of the stairs holding a cold drink. Once they were inside, Kevin also with a drink in his hand, he filled him in on the latest developments.

"We have some good news Kevin, our boys have played a blinder. The girl's father told them where they are in hiding, South West France." Kevin smiled, "Crafty bitch, she would have needed help to get there, her parents I guess. Never mind, I would have done the same thing. Let's find her, take the children and get back to business. What do you want us to do with her David? It's your shout."

"Get the kids back to the UK and then skin the bitch. I'm done with her. Leave her nailed to a tree for all I care."

"So it's definitely over then between you two?"

"Shut up you silly bastard, let's have another drink and a game of snooker, we have a bit of catching up to do." They headed through the house towards the snooker room.

"Who are we sending over there to bring them back?" Kevin asked.

"I have a couple of good guys, Keith Harding is a top man, you saw him at the meeting, former SAS but he doesn't discuss that side of life. The guys who know him well say that he was a hard bastard and a good soldier. He won a shit load of medals apparently. I am also sending Bob Brooker, he's a bit of a loose cannon but utterly ruthless and I'm sure Keith will keep him in check.

"Good for him, if they bring the kids back, I will stick another medal on him, or they can both have an extra twenty grand, see what they want." Kevin laughed. "Fucking squaddies, full of military discipline and comradeship, offer them a wad of money and they would shoot their family without blinking." The balls were all in place and Kevin broke with a resounding crack, potting a red.

"When can they be there?"

"They have been booked on the overnight Portsmouth to Le Havre ferry, and will then have a seven-hour drive down. It will take a while to find them, the place is filling up with Brits on holiday but the main thing is we are in the right area. They will be in the town by five o'clock tomorrow afternoon."

"How do we get the brats back?" Kevin went for another ball and missed.

"In the car and drugged off their face, it's a night ferry and we'll have two tired kids. I have a couple of guys at Portsmouth who will make sure that the car comes off with no questions, all sorted."

"Then what?"

"Then we have Byfield for breakfast. Now shut up and let me pot some balls, everything is sorted."

Stephen, Terry, David Willard, Jon Thomlin and Daniel Reeve sat in the Bristol pub where they had hired a small room. It felt slightly ironic to Stephen that the last time he had been in a pub meeting room he had been offered heroin and had agreed to be a drug dealer.

"Okay," he started, "what do we know?" Jon answered him.

"Well, it's good and bad news, Ellie and Harry are safe at the moment. They are staying with the girl in a small town named Monsegur in South West France. Myself and Dan are flying down there from Bristol tonight and we are meeting up with a guy who I know from the area. We will be in Monsegur at around one o'clock tomorrow morning." Stephen nodded before adding "I'm glad to say that the girl, Karen, phoned me today and I chatted to them both briefly, they seem in good spirits considering what they have been through. However, Karen wants an amnesty from prosecution, I'm waiting for a police response and when I have it, she will give me the address." Terry frowned.

"That's great news Stephen but we haven't got time for her to play games with us. The problem is that Karen's father has told the Broods that they are all in Monsegur so their guys are also hot footing it down there as we speak. They will be driving as they will need to bring the children back without anyone seeing. Difficult to do unless they have a private plane and a pilot who is willing to smuggle kids." Stephen stared at him, "Why would Karen's father tell them where she is?"

"They tricked the information out of him. Good news is that we think that they are staying somewhere outside of Monsegur and it's very rural around there. This is why we can't run straight in and save the day. We don't know where the house is, but neither do the Broods. Karen's father did not want to know further details just in case of these exact events."

"So, what are our plans now then? We need to make sure we get there before they do or we're right back to square one." Stephen's feeling of anxiety was once again growing. Jon continued with the plan. "Fly down, check out the area, find out if any children have moved into the area, a somewhat difficult task given the numbers of Brits on holiday and check out the local shops and supermarkets as they will need to shop. We are meeting up with Tony Hughes, my contact on the ground, later tomorrow. He is doing some groundwork for us. I am also speaking to Karen's father on the phone in a moment as he may know something else that will help us. In fact, let me go and call him now and I'll be right back."

He left the room, returning a few minutes later. "Okay, that was a difficult conversation, he feels an idiot having blabbed to the wrong people but he did speak with me after I had established my identity. The place is around five kilometers outside the town, he knows that it has a pool and a fishing lake but that's about the limit of his knowledge. Lots of places have lakes and pools around there, so we are still pretty much looking for a needle in a haystack."

"Ok and then what?" Stephen's frustration was growing making him curt with those who were there helping him. Jon understood the strain he was under and calmly replied. "We will have to evaluate a plan on the ground, don't forget that we will not be the only show in town."

David Willard then placed his briefcase onto the table before opening it and pulling out some notes. "Okay, this is what I have managed to get together, two of the Brood gang are heading to France by car ferry this evening, we believe it's from Portsmouth. The men travelling are known to us. The one of the most importance to us is Bob Brooker, he is an arms smuggler, extremely violent and a ruthless killer. He is going for one reason I am afraid, if Karen is found she will be dead within minutes. We suspect that the car that they are travelling in may conceal weapons."

"So why don't you stop them now?" Stephen asked.

"If we stopped them, we could blow another operation and the source of our intelligence will be uncovered."

"And meanwhile my children are at risk." Stephen glared at him.

Willard returned his stare. "National security is at risk, your children will not be harmed in France. Karen will possibly die and I can't stop that I am afraid. They flew into the area by private aircraft this morning and they are safe for the moment. We will find them and this will be helped by you getting their address out of the girl Stephen."

Jon and Dan stood and picked up their rucksacks. "We have to go chaps, we will do our very best Stephen."

"I know you will, thanks guys, good luck and please bring them home safely." Stephen shook hands with them both before they left the room. The door closed and silence reigned. Stephen looked at Terry.

"It's all out of our hands Terry, we are trusting your guys to get this sorted and I know they are some of the best."

"Stephen, I am doing all I can within MI5," David added, "I can't tell you everything but please trust me that things are moving forward."

"Thanks David, sorry for sounding ungrateful, I know that you understand how stressful this is and I really appreciate all you are doing."

"Stephen, stay strong and don't do anything else that the Broods ask, they are not running this show anymore." He picked up his bag and made his way out into the Bristol nightlife.

After dropping Terry off, Stephen drove back home. He looked at the clock on the dashboard, just past midnight. The guys would be in Bordeaux now, possibly driving down towards the children. He swung into the driveway, all the lights seemed to be on and Tanya and Chris sat in the lounge half watching nonsense TV.

Tanya looked up as he walked in. "I had hoped that you would phone Stephen, given that our children are in danger." She was very prickly, and Chris got up and headed for the kitchen.

"Can I make a drink for anyone?"

"Cold one for me Dad," Stephen replied, sitting down next to Tanya and drawing her into a hug. "I don't trust the phones at the moment darling and I hoped that I could tell you everything together." Tanya hugged him back, their stress was shared and neither wanted to upset the other. Chris came back in with a couple of cold beers and a wine and Stephen settled back to tell them everything that was going on.

"Okay, this is what I know at the moment," and he repeated every detail, remembering everything as if it had only been said a second ago.

# CHAPTER THIRTY-SIX

The plane touched down at Bordeaux, a small terminal annexed to the main airport which seemed to deal exclusively with budget flights, no frills but good prices and plenty of flights in and out. Clearing customs, they walked out into the large car park area where the car rental huts were illuminated in front of them. They quickly found Avis and picked up the silver Renault, a car which would blend into invisibility in the French countryside. Pulling out through the security barrier they joined the motorway circling the city, no traffic and a beautiful clear warm evening.

The satnav took them onto the Toulouse motorway and told them that in fifty minutes they would be in Monsegur. Passing the first automatic toll booth they cruised through the countryside, very similar to that in England if you discounted the numerous vineyards stretching out in every direction. Every now and then, these were interspersed with fields of sunflowers which, had it been daylight they could have appreciated, and had they not been on their way to save a woman and two children from certain death. They sat in silence, each considering the job they had in front of them. They were booked into a bed and breakfast a couple of kilometres outside the town, their story a couple of guys looking at property in the area.

The car ate up the miles on the near empty motorway and the exit they needed soon came into view. As they turned onto the smaller country roads, Monsegur was signed as fifteen kilometres away and they were ready for a drink and a rest. As they drove towards the town, they passed a large house in the darkness, it had a lake, swimming pool and two sleeping children and a young woman inside. Fifty meters from the people they were looking for and they had no idea.

The American voice on satnav guided them past a religious statue standing guard on the side of the road and then down a bumpy farm track. The house sat in splendid isolation at the end of the track and a single light shone from the kitchen window. As they drew to a stop, Dan saw a figure stand and soon the door opened to reveal his contact in the area, Tony Hughes. He shook hands with both men as he spoke.

“Good to see you both, come on inside and I’ll fill you in on what I’ve been finding out. We have the place to ourselves, the owners live in that annex,” he pointed to a small building to the rear. They followed him inside and into the large open plan living area.

“I have your keys and the other equipment, I thought that we would check it through in the morning before we set off.” Jon looked around the place, getting his bearings and a feel for the place before replying.

“Good idea, but I want a weapon in my room and so should you two. These guys are on their way and they’re as good as we are. Let’s not get caught with our pants down.” Dan nodded in agreement as he moved across the room to look out through the windows to check out the back of the house. Tony was a good mate but didn’t have their training so he was leaving nothing to chance.

“Whatever you want mate.” Tony agreed, “I have been doing some checks. The only hotel in Monsegur has a booking for the next few days, two guys from the UK on business apparently. The hotel is in the small market square and it’s not the kind of place where any secrets can be kept. The locals in the bar on the square were chatting about it, they thought it was a strange booking for this area, it’s usually all tourists around here. They must be our people. As for you guys, I’ve mentioned that you are looking for a property for renovation so are keen to ask questions about the area and who lives here. I thought that might help cover us when we start asking around.” They talked for a while longer going over their plans before Jon yawned and looked at his watch.

"Good work Tony, now let's get the hardware so we can get some kip. Up at eight for breakfast before getting a day's start on our friends. Hopefully we'll find our targets before they even get here."

The announcement on the ferry woke up the sleeping men, they had booked into an overnight cabin for the crossing. Le Havre was sitting twenty minutes across the spring light as they gathered their belongings together silently, both focused on what was ahead of them. Both men were hardened professionals and in any other circumstances they would not have liked each other, both far too single minded, too ruthless, too heartless. Neither had any family to speak of in the UK, no real friends, no one that they would trust except with some covering fire in a battle. They were there with two aims, find the children and kill the woman, end of story.

They strolled down the deck to find their car, an eight-seater people carrier, the sort that seemed to flood the decks of the boat, the type of car that you wouldn't look at twice, functional rather than sexy.

Driving through the port they found the road heading out of the city, and turning right they soon crossed the bridge leading towards the motorway system. Keith Harding focusing on driving on the right, looked over at Bob Brooker.

"If we keep out of traffic, we should be there in around six hours, we will need to stop for fuel and food on the way down but from this moment we do not leave the car unattended. If the weapons are found we are screwed."

"Keith, I know, I've been moving weapons around the world for years. Let's get down there and sort our shit out. We need to get out onto the ground and find where they may be. We don't need to be too subtle as I doubt she has told anyone that they are in hiding. She is unprotected and they'll need to shop, go to local markets, and other things so we just need to keep our eyes open."

"Agreed, how's your French?"

"Pretty good, I've spent time in Africa, they speak a lot of French there so I can get by."

"Same as. I'm going to stop around an hour from the town, we need to get the equipment out of the bodywork and I don't know what privacy we will have around the town. I have the medication for the kids as well, we need to get that in a fridge asap. The cool box can only do the job for so long."

Two thirty in the afternoon in a sunny market square in Monsegur saw the car park up opposite the hotel. It was a peaceful sight, a small group of locals sitting outside the bar drinking cold beers didn't give Keith and Bob a second glance. British tourists were two a penny around here. They took the bags out of the boot and checked into the typically French establishment. A small sign on the wall declaring 'L'hotel de Monsegur' was the only clue that it was a hotel. They booked in and found their rooms which were on opposite sides of the corridor, Keith had the view over the market square while Bob looked over the back of the small town. In any other circumstances this would have been a very relaxing place to stay but these two had work to do.

"Right, weapon and equipment check in my room in five Bob," Keith instructed as he closed his door and unpacked his small bag. He felt grubby after the long journey so quickly jumped in the shower and two minutes later, he was dressed in a smart white collared polo shirt and blue jeans. There was a knock at the door, and keeping the chain on, he opened it a couple inches. Seeing it was Bob he took the chain off and opened the door fully.

The weapons were laid inside the top drawer of the chest by the window. They were not heavily armed, two handguns, fifty rounds of ammo, a knife, kidnap kit of ropes, tape and plastic hand ties. The sleeping medication needed to knock the kids out for the ferry trip was safely stored in the minibar fridge. They were to be tied and gagged for the trip and once in Le Havre they would be knocked out, with a second dose being administered before arriving back at Portsmouth. In spite of the weapons, they were not expecting a fire fight, they just wanted to put the house under surveillance, grab the kids, kill the woman and get out.

Bob's eyes lit up inspecting the drawer. "That's what I'm talking about." He took the large hunting knife and felt the blade. "Brood wants her skinning and I'm going to do just that. We need to film it for evidence. There is a nice bonus for this one Keith."

"That's for you mate, you do what you need to, I couldn't give a shit about what you do. If it were me, I would just kill her quickly, I'm not into this skinning her alive bollocks." Bob laughed, "There lies the difference between us, for you this is just a job, for me this is a hobby that I enjoy." Keith looked at him, he didn't like this cavalier attitude to work, he was professional in everything he did and it worried him that he was with a psychopath rather than a soldier. Sometimes soldiers of fortune crossed the line and never found their way back. He made a note to not work with this guy again but in the meantime would do his best to keep things running smoothly.

"Bob, let's just get the job done and get back. I'm going out to have a look around, see what is going on in the local area this week. The market is on Friday and that could be our best bet for catching sight of them. Tomorrow morning we're meeting up with an old friend of Kevin Brood's, apparently this man was well connected in the sixties and seventies, he ran around with the Krays and Co in East London. His old man ran a pub that was well used and he followed in his footsteps. Kevin met up with him in jail years ago and trusts the guy. He is around ten minutes outside the town and might be able to offer some insight in to where to find people around here." Bob shrugged and headed for the door,

"I'm going to go and sit in the bar and see what gossip I can pick up....join me for a beer when you've finished filling your diary."

Keith left the room and walked out into the sunshine wishing that this job was already over. He had a bad feeling in his stomach, this job felt wrong as it had an air of revenge instead of just getting a job done. Maybe it was because he was tired and he hoped that it would pass. Whatever happened, the Broods needed to know that Bob Brooker had the potential to be a loose cannon.

The town looked pleasant, the shops and bars sat around a market square which was a covered area used on Friday mornings for markets where the local farmers sold everything from eggs and local honey to pottery and candles. There were four bars covering a few hundred square metres which was not a bad ratio. He entered one called the Sports Bar Cafe, which he hoped would be showing football or some other sporting event. He looked around at the battered chairs and tables to find not a TV screen in sight, nor was there any reference to any sport, not even a dart board. As he had no wish to spend any more time than necessary with Bob, he ordered a small beer and took it outside to watch the locals walk by. Some Brits were wandering around but not too many and the bar owner spoke no English at all which was a promising start. Maybe when this madness was over, he would sell up and move into an area like this. It had apparently worked for Ronnie Moore, Brood's mate. Keith was looking forward to seeing this old-time gangster from ancient history. His mind pondered as to what he would look like. He had seen plenty of the old school coming over to see Kevin or David in their pub in Kent, they still dressed smartly but were clearly a spent force, mostly in their late seventies or early eighties. They had paid their dues through countless prison sentences and were living on memories of violence that they could no longer deliver. He suspected that this Ronnie would be the same, drinking too much, smoking too much, talking too much of better times. It didn't really matter so long as he could help locate the kids and as a mate of Kevin Brood, he would humour him anyway.

The following morning, they drove over in bright sunshine to Ronnie's address through the countryside which lived up to its promise of green vines, yellow sunflowers and orchards of plum trees. Bob checked some written directions that they had been given before leaving the UK.

"We need to turn right before we get to the bridge and head towards the mayor's office. He lives in the fourth house on the left, a white house with blue shutters."

They both spotted the white house and pulled up outside. A selection of rowing and small motor boats sat in a large driveway and the house was typically French with all doors and windows wide open and not a hint of security. An old black lab came out to see who they were as a cat scuttled through the kitchen door. Keith knocked on the open door.

"Hello, Ronnie, anyone at home?" There was no answer and they then saw a bell mounted on the wall by the door and gave it a ring. An upstairs window flew open and a half-dressed man stuck his head out.

"Two minutes boys." He popped his head back in and reappeared in the kitchen a few seconds later.

"I wasn't expecting you until later this morning so I was just having a workout," he explained as they all shook hands. The guy was approximately seventy to seventy-five, average height and in great shape for a man of his age. He could see the surprise in their faces and grinning, invited them to come up and visit his office. The three of them went up and standing in the doorway to a fully equipped gym, looked at the array of machines and weights scattered around. It would have put most leisure centres to shame. Keith gave a whistle, "Bloody hell mate, you obviously wear the trousers around here. How do you get away with having all this stuff?" Ronnie laughed, "What can I say, she likes her old man looking good! Shall we go down and have a drink? Coffee or a beer lads, while the missis is out shopping?"

"Cold beer would be great," replied Bob.

"I will have a coffee Ronnie, so will he. We are working." Keith looked pointedly at Bob. Bob shot him a glare back but said nothing.

"Coffee all round then boys."

Bob sat at the kitchen bar silently sulking about his put down. He had things on his mind and not all of them were nice thoughts. He didn't like Keith and he knew the feeling was mutual. Keith was having his own worrying thoughts as they sat talking with Ronnie. He suspected that Bob wanted to be running this operation and the truth was that although he came with a good reputation, serious doubts were creeping into Keith's mind about his suitability and professionalism. He would need to warn David at the earliest opportunity. This was to come sooner than he thought as his phone rang. He saw the caller was David Brood.

"Hi David, how are things at home?" he greeted him as he left the kitchen and walked outside to take the call without being overheard.

"It has gone a bit cold over here Keith, we need you to warm us up with some good news."

"We're just at Ronnie's place, he sends his best to you all."

David laughed. "He's a good lad Keith, done a lot in his time and is still handy to know. Hopefully he will have some good contacts but I bet he can't speak a word of French. How's Bob doing? I was not sure about him at all but I was waiting for you to get to know him a bit before asking."

"Fucking liability David, he wants to run the show and sulks when I put him in his place. This will be the last time I work with him, he's a typical wannabe gangster and trigger happy from what I can see."

"Put me on to Ronnie for a second Keith and I'll need to talk with you again when I am done with him." Keith walked back inside and handed the phone over and watched as Ronnie listened. Eventually he passed the phone back to Keith and David gave further instructions.

"Keith, I am sending someone else out to help you, have you got any hardware on you?"

"Yes, of course."

"Take that little fuckers brains out. Ronnie will sort the mess out. Your new guy will fly in, should be there around five." With that he rang off.

Keith put the phone back in his pocket and looked at Ronnie, he noticed Ronnie was smiling and it gave him an idea involving no mess.

"Ronnie show us your weights again. I want to see how much weight Bob can bench press."

Bob laughed at the thought of showing off his strength to these tossers who thought they were better than him. "I'm in, load me up Ronnie. I want to do a one-twenty-five kilo bench but let me warm up first." Once back up in the gym, he lay on the bench while they put sixty kilos on the bar for the first warm up.

"Too easy boys, put on some more, I could do this smoking a fucking cigar," Bob bragged. They loaded the bar to eighty kilos then a hundred kilos and he was lifting it easily.

"Okay, one-twenty-five then boys, let's get this done," he ordered. Loading the weights onto each side of the bar, they looked at each other and nodded before lifting it into Bob's hands, still taking the weight.

"Ready mate?" Ronnie asked. "My bar," Bob replied. They let go of the bar and the one-eighty kilos pushed down towards Bob's neck as he tried to hold the weight. "Take the bar, take the bar," he panted at them in panic.

The two men watched as the Olympic bar sank onto his neck, he kicked his legs for a few seconds before going limp, the life crushed out of him. Keith looked at the body dispassionately.

"There you go Ronnie, and no mess to go with it." He emptied Bob's pockets and removed his gun from a side holster.

"You are a smart bastard Keith," Ronnie smiled. "Leave the rest to me, I didn't care for that man too much, bit of a loudmouth."

"Cheers Ronnie and can you ask around the area about this woman and kids? They're staying somewhere local so someone must know where they are."

Ronnie nodded 'The mayor will know something mate, I will ask him when I see him this afternoon, we're going out fishing. I don't speak a fucking word of French but he is okay with the English. I will phone you this evening, good luck with the new guy." They returned to Keith's car, leaving the body of the dead man up in the gym. Keith drove back to his hotel, wondering who Brood would be sending him. It needed to be someone who could toe the party line or Ronnie's river would be filling up with bodies.

Back at the hotel later that afternoon, there was a tap on Keith's door. He checked his watch, almost six pm, and checking the safety chain was cross the door, he opened it to see a woman standing outside. He was surprised to see it was Sandra Brook. Swinging the door open he greeted her 'Sandra what the hell are you doing here? Has David sent you as the replacement?"

"He sure has," she replied strolling into the room. "Firstly, I am the only person who he trusts enough to come out here and secondly, it is felt that if we are going to bring two sleeping children back to the UK a family set up looks better to the authorities." Keith wasn't sure what to think about this turn of events, would she give him the backup he might need?

"Good thinking, however if the shit hits the fan can you handle yourself?"

"Yes sweetheart. I can use a gun as well as the best of them, and I will be able to get a lot closer to the target than you ever could. Just trust me," she reassured him.

"I do Sandra, have a seat and I will give you a briefing."

"Is that what you boys call it now?" she asked him suggestively as she sat on the edge of his bed. "Well hurry up and get it over with, I am starving and you, my friend are buying dinner." Keith's phone rang, it was Ronnie.

"I've disposed of the rubbish you left here, and I've had a good chat with our mayor and we have two options. One is a place in a small village called La Violette where there is a holiday home which has just reopened. It looks as though a family have moved in and the locals haven't seen them before. The second is a larger place near a small village named Roquebrune. The owners have gone away for a while and a family are house sitting. He thinks that they have small children, it is not much but at least it is a start, I have texted you both addresses."

"Cheers Ronnie, we will check one out tonight and the other

tomorrow night. Take care mate and keep your ears open."

Keith climbed out of the car, it was a bright moonlit night which aided his vision but also meant he could be easily seen if not careful. He checked his watch, it was just after ten and hopefully the inhabitants of the house would have closed up for the night. He had already driven around the area during the afternoon and had quickly found the address, a large house with a sizable garden. It looked as though they had a lake at the bottom of an overgrown field but he couldn't be sure. It was perfect for snooping around after dark, they didn't seem to have dogs and the house was only overlooked by a farm to the back. He knew that these hard-working farmers were not party animals; they worked on the vineyards all day and would be dog tired come the evening.

He hopped over a low fence into the field and found himself knee deep in grass, the wetness from the coming dew soaking the legs of his jeans but it made no difference, he didn't seem to notice as he was in work mode and a small discomfort such as that meant nothing. He pulled a night sight from his leg pocket and surveyed the garden. It was clear apart from some children's toys scattered at the side of the house. Downstairs lights were on and someone was moving around. He climbed a larger second fence and found himself at the edge of the garden which surrounded the house. The tree line to his right looked as though it may be circling a lake and the frog chorus that was coming from that direction backed up the theory. He made his way down hugging the trees that formed the boundary. The tree line led him down to the lake where an old rowing boat sat tied to a post beside an area that had been cleared for fishing. Wild boar poked around somewhere in the distance and the sound of deer calling in the woods echoed into the night sky.

Having surveyed the boundary at this end of the garden and seen there were no other exits, he walked up to the house staying in the shadows. The smell of a BBQ was still in the air as he spotted the uncovered grill. The family had obviously had a drink and hadn't bothered to clear up leaving empty bottles of fizz littering the patio. It didn't look like the scene he had expected to see. He was anticipating seeing something lower key for a girl alone with two kids. He settled down behind a covering of bushes. From this vantage point he could see into the kitchen area and with a little more effort he could see the front door. This was a routine to which he had become accustomed, only he usually had a partner when on surveillance. The demise of Bob and the arrival of Sandra had ensured that this time, he would be flying solo. Sandra may be a brilliant operative, but she had never set up an OP and now wasn't the time to learn the craft.

Anyway, there was no imminent threat of compromise, there were no dogs, no threat of harm and if he was discovered he could just simply run away and get in the car. They would just think he was a snooper. He checked the area again. An SUV of some description sat in the large driveway and an occasional car passed by the front gates but nothing to cause concern. He placed his hand gun beside him within easy reach settling down for what could be a long wait. As soon as he could identify that Karen was in the house, he would wait for her to go to sleep before taking any further action.

Once he was sure that everyone was in a deep sleep he would sneak into the house and find which bedrooms they were using. The next day he would formulate a plan to take the children. Although he didn't like it, taking Karen alive was going to be impossible. He would shoot her ensuring that it was a quick kill. He respected what she had done and also had a grudging respect for the way in which she had evaded his search for her in the UK. Most people would have messed up and compromised themselves long ago. She had stayed in front of the chasing pack for almost two weeks, which was not a bad effort.

Movement caught his eye in the kitchen, a young woman came in and opened the fridge taking out a bowl of food. Keith guessed it was left over from the earlier BBQ. She also grabbed a can of drink, just one can which suggested that she may be sitting alone. He waited another forty minutes before she came back into the kitchen, and he peered through his night scope. He couldn't be sure if it was Karen, she was certainly in the right age group and had blond hair. He just couldn't be a hundred percent from this distance.

The lights were turned off and frustration crept in. If only he had positively identified her, it could have soon been over for the night. As it was, he would now have to wait until the morning to look at her again, unless she had left some ID out in the house that he could see when he was poking around later. He worked on the premise that people were in a deep sleep after around forty-five minutes and after this he would be in.

His waiting time up and no further activity seen, he approached a side window which hadn't looked secure during his initial observations. However, he had no need to worry as on checking the rear door to the house as he passed it, he found that it was unlocked. He smiled to himself thinking how easy his job was in rural France where people let their guard down. Slipping quietly inside, he moved across the stone kitchen floor looking out for dog bowls or anything to trip him up. Again, as he suspected, nothing.

He moved through into the large lounge, and checking his watch, saw it was approaching two o'clock and unlikely that anyone would be disturbing him. A handbag sat on the top of a welsh dresser, hopefully holding the clue he was looking for. He took it back into the kitchen and taking out his small pen torch, he opened the bag hitting the jackpot and finding her passport sitting at the top.

A British passport that looked well used. He opened the page and looked at the face of an attractive young blond woman. Samantha Geddes, Hatfield, Yorkshire. Wrong woman, wrong fucking house.

He placed the passport back into the bag and returned it to its place although he doubted that she would have known where it was in the first place. Gently opening the door, he stepped back into the early morning chill and headed back to his car and back to his room for some sleep. The place in Roquebrune would be his target for the following night and in the meantime, he and Sandra would spend the day finding any other leads there may be to finding their target.

# CHAPTER THIRTY-SEVEN

Stephen sat in his lounge, it had been twenty four hours since he had asked David Willard to speak to the CPS about immunity for Karen and he wasn't able to relax as he worked out every scenario in his head. Terry, Jo, Chris and Tanya sat in the lounge with him. Terry was in direct contact with Dan out in France who was in the process of staking out a house in the area. They were waiting for the CPS to get the paperwork in order so they could confirm with Karen that the house was the correct one. Once this was confirmed, he would go in and extract the kids. If Karen was to be given immunity, they would get her out as well, if not the French police would need to arrest her and then they would have to start the process of getting her back too. Tanya seemed to be making endless drinks, anything to keep herself busy as she flitted between emotions. Relief knowing that the twins were alive and the incredible stress of knowing it could all still go so wrong.

The phone rang and everyone looked at it before Stephen answered, he listened for a minute before just saying "Okay, many thanks," and cutting the call.

Tanya was pacing, 'What is going on Stephen, is it on?"

"Looks like it, David is getting the paperwork sent to us. By the time Karen phones we will be good to go."

"What time is that happening?"

"Tomorrow night I guess, that was the deadline she set."

"Fuck the deadline, you should have just got the number," Tanya told him, her anxiety making her snap at him.

"Well she wouldn't give it, so we have another few hours to wait. I have to be at work in the morning anyway, don't forget I am supposed to be delivering what they believe are the drugs, we still have that business to finish."

"Do you have to go in?" Tanya was irritated until Terry spoke.

"We need to close this part of the circle Tanya, we have to end what they started with Stephen." Tanya sighed, "I suppose so, it's just that even a minute longer without the children is too much." She walked over to Stephen and hugged him, "I'm sorry," she whispered.

The next morning, Stephen showered and dressed as he anticipated ending this saga. He picked up his sports bag which he had now filled with two very large bags of white powder. Tanya's pantry was once again depleted, but this time, of her very finest self-raising flour. There was no way he was going to let whoever was involved in the prison get away with it and so had to go ahead with a planned drop. He smiled to himself as he looked at the bag, he guessed that no other Governor in charge of a prison would be planning a half million-pound drug drop that day. He got into his car and sped off, half excited about the next few hours, and not being able to keep his mind from the fact that he could have the children back soon.

He reached the prison gates and parked in his designated space. Opening the boot, he grabbed the sports bag and walked through the gates and through security with no one giving him a second glance. He strolled directly to the gym and placed the two bags of powder into the dirty kit bin as instructed. He then left and went to the CCTV room where he was met by his security manager and a police sergeant. As they had agreed earlier, it appeared that Stephen had done all exactly as demanded of him by the Broods. They watched for five minutes before the gymnasium door opened. The gym manager, a young man selected for future development by Stephen personally, walked towards the bin. Stephen's heart was in his mouth. He liked this guy, and subconsciously prayed that it wasn't him. The manager walked past and started a cardio circuit leaving those watching the CCTV to breathe a sigh of relief.

The gym door opened again and this time it was the drug dog handler Simon Jacks. It was his job to search the prisoner areas before classes began for the afternoon sessions, so they didn't think there was anything suspicious about him being there. However, when he went directly to the bin and retrieved the packages, they knew they had their man. *You dirty corrupt bastard* ,Stephen thought to himself as they turned their focus to the cameras covering the corridors and wings. Jacks headed onto C Wing and up onto the 4's landing towards the cell of a known drug dealer from Liverpool. He quickly entered the cell and passed the package to the prisoner inside, all captured on the CCTV and discreet cameras.

Three security staff grabbed him as he left the wing and escorted him down to the Governor's office where Stephen and the police sergeant were waiting. The Sergeant wasted no time in letting him know what they were all there for.

"Simon Jacks, you are under arrest for the intent to distribute class A drugs to another person. You do not have to say anything, but it may harm your defence if you do not mention, when questioned, something which you later rely on in court. Anything you do say may be given in evidence."

Stephen said nothing, he just stared at Jacks who stared back at Stephen and shrugged his shoulders before trying to justify himself.

"They have been playing with you for weeks, the same way as they have messed my life up. I only did what you did and gave into the pressure."

"The thing is, Jacks I didn't give in. I did the right thing and reported it as you had the opportunity to do too." Stephen nodded to the sergeant who handcuffed Jacks before taking him away. He was led outside in the full gaze of the staff still coming on duty for the late shifts. In time he would be given twelve years in prison for his part in the Broods criminal enterprise. The trail of physical and electronic evidence was damning against him, and it would appear that he had been in the Brood's pocket for a while. That also explained why the drug dog was busy playing catch when Stephen entered the prison with a suspect package on the first occasion. Everything had been stage managed by the Broods.

Stephen reported the day's activities back to his DDC. It was a good operation all round but how different this could have turned out if it were not for Karen Matthews. Driving home he put on the ACDC CD full belt. The balance was swaying more in his favour and he was gaining back control.

At the same time David Brood's phone rang.

"Boss we have just lost all the gear meant for the prison. Jacks was nicked passing it to our man. Looks like a set up." David was livid, it looked like Stephen Byfield might know they no longer had his kids to threaten him with.

"Half a million wasted, what do you mean a set up? Get your arse to the club and explain to me what a lost half a million looks like. You were in charge of this one and it seems like you've messed it up big time. Don't keep me waiting." David ended the call and phoned Kevin instantly.

"I know that you've got to be back inside shortly Kevin, but we have had a little problem. That fucking idiot dog handler has been caught and we have lost half a fucking million pounds worth of stuff. The idiot in charge of the deal is on his way to the club to explain himself. Have you got time to meet him?"
Kevin wasted no time in asking for details, he knew he would hear those soon enough.

"Sure, are you coming?"

"Fucking right I am."

The club was shut and the young bar manager was restocking and auditing the store room when she saw David and Kevin walk in. The look on their faces were not a 'Good afternoon darling' sight. David looked over at her. "When that fucking idiot Bryan Cripps comes in, send him directly to the office. We are not to be disturbed."

"Yes sir." She carried on with her cleaning knowing better than to ask any questions. They sat and waited for another ten minutes before there was a knock at the office door. Bryan Cripps entered, hardly daring to look at the brothers, the sound of his own breathing competing loudly with the beat of his heart in his ears. Kevin got straight to the point.

"You have lost us half a mill Bryan. You have come here knowing that I am going to have you killed haven't you?"

"Yeah, cause I know that I am fucked, so what's the point in running?" The brothers smiled. Bryan had been a trusted soldier for them for over four years, never once letting them down.

"You've got bollocks Bryan, most people would have run and for that reason, I am going to let you pay off the debt."

"Are you serious boss? How am I going to do that?"

"Dead serious Bryan. Go and find Stephen Byfield and his wife and kill them both and the debt will be paid in full."

"When do you want it done by?"

"Yesterday. Now fuck off and do it or you most definitely will be next." David threw a package to him. "All the details that you require are in here. Get the job done this time, no excuses."

Bryan left a lot quicker than he had arrived. He sat in his car and looked at the large padded envelope. The weight told him that there was a gun inside. He quickly hid this under the car seat and put the Byfield's address into satnav. He would be there in two hours with a good drive. He took two deep breaths and headed off to plan how to pay his debt.

# CHAPTER THIRTY-EIGHT

Stephen arrived back home to find everyone still there, waiting for him. It reminded him of a maternity unit, everyone expectant, waiting for news. He hoped the result would be the same, the children delivered safely. He was quick to fill Terry in on what had gone on in the prison.

"That went so well Terry, we caught the bastard red handed. It was Simon Jacks, the dog handler and he's now in the process of being charged. When they searched his house, they found drugs, phones and bank accounts. They said it was a treasure trove of evidence so I hope some of it ties directly back to the Broods." Terry nodded, "Well done mate, I'm glad that's out the way, although now, the shit will really hit the fan."

"So now they know for sure that the drugs have gone Stephen," Chris was sipping another coffee as he spoke, "what do you think the reaction will be?"

"I think that I have become expendable. They will try killing me at the first opportunity I guess." He looked at the others, he didn't see much fear in their eyes, only a strong determination that comes when your choices were down to living or dying.

"Yeah that's what I was thinking as well," Chris took another sip of his coffee, "just that I think with the speed of events, that opportunity could be right now."

Jo looked up, 'You think so Chris? Do you think that they could be on their way here as we speak?"

Terry chipped in, "I would put money on it, about half a million in fact. Their world has started to crumble and they need to get back on top before they are finished."

They sat together for the next hour, planning how they were going to ensure they were all safe from any potential threat before Terry sat back in his chair. "We have limited choices and we are all in agreement that we are going to have to fight pretty soon, but we also need to eat. If we don't take the opportunity to eat, drink and rest we will be beaten before the battle starts and I for one am starving." Tanya stood up and going to the sideboard, opened a drawer and pulled out a pizza menu.

"This place is good, anyone mind having a pizza? It's quick and simple and they normally deliver in around half an hour." Everyone nodded their agreement and she phoned through their order before they continued to discuss how they could protect the house and protect themselves. Terry with his military background took the lead on this.

"Firstly, let's do the basics, lock every external door of the house and make sure all downstairs doors are secure as we are going to camp out upstairs for tonight. I don't want anyone moving around down here without us hearing them. Also, close every curtain to stop them watching us. If there is anyone out there, I don't want them knowing who we have in here. Secondly, I want us all armed, get whatever you think you can use. What have you got in your garden shed Stephen? Garden forks are a decent weapon, kitchen knives are good for closer quarters. Anyone have anything else useful?" Stephen looked over at Chris, "What about your old shotgun? Have you still got it?" Chris stood up and headed for the door, "yup, not sure if it still fires but I'll go and get it." They all dispersed to various parts of the house and garden gathering anything that could be used as a weapon before all meeting back in the kitchen and laying everything out on the table.

"Okay, all doors locked and no one to go outside again tonight, no matter what the reason." Terry looked at the others as they nodded. Let's go back in the lounge and wait for the pizzas. Me and Stephen will take first watch until 02.00, then Chris and Tanya until 00.40 then me and Jo until 06.00 then we reassess the situation. Again, they all nodded and headed back into the lounge before Terry continued. "We will use the main bedroom as a base because that means that if we are attacked, they will have to come up one at a time and the pitchfork will slow them down a bit. If it looks like they are going to overrun us, we all attack at the same time and overwhelm them."

Tanya checked her watch and saw it was already seven thirty. "They're a bit slow today with the delivery, it's been nearly forty-five minutes since I called them. I'll phone them again."

She disappeared into the kitchen to phone in peace and they had just told her the delivery should be with them shortly when Jo walked in. Tanya smiled at her friend, they had been through so much together in the past year and she could see the anxiety on her face.

"Are you ok Jo?"

"Not too good, probably about the same as you, very scared about these threats. It just brings things back to me, being taken by that awful man last year, I can't go through that again." Jo came and stood in front of Tanya, looking into her pale face, "But how selfish am I, here's you with your children missing and your husband with his life in danger, yet again. You must think I'm awful worrying about how I'm feeling with all this going on."

Tanya hugged her. "Don't be silly, we're in this together, as we have been throughout everything. We are here for each other and once this is over, we can all try and get back on with our lives which I hope will be forever more boring and uneventful." They both laughed at this and gave each other one last hug. Terry limped in. "What are you two whispering about? What's happening with the pizza Tanya, I'm bloody starving."

"They say that he should have been here by now," Tanya replied at the same time as there was a knock on the front door. She walked out into the hallway, followed by Terry and looked though the security hole in the front door.

"That must be him, there is a guy with a pizza bag, but he's come in his own car and not on a scooter, how odd." She opened the door before Terry could stop her and picked up her purse as the world drifted into slow motion. She looked up into the delivery guys eyes and knew it was all wrong as the adrenaline filled look cut through her. The anticipation as hunter meets the quarry was tangible, they could smell and taste the electricity that flowed through the door as slow motion became a blur. She was pushed back so hard that she fell and smashed her head on the wall behind her. The Pizza bag was thrown onto the stairs as the man pulled a gun from his waist band. The others, hearing the disturbance, ran to the lounge door and froze. The gun was two inches from Tanya's face as pizza guy turned to them.

"Back away all of you. Stephen Byfield, you are a dead man." He took one pace back and leveled the gun at Stephen. "The rest of you sit down, or you will die where you drop." Before he had the chance to utter another word the kitchen door flew open and Jo unloaded two barrels of the shotgun directly into his chest. Her face partially hidden behind gun smoke, ears ringing and dazed senses trying to calculate what had happened, she lowered the gun barrel to the floor.

"That's for my husband, you filthy bastard," her voice shook as she looked at the man who had slumped dead onto the hallway floor, blood oozing out from the gaping wound in his chest. She dropped the gun and fell onto her knees sobbing as Terry turned and crouched down next to her, wrapping his arms around her. The house became silent, with the haze of gun smoke and the familiar smell of cordite that Terry had lived with during his service days. Ears ringing from the explosion of the shots, all eyes transfixed to the lifeless body on the floor, everyone remaining motionless.

"Phone the Police and an ambulance," Terry eventually broke the spell. "We need to get this examined before we are in trouble. Jo, leave the gun on the floor and touch nothing. This was the bastard who drilled out my knee, I would recognise him anywhere." He stood back up with some difficulty, "Everyone back into the lounge so we don't touch anything, we'll wait for the police to deal with it." They backed away still transfixed by the scene in front of them. The phone rang, shocking them back into the moment. It was the long-awaited call from Karen, oblivious to the drama they were in the middle of. Stephen answered.

“Any news?” she asked without preamble.

"Hi Karen, it’s a bit hectic here but yes, you have got what you wanted so we just need your address to get you all home.”

“Send me the documents, I need to see them first. I’ll give you my email and I can pick it up on the laptop here.” Stephen headed out of the lounge towards his office. “Wait while I send them to you, are you all safe?”

“Yes, we’re fine. It’s just getting dark here, so I’m hoping we can do this tonight as I’m starting to get a bit jumpy here on my own with the kids.”

“We will pick you up as soon as we know where you are,” Stephen promised as he pressed send. Karen heard the ping of incoming mail on the family laptop, and she opened it and studied the wording. There it was, the get out of jail free card. She sighed with relief.

“Okay, here is the address.” Stephen scribbled it down quickly before giving her further instructions.

“Stay where you are and our men will be with you shortly. They will have a password which they will give before you let them in. The password is Resolution. Anyone who doesn’t have the password consider as a Brood. Do you understand Karen? The Broods have their guys in the area too so it is imperative you know who is who.”

“Yes, I understand, just make sure it is your guys who get here first, I hate to think what the Broods will do to me if they get me.”

# CHAPTER THIRTY-NINE

Reassured that rescue was on its way, Karen prepared her things and got the children ready to leave when help arrived. It was past their bedtime and they were confused as to why she was getting them dressed instead of into their pajamas. She tried to keep the fear and anxiety out of her voice as she explained.

"We will be going home soon, just do what I tell you for the next few hours and then you will be with Mummy and Daddy again. I just have to make sure it is safe for us to leave." She checked through her own things one last time and realized she had left her watch by the pool. She turned to the children sitting side by side on the sofa, watching her with solemn faces and large round eyes.

"Just stay in the house for a second, I need to find something quickly." She left by the front door and walked around the side of the house, the intruder lights lighting her path. She reached the pool area and checked on the table where there was no sign of the watch. Then she remembered, she had left it on the bar, taking it off before playing table tennis that afternoon. She opened the door and walked across the pitch-black room to reach the light switch. A voice came from the far corner,

"Fee! Fie! Foe! Fum! I smell the fear from a surrogate mum." The lights flicked on and there stood Keith, a large shining blade glinting in the light.

"Give me the children Karen, I have gone to a lot of trouble to pick them up."

"Fuck you!" She turned and ran, slamming the bar door behind her. She had a bit of a head start and needed to make it back to the children. She could hear the gravel crack behind her as he gave chase and leaping a small step, she picked up a large pot and slammed it into his chest knocking him backwards, just giving her the time to get into the house. She grabbed the children from the sofa, yelling at them "Quick, into the den." This was the less frightening name given by Karen to the panic room. They rushed down the stairs and into the room just as the front door was kicked open. Keith watched them disappearing down the stairs and shouted after her.

"Go on run. Where are you going to go, you stupid bitch?"

Karen slammed the heavy metal door closed and bolted it, before collapsing onto the stone floor, gasping for breath, the children crying in bewilderment and fear.

Bam! Bam! The door was kicked in rage as Keith realized he couldn't get through it. The noise stopped for a minute before being replaced with the sound of a sledge hammer smashing into it. The door vibrated but held firm. It was as if a giant was outside trying to beat down the walls and every thud shook Karen's confidence that the door would hold. Again, the banging stopped as Keith shouted through the door to her.

"You just wait there lady, I will be back and your little metal door will make a good headstone." She could hear him walking outside, the gravel under his heavy boots crunched menacingly, making him sound very close. Occasional thumps of the hammer against the three-foot-thick walls made them all jump, then silence. The kind of silence that seemed worse than the noise, the kind of silence that makes you wonder what was happening, the kind of silence that encourages you to make the next move.

She looked at her watch, it was now an hour since she had spoken to Stephen. Where were Byfield's men? Being down in the panic room, she wouldn't hear them and they may not find her. When the Broods came back with the tools they needed to finish the job the children would be taken and she would be killed, and it would all have been for nothing. It was almost too much to comprehend. She waited another hour, everything still silent. Desperation was tugging at her senses, and the silence made her decision for her, she had to act. Quietly sliding back the bolts, Karen opened the door and peering around the corner she came face to face with a balaclava clad man carrying an automatic weapon. He grabbed her and threw her back through the heavy door, two other men following as she fell backwards onto an old sofa, begging for the children's safety. Harry launched himself at the lead man in an attempt to protect Karen. He was crying and screaming as he tried to push the man backwards but he soon realized that it was futile as he was swept off his feet into the arms of the attacker.

The last man through the door closed and locked it before all three removed their balaclavas. The lead man put Harry down and took Karen firmly by the shoulders forcing her to look at him.

"Resolution! Resolution! Resolution!" he repeated until he saw the words sink in and felt her body relax. Karen threw her arms around the man. "Thank God you are here, I thought that we were dead." Ellie who had been screaming at the top of her voice stopped when she saw Karen hug the man and Harry stopped pummeling his back. Dan turned and looked at Harry, giving his back a rub as he did so. "You pack a hefty punch big guy, your dad will be proud of you when I tell him." He turned back to Karen,

"We're not out of the woods yet, we saw the drama from the lake, we just couldn't get up here in time without creating a bigger drama. The Brood's man will be back, he has obviously gone for tools and backup. We need to stay here for a bit but don't worry, just leave it to us."

Karen and the children were moved to the back of the room behind a solid wooden table, tipped on its side and cushions were laid on the floor for them to get a little comfort, not that this was on their minds. Karen and the children whispered in the darkness, but the men said nothing, they just sat and waited. A chill crept into the room, goosebumps sat on top of goosebumps, fear had given way to anxiety and in turn back to fear, Karen's emotions were on a rollercoaster, she needed to be free from the Broods but the thought of returning to England churned her stomach as she knew someone somewhere would still be watching.

Through the blackness the sound of a vehicle coming across the driveway heightened tensions. Scuffling feet and a whispered conversation could be heard as something was attached to the door. A woman's voice could then be heard, very calm and reassuring.

"Ellie, Harry your mummy has asked me to come and get you. Open the door, the bad man has gone away and I am here to take you back home." Harry, feeling very brave now answered her.

"What's the password? My daddy knows a secret word and if you don't know it, you are bad people." One of the men moved backwards towards the children and whispered quickly "Shhhh."

A gruff voice barked back, his impatience flowing through the door and all pretenses gone.

"You have two choices Karen, open the door and walk out with us or we jack the door off the hinges and you take your chances with us, it's up to you."

"If you want the children you will need to kill me first so come in and get me," Karen yelled with pure venom. The electric jack began to buzz, as the wooden frame around the door started to buckle and splinter. Dan had already killed the lights leaving the room in darkness for the past hour and as the frame broke and the door crashed forwards, it created a cloud of dust mixing with the blackness of the basement. One second later Keith and Sandra were illuminated with a powerful blinding torch as they tried to pick their way through the room. A hail of automatic fire cut them both down where they stood, both bodies dropping amongst the debris they had just created.

"Let's go," Dan instructed. "Bring the children and stay behind us, there may be others outside." They raced outside shielded by the men, leaving through the large entrance gates and stepping into the small, single- track road. A black Range Rover swept up and all four doors were opened as they all piled in. The leather seats and warm interior made them feel very secure and with the engine purring, they pulled out onto the main road heading towards Bordeaux Airport.

# CHAPTER FORTY

Stephen Byfield's phone lit up, he answered quickly and stared intently into the distance as he processed the information. He turned to Tanya and smiled as the news sank in. "Thank you so much for everything, we will see you there." He put the phone down and punched the air,

"They are safe, we can meet them at North Holt airport. They will be here at two o'clock tomorrow morning."

He was soon brought back into the reality of having a dead body in his hallway and the blue flashing lights of the two police cars followed by an ambulance flickered through the windows casting shadows through the rooms still unlit. Stephen opened the door and saw three armed police standing behind the front car. One shouted at him "Place your hands in the air and take two steps forward."

Stephen obeyed the instructions and soon found himself lying face down on the driveway and the others soon followed before a rough search was conducted. No words were spoken as he lay with his right cheek pressed into the gravel leaving a mosaic imprint. The evening chill and dampness in the air left him shaking, his clothing sticking to his sweaty skin. The adrenalin still flowing, he had not had the chance to slow down and the reality now kicked in. They had killed a man in the hallway of their house. They had a deadline to meet the children and this was the first time that the gravity of their actions had kicked in. They had killed a man and still expected to be home in time for the reunion. It couldn't possibly happen. He felt angry, suddenly he was no longer the victim, but instead was a hunted man and the police certainly had him in their sights.

He sat in the back of the police van, the anger had passed, but he would challenge anything they could throw at him. A police woman looked in at him and smiled before mouthing the words "Don't worry."

More police arrived and after what seemed like a lifetime the vans started to pull away, Stephen could see that they had all been kept separate and his van was the last to leave. As it pulled through the gates and out of the drive onto the road, he could see a stretcher bringing the body out. The overriding question was if it was definitely all over or if there was worse to come.

As the vans swept into the police yard, a harshly lit forecourt welcomed them as they were taken into the station one at a time. Again, Stephen was last. He was escorted in front of a high desk where a young sergeant looked at him before starting the booking in process. He was friendly and very cheerful considering the circumstances they were there under.

"Mr Byfield, we need to get this started. I understand that you have an important appointment later this evening. I promise that you will all be out of here within the hour, how does that sound?" Stephen nodded, not quite sure why they were all taking a murder so well. "Thank you, Sergeant, that would be much appreciated."

Sat in the chilly cell he could hear the others talking through the doors, his mind drifting to what was going to happen to them all.

The sound of the cell door opening made him jump, he hadn't heard anyone coming towards the door. He looked up and saw David Willard framed in the doorway, a smile on his face.

"How ironic Stephen. Get your stuff, we've places to be and children to see."

David Brood's phone rang. He listened intently and without speaking until whoever was talking had finished. Brood did not answer but just terminated the call. He slid the phone across the polished wooden table and stared up at the ceiling as if searching for an answer that couldn't be found. He turned his head towards Kevin, "Big trouble Kevin. Bryan is dead, so are the guys in France and the kids are out of our hands. Byfield's lot have royally screwed us over. Any suggestions?" Kevin gave a humourless laugh, "We've really fucked up this time, there's nothing more to say. Just prepare for a visit from the old bill, as without a doubt they'll be heading our way. Is everything in order at our end?"

"Yes, I can only hope it is. Everything we have is now in a safe deposit box in the city according to Susan, but even so, I think I will be joining you behind bars brother. Let's just hope it's a short stay."

"Fingers crossed mate, depends on who squeals. Speaking of which, I'd better fuck off back to my open prison while I can still go there. I have some business to take care of before the old bill come knocking on my cell door. See you around David."

"Hopefully outside rather than in," David replied with little hope.

The small plane touched down at the far end of the North Holt runway and taxied towards the waiting group. The passengers on board were two government officials, five police liaison officers who had flown out to Bordeaux one hour before flying back, and a senior police inspector from the Met Police. They were accompanied by Karen, Harry and Ellie, not to mention the three sleeping men in the back row of seats who were ready to slip back into the shadows as soon as the plane landed.

A small hanger sat twenty meters away where Stephen, Tanya and Chris stood peering through the vast arched opening at the end at the runway illuminated with its red and green lights. The hanger was large enough for a private aircraft to drive into but too small for the military planes which used another larger hanger. Two ambulance crews waited patiently sitting on top of an old wooden crate, chatting and sipping on steaming drinks. Next stop for them was Great Ormond Street hospital, London with a precious cargo.

The vending machine by the opening clunked as cans were chilled for the thousandth time. Anticipation pulsated through the darkness in the hanger, those waiting inside barely able to talk and the only chatter rhetorical. A number of vehicles sat on the runway, engines idling, exhaust fumes painting patterns in the distant rainbow lighting.

The aircraft steps were driven alongside the plane as it stopped by the hanger door, and after what seemed like an eternity, the door opened revealing an attractive air stewardess looking out towards the hanger. Stephen and Tanya stood in the shadows looking up at the plane, Tanya with tears flooding down her face in anticipation, the blackness of the night leaving the airport lighting to illuminate the scene. Consequently, it made it impossible for the children to see their parents as the hanger lighting was turned off for airport security.

The first person off the plane was a blond-haired young lady, who was escorted by a police officer and handcuffed. Karen walked slowly down the aircraft stairs looking anxiously in all directions, her hair blowing in the suction from the aircraft engines. Once at the bottom, she glanced behind her towards the aircraft door as if looking for something now out of sight. The interior of the police car was illuminated as she was placed into the back seat and they were close enough to see that she was talking to the driver before the doors closed and she disappeared into the darkness. The vanishing break lights were the last evidence that she had even been there.

Three men then came down the stairs purposefully and climbed into a waiting black Range Rover, no interior lights this time and no talking. They disappeared in seconds leaving the anxious parents to greet the children they had rescued.

An airport vehicle turned in the distance illuminating the plane, its silhouette standing out boldly as a woman with a child on either side came down the stairs and stood at the entrance to the hanger with the lights of the distant truck behind them. Stephen momentarily froze as the image from his recurring dream played out in front of his eyes. The children were waving at him but behind them, Stephen could see the headlights of a truck hurtling towards them from behind the plane, dust kicking off the wheels as the vehicle raced towards the unsuspecting people. At the last moment it turned off towards a military plane further along and he snapped out of his trance as the hanger lights were turned back on.

They all rushed towards each other, yelling, crying and laughing, arms out stretched ready to embrace.

"Mummy! Daddy! Grandad!" the twins yelled as they leapt up into their arms. Unwilling to interrupt the reunion, but needing to ensure procedures were followed, the Police Inspector ushered them back into the depths of the hanger before explaining what would happen next.

"Okay, we need to get this right Stephen, Tanya," he looked at them both. "I do understand that you want them home now, but as we explained to you earlier, we do need to ensure that the children have the best medical care as they have been through a lot and none of us are sure exactly what they have endured."

"Sure, as long as we can be with them all the way if that is okay," Tanya replied drawing them both closer to her, unwilling to let them go again, even for a second.

"Absolutely," he reassured her. "We will also need to have a chat with them about what they've experienced in due course but that can wait for now until we've had them checked over."

Ellie broke free from Tanya's hugs and looked around. 'Where's Karen?" she asked, "she said that she would be here with us when we got back." Tanya crouched down so she could look Ellie in the eye. "Karen has had to go see her mummy and daddy as well sweetheart, so don't worry, she's nice and safe."

"Can we see her Mummy, can she come and stay? She played some cool games with us, can we show you them?" Tanya hugged her tight again,

"Of course you can darling, we just need to go to a special hospital for children before we go home. We have to make sure that you and Harry are fit and healthy so the doctors are going to have a little look at you but Mummy and Daddy will stay with you all the time." Harry looked at Tanya, a look she knew only too well in his eyes.

"We are not poorly, Karen gave us lots of dinners and we went to bed early in France, we were very good. Karen took us away from the bad people and she is nice," he emphatically stated. Tanya glanced up at the police inspector who raised his eyebrows at her.

Karen sat in Chelmsford Police station and looking around her cell she wondered where life would take her now. The door opened and a smartly dressed man stood in front of her. He smiled making her think that maybe things weren't as bad as they seemed. He came in and sat down on the cell bench next to her.

"Okay Karen, I think we have all we need to deal with this case and I also note the promise that you have been given regarding freedom from prosecution. However, that only covers what has happened in the past so any events from today will be dealt with as a criminal matter, make no mistake about that." Karen gave him a small smile, "I don't expect to ever be involved with anything like this again," she replied, "although I am seriously not safe at the moment, I have upset a lot of people."

"You certainly have. David Brood is being taken into custody as we speak and will be remanded in prison along with a number of the gang. I would suggest not going directly to your parents until the dust settles so we have arranged for you to stay at a safe house under our protection, if this is okay with you?"

"Sure, I don't want to put my parents at any further risk. Where will this be?"

"Hastings, a small town on the south coast. It will be close enough for you to meet family should you choose too. We will not stop you doing anything you wish to and we will not be living in the flat with you but we will however have panic alarms fitted should they be needed. But all this comes with a condition...."

"Which is what?"

"You will need to give your evidence at the Old Bailey when it comes to court. Can you do that?"

"They would kill me in a heartbeat if they found me so of course I will testify against them. I knew David wasn't an angel when I was with him but taking those children was a despicable thing to do and as for getting his people to kill my friend, I will never forgive him for that."

"Splendid, a car will be here in an hour to take you to the safe house. Once there, everything will be explained to you. We will probably not meet again until the court case so good luck and stay safe." He turned and left the room and shortly a young female police office came in with Karen's belongings and a microwave meal. "I thought you might want this, you've had a long night." Karen sat with the small tray in front of her, thinking of what would happen next. She needed to see her parents and mend all the hurt that she had caused, but she wished most of all that she could speak to Stephen and Tanya about the children and apologise for her part in their abduction.

# CHAPTER FORTY-ONE

Kevin Brood sat in his cell, back in prison for the past twelve hours his mind was racing, considering all scenarios facing him. The family were in big trouble, the police would, without a doubt be planning to raid all known haunts of the Broods. Everyone would be taken into custody and the Senior Management of the Brood company would not be granted bail. They could expect months on remand before any sniff of a court case being presented against them. He just hoped that the contingency plans put in place by Susan Turner were robust enough. She needed to make sure that there was no trail leading from the Broods to the security deposit building but he trusted her implicitly. As thoughts of the demise of his business went through his head, his door burst open and three officers walked into the cell issuing him with instructions. “Follow us Brood, don’t pack anything, you are leaving here now and your property will follow.”

"I ain’t going nowhere without my stuff, so fuck off out of my room while I pack. I will go, I couldn’t give a fuck about going, but I am taking my stuff.”

“No you’re not, so you choose how you are going to go, walk or we will drag you out. Make up your mind.”

“Go and get half a dozen friends because you are going to have to fight me. I am going to make you bastards work for your money.” The biggest of the officers stepped forward, “You think that you are a big shot old man but I don’t need any friends, I don’t even need these two. You want a one on one, I’m your man.”

Kevin was surprised, the guard was being deadly serious and this was the first time anyone had squared up to him. He thought he would give him another chance

"Why would you want to do that son? Why are you giving me the chance to hurt you badly?"

"Because you can't Brood. You are finished."

A cold chill of realisation swept over Kevin as he suddenly felt his age and his overrated confidence was stripped away. He had been fronted out by a young gun and he knew that he couldn't compete. "Okay Rocky, I'm ready. Take me to whatever prison you like. You have big balls son, you want a job?"

"I already have a job, now get a fucking move on while you can still walk." Kevin knew when he was beaten and headed out of his cell. The walk towards the prison van was torturous, his pride in shreds, his reputation over, and he felt he had to act. He had to do something or he would lose face for good and that would never do.

Brood spun on his heels and punched the big officer in the face but he didn't go down, he just stepped back a pace and looked at Brood. "Leave us to it," he said to the other two officers, "he's had this coming, this bastard had my best mate cut open." He dragged Brood behind the gymnasium wall and pounded his face. Brood had no chance and stumbled to the floor. Holding his hands up, he begged, "Enough son, I have had enough."

"I haven't even started yet you fucking scum bastard," the officer sneered at him and pulling him from the floor he smashed a large fist into Brood's mouth. He felt his teeth shatter and again Brood fell to the floor spitting blood and teeth onto the dirt ground. He felt rough hands pull him to his feet. "Get up!" came the order as the other staff intervened before the beating could go any further.

"Enough Andy, let's get him out of here." The officer looked at Brood before giving him a warning. "You have got a lot more of this coming shit bag, so you'd better be ready." Brood half walked, half stumbled to the van where the Duty Governor was waiting. This was an unexpected turn of events and the staff were mumbling between themselves as they realised that they were in deep trouble. Regardless of who he was, the staff had committed an assault.

"Do you know why you are going Brood?" the governor asked him before stopping. 'Bloody hell, what has happened to you?" Brood looked at the officers, "I had a funny turn, got off the bed too quickly and toppled over, no dramas Governor. I don't need any medical help, I just want to get to my next nick and settle down." The Governor looked at the staff and shrugged his shoulders.

"Put him on the van lads," and off Brood went, into the morning traffic and back into another high security prison.

He looked around the cell in the van with barely enough space to move, and he called out through the door to the big officer who was sat in the back with him.

"Andy, Andy are you there?"

"What do you want Brood?"

"I saved your job back there, you owe me."

"I owe you nothing Brood and if it was down to me, I would be in that cell on a murder charge. This isn't over Brood, you will need eyes in the back of your head where you're going, remember that."

"I know a lot of people Andy. Trust me I could have your address within half an hour of being in the next nick and I could have your house burning by tonight."

"I already know your address Brood, yours could be burning now so shut the fuck up!"

David Brood was considering having a swim. He knew that trouble was on the way but could never have realised the intensity of what lay in wait. His home was a million miles from a prison cell and the phone call that he had just had with his legal team gave him some confidence. It would seem that Susan Turner had done the housework and any evidence against him would be on a lower level meaning that a period of time on remand would not be necessary.

The armed police in the driveway had other ideas. The first David knew of their presence was when his front door exploded and disintegrated into the hallway. A tight team of armed police stormed through the door carrying ballistic shields and automatic weapons. He dropped onto his knees before being asked, his white bathrobe looking ridiculous within the setting of a war zone.

"On your front, now!" barked an order. Brood dropped down, his heart thumping and a tightness in his throat made it difficult to get his breath. He was handcuffed before being dragged to his feet and marched into a police van and into custody. He looked down at the grubby, grey floor, his white slippers and bath robe being the last hints of luxury that he would see for a while. Gaining his composure, he shouted to the police officers in the front. "You have got nothing on me at all, this is a big mistake, mark my word."

"Mr Brood, if I were you, I would save your bull shit for your legal team, you have no idea what we know about you." These words stung his senses, what did they mean? All bases had been covered, so what did they know? He concluded that it must be a bluff and he would wait until he had his legal team with him.

They pulled into the police station where the harsh lights and smell of fresh paint invaded his senses. David was lined up in front of a high desk where a police officer stood behind a computer terminal tapping in unseen information. A series of monotone questions were asked, the gravity of the situation seeping in with each answer. All demands to see his lawyer were ignored and he felt stuck in a maze where every question he answered seemed to take him deeper into the puzzle. Within a few minutes he was processed and led into a cold unfurnished cell where he was at last given the information he needed by the custody officer.

"Your brief is on his way in, he has some clothing for you so you don't look like you're on a spa weekend. We'll be talking to you within an hour."

The door shut and bolted, he lay on the hard, solid plastic bed and after what seemed like an age his door opened again revealing his solicitor, an old family friend, Ken Carney. David sat up.

"Thank God you're here Ken, what the fuck is going on? The call we had this morning sounded like I would be out on police bail in a heartbeat but instead I have had the full SWAT squad treatment. What are we missing?" Handing him a bag containing trousers, shirt and shoes, his solicitor answered him.

"Not entirely sure David. It would appear that they have slightly more evidence than we anticipated but the police are not disclosing everything just yet."

"Is that legal?" David asked as he quickly changed out of his swimming robe.

"I am afraid that they can do this if they choose." The cell door was pushed open and a young police officer nodded towards them both.

"We are ready to interview you." Ken looked over at David, "You ready?"

"As always."

They entered the small interview room, the tape machine buzzed as the interview started. Once the police had conducted the opening statements, the solicitor started the conversation.

"My client intends to give a no comment interview. We would welcome the opportunity for Mr Brood to be able to go home and carry on with his life until these scandalous accusations are dealt with." The officer conducting the interview looked at the solicitor.

"Mr Brood can exercise his right to a no comment interview, it will make no difference to us. We have a significant amount of evidence against him which we will disclose when we are ready." He turned to Brood,

"Mr Brood, can you please tell us what you know about the abduction of Ellie and Harry Byfield?"

"No comment."

"Can you tell us about the murder of two individuals in your social club and being an accessory to murder of a third?"

"No comment."

"We have evidence to support your involvement in these crimes which I will bring to your notice shortly."

"No comment." David's head was spinning, how did they know about these things? They were on a strictly need to know basis amongst his team and he thought he could trust all those close to him. The officer's next question puzzled him.

"Tell me about your employee, Susan Turner."

"No comment," he replied, worrying that they might have arrested her too and hoping she would not disclose anything.

"Oh, so you know that she actually works for MI5 David and not you?"

"No comment." He felt sick to the base of his stomach. The solicitor asked for the meeting to be stopped in the interest of him taking instructions from his client. The two officers stopped the tape before picking up their files and heading for the door.

"Sure, take as long as you like, we have plenty of time."

Ken Carney looked at Brood. "David, what haven't you told me? I thought you said there was nothing for the police to find and all your dealings were above board."

"Maybe I have underestimated the stupidity of two ego-maniacs. We have been set up Ken. I am afraid that if Miss Turner is in fact what they say she is, they have everything and I mean everything and none of it will pass muster."

"For the sake of God David, why didn't you consider telling me about this and that evidence existed?"

"I thought it was well and truly hidden, I implicitly trusted the members of my board, that's why. What now?" Carney closed the file in front of him and stood up.

"Custody I'm afraid, you will be going to prison on remand and high security at that. You will be gone today without a doubt and there is absolutely nothing I can do. You have misled me David, and you are on your own. I was willing to get you out of a few dodgy business deals but triple murder is another thing altogether and I will not be part of it." David jumped up thrusting his face close to that of his solicitor.

"You fucking dog, you took our cash when the going was good, and now you might have to work for your money, you are turning your back on us." Carney calmly took a step back before replying.

"David, the family is finished, you are no longer a power to be reckoned with and you no longer have a hold on me or my family." He turned his back and left the office. Turning to the officer outside the door, he confirmed "I am finished with him, take him back to where he belongs," before marching down the corridor and out of Brood's life.

# CHAPTER FORTY-TWO

The Somalis on C wing HMP Birchwood were waiting for two new receptions. The prison drums had been beating, never wrong and somehow always an hour ahead of the event happening. The Brood brothers were on their way. Two Category A cells on the third landing had been prepared, it was an unusual occurrence for two Cat A brothers to be together on a wing but apparently it was happening.

Errol Brown a prisoner well over six feet tall, serving a life sentence, pushed his broom along the landing. He stopped next to two young officers drinking a cup of tea by the wing office.

"What's happening boss? I have got the two Cat A cells ready and they have been searched by the dog team. Who is coming? I have heard it is the Broods?"

"Fuck knows Errol, you could be right mate," one of the officers agreed. "Whoever it is, they will be here this afternoon." Brown nodded at the staff and carried on sweeping the imaginary pile of dirt until he passed the end cell. The door was open as usual and four men were chatting inside, two on chairs and two slouching on the beds. One of them looked up at the sound of the sweeping.

"What's happening Errol?" He looked in and saw four tall, slim built Somalian men with thin chiseled faces and hard murderous eyes. These men had grown up on the tough streets of the Somali capital, fighting for their lives against war lords and American Special Forces. The cell was sparse, with no display of the wealth they had accumulated as major drug dealers over the South East of England and no sign of the property they had taken from other prisoners during their reign in Birchwood.

"Those old white boys here yet Errol?"

"Not yet boss, probably this afternoon."

"Nice. Here, we have a little something for our boy." One of the men threw him a small thumb nail size package, "Just remember who looks after you brother." He looked at the package in his hand, he had tried to stop taking heroin so many times but it was a hopeless fight. These men controlled the drug trade in the prison, they had four staff on their pay roll and the flow of drugs and mobile phones was relentless. Brown returned to his cell and pushed his door closed. Taking his pipe from behind his single locker, he prepared his hit. Sucking the drug deep into his lungs he fell back onto the harsh green blanket on the bed into a few hours of oblivion.

He was woken up by one of the staff he had spoken to earlier.

"Errol, for fucks sake mate, what have you been up to? You been smoking that shit again you fucking idiot. Sort your shit out and get out here, I have a job for you." He sat on the side of his bed, head down wondering why he had messed up again. But he knew the answer, it was fifteen years until he could face the parole board and the heroin didn't really matter, his life was over anyway. No family, no home, no friends. In truth after the past seven years in prison he didn't want to be released. Life was easier here, he had a job, home and people to chat to. What more did he need?" He looked up,

"Yes Mr Coppell, what can I do for you?"

"Firstly, you can stop taking that shit or I will have that job off you. Secondly, your two Brood boys are on their way up from reception, so you'd better tell your boys."

The reception department at HMP Birchwood was modern by normal prison standards and it was not so different from the police station where David Brood had just been moved from. He sat in a small cell by himself, wondering what was awaiting him when a familiar voice cut through his thoughts. Another van had arrived and the prisoner was standing in front of the reception desk. David could hear the conversation.

"Name and Number?"

"Kevin Brood A3245DC. Where is my property?"

“Following on, it will be here tomorrow. What has happened to your face?”

“Fell over. What wing am I going on?”

“C Wing, we have put you with your brother.”

“David? When did he get here?”

“Twenty minutes before you, he is in holding room four, you’ll be in five. We will have you both on the wing in twenty minutes.”

“Sweet.” David heard the footsteps of them walking to the room next to his and it wasn’t long before he heard Kevin again. “You there David?”

“Unfortunately, yes, I think we are screwed Kevin.”

“What are you talking about? Be careful what you say mate, the screws will be listening.”

“It would seem that Susan Turner was working for the other side and everything we gave her is in the possession of the Police. I don’t know much else, only that the snake of a solicitor Carney has deserted us as well. Not a good day mate.”

"No, I can agree with that. Okay, say nothing else mate, it may be that they are going to put us on the same wing, which is unusual and a real result. We can chat then but just listen to my advice for once when we get there. I know these places and you will have to go through a longer process than me. When you speak to the doctor tell him that you need to be on the same wing as me, you feel depressed and I am the only one you can talk to. You know the score.”

“No problems.” Thirty minutes later the initial reception process had been completed and David was dressed in green overalls with a yellow stripe running down them. Apparently, it was for easy recognition of Category A prisoners. He was given a pair of black slip on shoes a size too big and a pair of gray prison socks which felt like they had been worn a few times too many. The blue prison boxer shorts given to him made him cringe. Never in his worst moments would he have ever considered wearing used underwear.

Kevin caught sight of him from his room door window as he

passed the cell and called out to him.

"Don't worry David, we will be out of these pyjamas in no time, I will make sure you get your sexy silky boxers and socks back. Get into your new cell and settle down. It will be a single cell so no sharing but I'll be along to chat with you as soon as I can."

David Brood was escorted to C Wing. A rattle of radio messages gave the staff permission to move him and they walked at speed through the brightly lit corridors, every move scrutinised on CCTV until they reached the wing. All prisoners were locked in their cell and the wing was silent except for the sound of a hundred different tunes drifting under cell doors. The wing resembled a massive warehouse for people and standing on the first landing you were able to look up and see every cell door, all painted in the same shade of blue, with massive air vents dominating the high white ceiling. It was a soulless building filled with two hundred lost souls. A waft of cannabis swept through the air as David was taken up two flights of metal stairs, the grime imbedded at the edges from years of abuse and poor cleaning, and onto the third landing. Again, it was silent and as he passed a number of locked doors, names and numbers outside each cell, he could see unrecognizable faces peering through the door hatches, assessing the new guy as he passed by. He had the feeling that he was expected. "Cell 3.25 is your home for the moment," announced the old officer who had seen too much during his thirty years working on prison landings, as he unlocked the door.

"Put your stuff in there and get sorted out. The tea meal will be ready in an hour. Three words of advice Brood, don't borrow anything, don't lend anything out and above all, watch your back, it's a different world in here." The door closed with a metallic clang, leaving David looking around. A steel toilet heavily stained sat in the corner, partly concealed by a low partition wall. An old battered twenty-inch television sat on a built-in shelf, which initially looked promising but the back was broken and it didn't look as though it would work. A small white kettle stood on another dirty shelf with the stains from a million cheap tea bags decorating the top and a thousand cigarette burns completing the look. The barred windows were heavily vandalised and with a dozen names scratched onto the thick plastic, the sun struggled to find its way through. The same windows had no way of opening and an inadequate ventilation system either side seemed useless with no hint of fresh air coming through. The walls were stained with blobs of tooth paste where photographs had been displayed by the last resident. The back of the door was painted in a dark blue. At least it would have been blue had a million names and towns not been scratched into it. A single metal light switch and emergency alarm were located to the left of the door frame. He had been warned that he could only push this alarm for life and death emergencies. Anything else, he would have to wait. The bed had a built-in solid plastic base with a flimsy two-inch mattress. He had one pillow and a small bundle of two sheets, pillow case and a small green towel. He made up his bed and looked around in disbelief. Just a few hours earlier, he was considering taking a swim in his private heated pool, now he was thinking about how he would cope with nothing.

# CHAPTER FORTY-THREE

It had been a week since the children had returned home from a couple of days in Great Ormond Street hospital. A barrage of examinations and psychological tests had been taken and it was thought that in time the memories would dull. Karen had played a large part in the lack of scars. She had treated the children as though they were her own and they had suffered little during their two-week ordeal and had considered Karen a member of their family. Stephen and Tanya however, had mixed feelings. Although ultimately, she had done the right thing, it had to be remembered that she was partially responsible for the kidnap attempt.

All three children were in bed, it was nine thirty and Stephen was pouring Chris and Tanya a glass of chilled,white wine.

“Cheers everyone, let’s hope that we can now get on with life again." They chinked glasses as Stephen continued, “Back to work again on Monday worst luck, but at least I don’t have to go back into a prison for a while.” Chris nodded, “Bit of a strange assignment though Stephen, I know that you are good at uncovering wrong doing, but to head up a small team dedicated to corruption, is that normal?”

“No, it’s not normal in regard to the fact that even I don’t know what I am going to be investigating. It’s exciting though, and I’m sure all will become clear on Monday.” Tanya smiled at him.

"I’m just glad my husband is out of prisons for a while, I for one have had enough drama to last me a life time.”

“Me too,” Stephen agreed. “I could be out forever Tanya, the new governor starts in charge next week, Terry knows her so he is happy. They've worked together in the past.”

"What, never back into a prison?" Tanya looked surprised, "You didn't tell me that."

"No, I haven't really had the opportunity, I just had an email from a guy in Government this afternoon. I didn't know either but it would seem I have been promoted for this new role and it looks like a bigger job than I thought. I have to report to an Office in Whitehall at midday on Monday, so higher up the command chain than I anticipated."

"Wow, well I'll drink to that," said Tanya, taking another sip.

David Brood's cell flap opened and a face peered through the glass, it was Errol.

"Mr Brood, they are serving tea in ten minutes and you are getting chef's choice. Today that is pasty and mash, not the greatest meal but it is all you will get. Do you want any burn? I can lend you some until Friday."

"No thanks, I have stopped."

"Do you need anything else, you know, weed or anything else? If so, come see me."

"I'm fine thanks, is my brother here yet?"

"Yes, he is in with the Governor, he hasn't got up to his cell yet and it looks like he is having a right go." David smiled, "Typical, will someone unlock me for my meal?"

"Yeah, they have just started unlocking. Remember, my name is Errol, anything you need, I'm your man." Minutes later his door opened, the same older officer pushing the door open. "Tea, bring your bowl as there's soup as well." David walked down the two flights of stairs, plastic plate and bowl in hand. The wing looked very different now with prisoners everywhere of all ages and races. The smell of the food spread over the first landing. He saw a queue and joined the back of it, around ten people were in front of him and he could see a hotplate area with people serving food. Errol was at the end handing out slices of bread. He reached the front of the queue, "Name?"

"David Brood."

"Brood, chef's choice." A pasty was tossed onto his plate

quickly followed by a scoop of gray mashed potato which looked disgusting.

"Veg?" a gruff voice came over the hotplate area.

"No thanks." The veg went on the plate anyway. David looked up at the prisoner behind the hot plate.

"I said no." The stocky food server put down the ladle and walked out to the front where David was standing. Around five foot ten and packed with muscle, tattoos covering his neck and arms, Alex Bell was every inch a dangerous man.

"Have you got a problem with me old man?' It was the type of question Bell normally followed with aggression. The staff heard the commotion, some came closer sensing that trouble was imminent and the wing manager told a new officer to stand by the alarm bell and push it when something happened. All the staff knew the trouble that this guy could cause, he had been given the job serving food after six months in segregation for violence when he had promised to turn over a new leaf.

The Governor in charge of the wings had put his neck on the line and had told the wing manager to employ him. Everyone else had disagreed with the idea, but what could they do? This jumped up little Governor with five minutes experience thought that he knew everything so here they were, face to face with a problem of their own making. And David Brood was on the edge of getting badly hurt and realized it. He was used to employing thugs to deal with violence for him, unless it was on his terms.

"Sorry, I wasn't thinking."

"No, you weren't thinking old man, fucking Cat A prisoners, I shit on them." A hand clasped onto David shoulder from behind, "Is there a problem brother?" and relief flooded in as he realised it was Kevin. He was staring at Bell as he repeated his question, "Is there a problem?" Bell glared back at him before bursting out laughing.

"Fuck me, I do believe it's the Chuckle brothers." The other servers laughed but Kevin didn't, he had been here before. Grabbing the heavy serving ladle from the soup bowl he smashed it into the face of Bell, blood spurting against the tiled wall. He followed this up by grabbing his head and crashing it into the steel hotplate while Bell was still disoriented. Without pausing for breath, he took the large metal container of soup and poured it over Bell before hammering the empty pot into his face, Bell's forehead exploded with a deep bleeding wound as he begged Kevin to stop.

"No more Mr Brood, I have had enough, I'm sorry." Brood looked over at the staff, "Press the fucking alarm bell and you will have a riot on your hands," and with that, Kevin Brood was back on top. He took David's plate and served him a fresh meal. "There you go David, welcome to my world."

Errol stood at end of the hot plate with the bags of bread in the bread tray. "White or brown boss?" Kevin looked at him in surprise.

"Bloody hell Errol, haven't seen you since you killed that guy who stole my money, how are you keeping? I trust that we are still giving you a nice monthly allowance?"

"Yes, thank you Mr Brood, nice to meet up with you again."

Before Kevin could sit down with David to eat, an officer unfamiliar with the Broods walked up to him, and taking hold of both his arms, tried to lead him away. "Come on, you're coming to the block." Kevin shrugged him off with little difficulty, "I'm fucking going nowhere." The officer reached for his baton to apply some persuasion when the wing manager appeared. "It's ok, let him go back to his cell, that prick had it coming." They both walked away taking Bell to the infirmary and leaving the Broods to sit down to eat while the rest of the inmates continued with the routine of meal time queuing now the show was over.

Up on the landing above, the Somalians stood watching the commotion before disappearing back into the end cell to bide their time. When the wing was locked up and staff went for their breaks, it would become a different place, silent, as everyone became caught up in their own thoughts. The thought for today would be about the Broods. Kevin had humiliated the wing bully, dictated what he would and wouldn't do to the staff and had laid a marker down to the Somali gang. He knew who they were and what they could do and was preparing for a war to claim leadership, he just needed soldiers to fight with him.

The Somalis were part of a three-hundred-strong gang from Woolwich, London and they controlled drugs, prostitution, and protection across much of the south of England. They had just moved into Scotland with violent results and were estimated to be making five million a year from the sale of crack cocaine alone. They had been careful so far not to involve the Broods in a turf war, but this day would come.

The Broods were old school, a family grown up in the shadows of the Kray twins. They were hard people descended from an Irish travelling background. They had earned their reputation as the most notorious criminal gang over a thirty-year reign of violence. Kevin revelled in the life, he walked it and talked it but David however could see that times were changing. The old-time gangs were becoming archaic, the format of one godfather leader was historic, and violence, drugs and protection were a prehistoric club to the head. The Broods were way ahead of UK gangs in their structure, but even they could not compete with the modern enterprises.

The Somali gangs acted like Microsoft, Google and Apple all in one. They had a CEO and a full management team that developed strategy and they didn't stay still for two minutes. Their methods for delivering maximum profit lay between cyber-crime and old-fashioned drug sales. They were everywhere, hundreds of thousands emigrating from Africa to the UK. Hard cities such as Liverpool, Glasgow and London were under Somali control, in the 1980's this would have been unthinkable, but now it was fact.

Another major difference lay in the background of these gangs. The established white and black gangsters had become bloated on a soft western lifestyle but these guys were from the war zones of Africa. Death was nothing, respect everything, but above everything came profit. These gangs worked twenty-four hours a day with teenage thugs working shifts to ensure that they were able to deliver at any time night or day. It was relentless and the old school gangster could not cope with this tide of imported violence.

Kevin and David stood on the third landing chatting and looking over the railings towards the server area where last night's violence had taken place. David was still acclimatising himself to his sudden change in lifestyle and the fact that such violence could erupt over a plate of vegetables.

"What happens now then Kevin? Everyone knows that we are here, that's for sure."

"What happens now is nothing David. The Somalis have been running the wing up till now and will be talking about us. They will arrange to meet us and work out a deal. We will run some rackets, possibly phones and they can keep the drugs market. We will all keep out of each other's way until we upset each other, just like outside. Then we have another war and so it all starts again. We just need to recruit enough soldiers to be able to keep their arms at arm's length."

"So who exactly is on our side? From where I stood last night, it seemed like me and you against the rest."

"Errol and that idiot Alex from yesterday are our boys believe it or not and we also have five guys from a firm in Southampton who are handy. There are another dozen from East London who hate those black gangsters and are looking for a bit of pay back."

"So around twenty then? Seriously?"

"Twenty's plenty David," Kevin laughed as he turned and went back into his cell. He remembered something and turned back round,

"Oh yeah David, we can get these poxy pyjamas off this afternoon. I had a row with the security governor, and the result is that we are not Cat A prisoners anymore." He kicked his door shut still laughing.

Errol pushed his broom along the landing for the twentieth time that afternoon, the Broods were chatting again outside Kevin's cell as he brushed past them. "Looking good in your own clothes again gents."

"Thank you Errol, feels much better." Kevin grabbed the handle of his broom as he went to sweep past them again, "You have obviously got something to say old son, you have virtually lived on my doorstep for the past thirty minutes, so spill."

"The guys want to meet up with you Mr Brood, I didn't want to pass messages from them but you know how it is."

"When and what time?"

"In the gym for the afternoon session, around three. I have put your names on the gym list."

"Very thoughtful Errol, I fancy some weights actually, what about you David?" David who was still trying to work out if Errol was working for them or the Somalis nodded.

"Sure, a bit of exercise will do me good and pass some time."

"Can I tell them that you will be there?" Errol was eager to ensure he pleased everyone and he was walking a fine line between the two sides. Kevin nodded, and he swept off down the landing to deliver his message. Kevin turned to David, "See David, you may be good at the corporate stuff in business but I know how these places run. Get your trainers ready old boy."

A procession of chattering prisoners walked towards the gym, David and Kevin stayed at the back as they didn't fancy being jumped by these guys in the middle of a big pack, it would be suicide. They noticed the four Somali men were at the front, but they kept glancing behind them assessing where the threat could come from. David looked nervously around,

"Great way to do business Kevin. If we get there alive, we may be able to reach an agreement on something. For fucks sake, your world is messed up." They walked through the metal gates of the gymnasium where one physical education officer was watching the changing rooms while the other counted people into the gym.

"Thirty-four in Jon," the latter reported as everyone rushed to get changed. One hour wasn't long when they all had to share the equipment. The Somali guys were not getting changed, they sat on the wooden benches staring at the Broods.

"Don't think that we are going to get much gym work done," muttered David.

The gym officer came in and looking around, saw the Somalis sitting on the bench. "Come on you lot, on the gym floor, now."

"Jon, leave us to chat this out please, it will save you guys trouble later," Mo, the larger and obviously leading Somali spoke calmly to the officer, and smiled as he spoke. The officer nodded and walked back out into the main gym sports hall. Mo turned back to face the Broods.

"Okay, how do you want to play this one? We've been running this wing for the past year, no problems; you guys have arrived and have caused some trouble already. It seems like the wing isn't big enough for the both of us so you are going to have to leave. Simple."

"Not simple," said Kevin, "We are here, we aren't moving and I have enough back up to cause you all the problems that you need. We want the phone business, you can have the rest." Mo stood and moved a step closer to the Broods,

"We are Somalians, we don't do compromise like that. We run the drugs and phones, you run nothing. Watch what happens to your boys if you don't play our rules." Kevin hadn't expected such a strong stance and he was taken aback. He tried again.

"We want the phones, that's all, you can have everything else."

"You will move yourself from the wing by the weekend or we will shut the Brood family down for good, understand?"

"So we can't talk a deal?"

"We don't deal with anyone, we want everything, simple." Mo turned and led his gang out into the sports hall, meeting over.

The Broods returned to the wing, Kevin deep in thought. This was not how the script normally went. Before they parted to return to their cells, David had a request for Kevin,

"Kevin, talking of phones, can you get one for me? I have some unfinished business outside that my sudden arrest didn't allow me to deal with."

"It will be in your cell within thirty minutes, let me know when you have used it and leave it under your pillow. I have a guy who will collect it from you." Kevin's thoughts were elsewhere, he could only see one solution to the Somalian problem; he would have to provide a show of force so great that even these African warriors would have to change their minds.

While waiting for the phone, David headed down for tea break. As he queued at the hotplate, he noticed that whatever was on the menu for that day, the smell was the same as the previous day. He passed his blue plate over the counter, the days of chef's choice were gone. Now that the Broods were a recognised force on the wing, he could choose whatever he wanted. The men serving didn't openly suck up to him but he seemed to get the best selections of whatever was available. He picked up the two slices of bread from Errol and walked back to his cell. On the advice of Kevin, he had selected chicken ribs and chips. A preprocessed lump of something sat on the plate and he poked at it before eating it. Disgusting, but better than the empty pasties they had supplied on his first night. Having finished what he could eat of the culinary mess, he reached under the pillow and felt for the phone. The wing would be locked up as soon as the last person had received their meal and he could then have a whispered conversation without risking anyone disturbing him. He played through in his mind what he would say.

Finally the last door banged shut and silence consumed the building broken only by distant music and the odd burst of laughter from the departing staff. He took out his address book and thumbed through until he came to Ernie, someone who he had worked with on a number of occasions and could trust. He pulled his sheet over his head as if sleeping and dialed the number.

"Ernie, its David. Karen is back in the country, find her and phone me back when you do. I will only be on this number for a couple of days so you need to work quickly. I know how she works, she will need to see her parents and she will also get in touch with the Vet's surgery, that place is her life and she left in a hurry. She is bound to have left something there that she will need to pick up."

"No problem David, I will get onto it straight away, text me her parents' and vets' address details if you have them. The police will have her in hiding but she has been on the run for a while so she's bound to break cover."

"Cheers, remember she is smart, she out ran us for two weeks after all. Speak soon." He rang off and hid the phone in a hollowed-out pocket in the foam mattress.

# CHAPTER FORTY-FOUR

Karen looked around the sparsely decorated first floor flat. The staircase leading up to it had the smell of damp and the white door on the right of the landing had the number 12A screwed onto it. The lounge was large with a wide bay window overlooking a residential street with the sound of seagulls resounding everywhere. The flat sat a hundred meters from the beach and the strained, musical melodies could be heard from the occasional ice cream van. A small hallway led to a bathroom with a grubby looking green bath complete with shower curtain and a showerhead attached to the taps. The toilet sat directly next to the bath with a basin squeezed in between the toilet and the door. The double bedroom sat opposite, again with a bay window facing the street. Patches of damp could be seen coming through the flat roof over the window. A tiny kitchen perched in between the bedroom and lounge where someone had tried to attach swing doors for an inexplicable reason and they clearly had no idea what they were doing. Poorly put up, they didn't close properly leaving a six-inch gap between the two. It was not a bad hideaway but not somewhere that she would choose to live.

She sat staring out of the lounge window considering what to do. She needed to get back to see her parents and she had left some personal items in the surgery as she had never expected to be away so long. It was all a risk but she knew that she would have to take it. She could meet her parents anywhere that was safe, but she also wanted to clean out her locker, nothing of sentimental value but her book of contacts was still sitting in her old bag. If the Broods got hold of this, they could hunt her down again or threaten any one of her friends in order to get to her.

Decision made, tomorrow morning she would go to the train station and get it done. The surgery was in walking distance from Colchester station and she could be in and out within twenty minutes. Hopefully if she arrived before eight o'clock the receptionist would be there to let her in and there wouldn't be too many people around to ask awkward questions. She spent a sleepless night tossing and turning, running through all the options in her mind. In the two weeks on the run she hadn't taken many unnecessary risks which was why she had stayed ahead of the game. This time she would be returning to a known location.

The train rattled from Hastings to Victoria, followed by a quick tube ride to Liverpool Street Station. Here it was around a one-hour journey from London, and with over a hundred trains a day on this line, she could be back in Hastings by mid-afternoon.

Sitting back on the early train she silently planned the morning, hoping that she would be there by seven thirty. Karen took out a magazine and hid behind it, she mustn't screw up now although no one seemed to give her a second glance. She appeared to be surrounded by the normal commuter type people who were bored to death of life. Sex only on a weekend if they were lucky and a group of friends that bored the shit out of them. Vegetating until the day that this pointless working charade was over and they could retire and bob along until they shuffled off the planet. Karen grimaced at the thought and also considered the irony that she had met David Brood during the same journey, which seemed a lifetime ago now. If only she'd known then what she knew about him now.

Checking her watch, she took a deep breath, seven twenty-five. The train slowed and pulled into Colchester, the doors opening and allowing a stream of people to get on and off. Stepping out onto the platform a shiver ran down her back, this was the closest she had been to where this horror show had begun and feeling uneasy, Karen pushed her ticket into the barrier and set off in the direction of the vets. A twenty-minute walk then she could grab her things and be out of there.

Deep in thought and unaware of all else surrounding her, she soon found herself in the leafy road leading to the practice. She looked around and apart from a few cars on early school runs, the roads were empty. Hurrying over the damp tarmac and into the driveway of Godman and Partners Veterinary Practice, she took another deep breath and approached the entrance foyer. The door was shut but she could see Sandra, the receptionist working behind the desk. She pushed the bell and was buzzed in, to be greeted by Sandra wearing the largest grin Karen had seen for a long while.

"Karen, we have been so worried, what is going on? Where have you been?" Karen gave her a quick hug.

"I will explain later as I can't stay. I just need to grab my things so tell everyone that I will phone later this week. I am fine though thanks, and it's lovely to see you again." She hurried into the staff room and opened her locker, finding everything just as she had left it. That was a huge relief. Quickly gathering it all together Karen rushed back past the reception desk. Seeing Sandra was gone, she thought to herself that she must have gone to make a drink, which thankfully would mean no more questions. Pushing the door, Karen realised that it was locked again so she called out, "Sandra, can you buzz the door sweetheart, I need to dash." There was no answer, "Sandra," she called again, louder this time so she could hear her in the kitchen.

A crash from the operating room startled her, and she wondered what Sandra was doing in there. Karen felt a flush of anger crossing her face in her exasperation, Sandra had been told countless times to stay out of the operating rooms. She was employed to answer the phones but often found the alure of the more interesting surgery difficult to resist. Pushing through the door into the theatre, she tripped over something and was momentarily irritated that anyone could have left something on the floor to trip over. Looking down she found herself staring open mouthed, eyes bulging and a scream stifled within her throat. She gasped and a sob escaped her as she observed Sandra's body. Laying in a grotesque position, it looked as though her neck had been snapped. A trickle of blood seeped from her nose and gently spread its way towards the operating table. A soft noise behind her made Karen spin around. Still dazed, it took a couple of seconds for her fight or flight reflex to kick in, and when it did, she tried to run for the door but it was too late. A blur raced towards her, quicker than she could process and Ernie grabbed her around the throat. She froze in terror before he punched her hard on the jaw and legs buckling, she fell on top of the lifeless body, before been dragged back onto her feet and thrown onto the operating table. She tried to struggle but was punched again and this time she blacked out.

The fog in her head beginning to clear, Karen tried to move but found she couldn't. She was secured to the table by straps on her arms and legs with an intravenous drip hanging from her arm. Ernie had used these many times during his time in the special forces. He looked blankly at her, emotionless as if he were simply a professional carrying out a routine task, a robot programmed to kill.

"This stuff will kill a horse in a second," he told her looking up at the drip, "but I guess you already know that Karen. You may have led everyone on a merry dance but you won't get away from people like me. Nothing personal but business is business."

"Please, you don't need to do this to me, let me go," Karen pleaded. "You will never see me again, I promise."

He remained without emotion, without empathy, employing just the cold, calculated actions he used whilst stalking and killing the enemy, Ernie took his phone from his pocket and dialed.

"Mr Brood, I have her. You asked me to phone you once I had her under restraint. What do you want me to do with her?"

"Put the phone to her ear Ernie. I need to hear something."

Ernie placed the phone to her ear and bleeding mouth.

"Karen, it's David. One question, why did you do this to me?"

She sobbed, blood dripping from her mouth and nose, making a pattern down towards her slender neck.

"I just couldn't see the children hurt David, I couldn't live with that," she broke down, struggling to get anymore words out of her mouth. "I wouldn't have been able to live with myself if I had not helped them." David sighed and looked around at where he had ended up and what he had become. Was he any different to the other monsters that roamed these landings? There had to be more to life than taking life. How many did he need to take, how many more families did he have to break? His life was fucked now so why carry on? He came to a decision and spoke again to Ernie.

"No Ernie, let her go, I have done enough damage. Thanks for the good work, you will be paid whatever." Ernie put his phone away and looked down at Karen,

"Your lucky day Karen, go home, your debt has been paid." He undid the straps before turning and walking out of the room. She heard the main door as it buzzed and clicked shut again behind him. The noise of the morning traffic began to build as she lay there, unable to move through shock and fear. Eventually, sliding her legs from the edge of the table, she looked down at Sandra's body.

"Sandra, I am so sorry, please forgive me."

She heard the main door open again and someone chastising the fact that Sandra had not turned up for work. The operating room door opened but Karen didn't look up, she didn't care anymore, she had seen too much pain and suffering and she was the facilitator of so many deaths. She let the pandemonium wash over her as those around her dealt with the latest.

# CHAPTER FORTY-FIVE

The landing staff had noticed a change in the atmosphere around the wing, it seemed strained and snippets of information were drifting through, indicating trouble was approaching. A couple of the more popular members of staff had been told to stay away from the wing during lunchtime. It wasn't an option, they reported it but stayed on duty. Again, a prisoner had approached them that morning to warn them of the coming danger but they had shrugged it away, this was their job, what they were paid to do and quitting wasn't an option. The union officials were, however, seeing if they could sideline the trouble before it started. Sitting in the governor's office the union chairman faced him across his desk.

"Governor, this wing needs to be shut down and searched immediately. You need to separate the ring leaders and move them out to another prison. We will lose the wing if you don't act." Here he hit the table to push the point, "And this could happen at any moment." Martin Cale had been the Union Chairman for the past five years, the staff and prisoners respected him and he had a reputation for making the right decisions. He also had the ear of the Governor. He wasn't a trouble maker and avoided putting staff in danger. A short stocky man with thick, tattooed arms, his short hair and thick black moustache made him look formidable but in truth he was a caring person who had a heart of gold. The governor listened before giving his own thoughts on the matter.

"Martin, it's lunchtime in five minutes, let's get through the next hour and I will phone Area Command this afternoon to get people moved. In the meantime, we will do a controlled feeding for the meal, no more than ten out at a time, and obviously keeping the main players apart. Can we run with that?" Martin shook his head.

"All due respect Governor, we need to lift these people now and put them in the block to show the staff that we are taking this threat seriously." The governor thought for a few seconds before agreeing.

"Okay, Martin. The prisoners in the workshops and education will be returning as we speak, let's get them back into their cells and then we will lift and shift." Martin stood up,

"Well done Governor, I will leave it in your hands." He left the office and walked back towards the wings. He heard the roar going up while he was still fifty metres away and the radio strapped to his belt shouted out. *'Alarm Bell A and B Wings, all staff to attend!'*

The rumble of feet and clanging of the wing gates being thrown open as staff attended was a familiar noise within the prison. A second roar from the prisoners milling around the wing also wasn't unusual. The fact that it was happening on two wings at the same time worried him greatly.

The Brood's plan was coming together but they had realised that news of potential unrest had slipped out so they had needed to act fast. Kevin knew that this afternoon would be too late, the game would be up and he would be on his way to another prison so it was now or never.

As the prisoners came back onto the wings, an organised attack on the Somalian prisoners took place. Gangs of the Brood's prisoners stormed forward, fists and boots flying, but the African warriors were ready for this and the days they had spent organising and making weapons were suddenly worthwhile. Every black hand held a lethal homemade weapon, razors melted into toothbrush handles for slashing, long screws embedded into snapped mop handles formed stabbing weapons and pool balls in socks that could club a man unconscious in one blow. Every man knew his job, to destroy anyone who got in the way and to club the Broods back into the stone age where this type of gangster belonged.

The violence covered all areas of the ground floor landing, some prisoners having toe to toe fights, others bundling each other onto the floor where a hail of blows and boots awaited them. The staff could not cope with the scale of the violence, they tried desperately to separate the fighting gangs and they tried to push and cajoled other prisoners towards their cells, but soon the violence was directed towards these Officers. Under such a barrage of aggression the staff had to withdraw from the wings and the prisoners were left to fight it out.

David and Kevin were watching from above and they could see that the fight had got out of control. Many prisoners were on the floor bleeding and the Brood's gang were being forced back towards the end of the wing. Their backs against the far wall ensured that they could no longer retreat and like the Spartans from '300', they had to stand and fight the enemy or die a coward.

The Somalian gang had indeed been well prepared and they were hard men who knew violence as part of their lives. They pushed forward, twenty of them against ten of the Brood's who still stood, ready to fight. The rest were injured beyond the point of continuing the fight or had melted away as they realized defeat was inevitable.

Kevin watched the last of his soldiers fall bleeding to the floor before turning to his brother, "David, let's get out of here, follow me." He led the way to an empty cell, with no cell card on the outside where hopefully they would be able to escape detection for a while until the officers had regained control.

Kevin pushed the cell door shut and hearing the click of the lock, he gave a deep sigh. "This has gone tits up David, climb under the bed and keep silent. They will come looking for us so we need to ride this out." Kevin looked around and seeing the cell was empty except for the dirty bedding still on the two beds, he shuffled himself under the other bed. He looked across at David. "Not a word brother, we need to stay here until the staff get back onto the wing." The Brood brothers were finished, each of them submissive and cowering under a cheap broken metal bed. Cowardly and shaking, Kevin silently prayed that the very prison staff who he had corrupted and used for his own pleasure in the past would now come to his rescue.

The sounds of battle had diminished on the ground floor, although screams of delight still rang out as another office was ransacked, but the real work was complete. Mo, the Somalian gang leader stood looking out of the gate towards the staff, debris strewn around his feet.

"Come in here, you get the same, understand?" He looked an imposing figure, a small razor-sharp knife sitting in his right hand and a home-made javelin in the other. The wing was in turmoil, the offices had been ransacked and documents were thrown around or burned. The healthcare medication hatch had been smashed open and every tablet and liquid was in the process of digestion. A huge barricade was growing, preventing access for anyone trying to enter the wing but also preventing rescue for any poor souls wanting out of this hell. He turned to the others behind him and ordered, "Find me the Broods!" They turned like obedient blood hounds and followed the scent, the scent of fear.

Hiding under the beds like children, the Broods could hear a mob baying for their blood. Cell after cell was searched as footsteps came thundering down the landing moving closer and closer, the sound of rubbish and glass crunching under menacing feet. The cell flap on their door was opened, and hardly daring to breath, they lay motionless hoping that the mob would pass on but in the next instant, the observation panel glass smashed through. They had been seen. As the shout went up, Mo approached the cell and stared through the smashed opening.

"Brood, you fucking batty man, hiding like a fucking baby. Your boys are gone Brood, you are the only ones left." Kevin climbed out from under the bed and dusted himself down, David followed.

"Come in and get us then you black bastards," he invited in one last show of bravado. Mo laughed, a truly terrifying sound.

"Oh no man, we don't need to do that. We are going to cook your white skin right where you stand."

A huge bonfire was made outside of the cell and a liquid was squirted through the broken panel. The smell was unmistakable, the bastards had got hold of petrol from somewhere and bedding soaked in fuel was pushed purposefully through the hole where the glass panel was once held firm. Bed sheets, pillow cases and old duvet covers littered the cell floor, the fumes overpowering. The mob outside were screaming as they all bayed for a ring side seat.

David pushed the cold-water tap, hoping to douse the linen but nothing happened. The water had been shut off. A glass jar filled with petrol with a burning rag pushed into the top came crashing through, smashing onto the floor and spewing out flames. The bedding erupted into a volcano of fire and choking black smoke.

The Broods moved to the vents on the window in the back wall trying desperately to suck in any air as the heat behind them started to singe their clothes and hair. Turning around, Kevin looked back through the blazing cell as David fell onto the floor unable to breath. The last thing Kevin saw was Mo, laughing at him from behind the door. "Smells like pork for dinner," he shouted as Kevin collapsed into the wall of flames, clinging onto the smoldering body of David. He screamed one last agonising scream as the flesh melted from his face.

Then it was over and the wing dissolved back into silence, each man returning to what was left of their cells, to pack up their property and await the staff who were now storming back in to take control. Mo looked down at the encroaching staff from the top landing, and launching the spear towards the watching staff, he let out a scream of victory before wandering back into his cell.

# CHAPTER FORTY-SIX

The fresh morning chill bit into Stephen's cheeks as he walked past the House of Commons on his way to Whitehall. Standing outside a large, imposing entrance way to an even grander building, he entered through the revolving doors, showing his identity to the young attractive lady with a velvet soft Irish accent. She stood and walked round to the front of the desk before asking him to follow her. A beautifully painted finger nail pressed the button in the lift to the second floor. She didn't speak to him during the time it took for the lift to travel and kept her eyes on the floor. Stephen guessed that she had done this same journey a hundred times and was bored by the process. They reached a large oak door outside office number twelve. Pushing the door open he could see another three men sat back in leather chairs, sipping coffee in silence. A busy looking notepad with an expensive pen resting across it were the only items resting on the large antique oak desk and the captain's chair behind had a look as if someone had hurriedly pushed it backwards and left the office. A double sash window overlooked the rooftops, spikes on the outside window ledge keeping the pigeons at bay but an occasional flutter of wings crossing the courtyard below betrayed their presence. Declining the offer of a coffee, he took the spare leather chair to the left-hand side of the office. Its cold surface chilled his hands as he settled back, silently acknowledging the other men as he casually checked them out. He didn't recognise them but noticed that at least one of them had a Met Police briefcase at their side.

The door opened again and a young, smartly dressed man walked in and took the seat behind the desk. This seemed to take the waiting party by surprise; Stephen guessed that they all expected an older, plumper politician of some type. Glancing down at the note pad he muttered to himself before addressing the meeting.

"Good morning gentlemen, let's get this on the road. I am sure that you are all eager to find out why we are all sitting here." They all nodded.

"You have all been selected by MI5 to lead on a very delicate matter involving Members of Parliament and senior members of the Met Police and Prison Service. You all have specialisms which will be needed over the coming year." He looked at the faces staring back at him with a mix of excitement and wonderment. It made him give a brief chuckle before continuing.

"My name is James Childs, my background is with the Security services for the last five years and the British Army for the twelve years prior to that. I have been tasked to investigate issues that if they became public knowledge, would bring the country to its knees." Again, he looked around the room before taking a long drink of water from a white plastic cup.

"Senior members of Government, the Prison Service, Armed Forces and the Police are involved in the dealing of weapons and drugs to terrorist organisations and organised criminal gangs. Potentially they stand to make millions of dollars each and cause the deaths of thousands of innocent men, women and children. These people are plotting to commit acts of terrorism and more worryingly they intend to have a senior member of the cabinet assassinated."

"How do we know that this information is true?" Stephen couldn't help but ask the question.

"Partly down to you Stephen." He kept the gaze directly at Stephen as though to read his expression. "We had inserted a member of our team into the Brood family. Details of stolen arms and ammunition came to light a few months ago, and the influence that some senior prison service board members were having amongst the hard-line Muslim prisoners within the special units at high security prisons filtered through at a similar time. It has snow balled from there."

Stephen nodded. "A day without the Broods would be a good start."

Childs was quick to reassure him. "The leaders are dead and the gang members are either dead or in prison. The Broods are long gone so let's move on to bigger fish." Stephen nodded again and Childs continued with the briefing.

"So, we are leading a small discreet team to investigate and smash this corruption. I trust that you are all in agreement that this is in the interest of our nation, therefore security of all information is key. Any leaks will have come from one of you gentlemen. Do not be the one who breaks our confidence." It was the type of warning that was disregarded at peril and all four men listening nodded in serious agreement.

"Right then, if you are all okay with the task, I will leave you for today. My colleague will arrive in five minutes to go through the details of the operation and I will see you all again here at ten tomorrow morning unless there are any questions?" There was silence. "I repeat, no details regarding any matters relating to our work will be discussed with anyone. Failure to obey this instruction will result in serious consequences. Understood?"

Again, there was a silent acknowledgement. He sat for the next few seconds surveying the room before leaving the office. The remaining men looked at each other and exhaled. "Bloody hell!" one of them uttered.

# CHAPTER FORTY-SEVEN

Stephen and Tanya sat on an IKEA sofa in the Child Protection office based in an ugly council building in the centre of Birmingham. The day had a grey, autumnal feel to it, the sort of day where you suddenly realised that you were facing months of semi darkness. Tanya had already given the woman in front of them a once over and she hadn't been impressed with her first observations. Although the woman looked reasonably bright, it didn't seem appropriate to be discussing the progress of their children with a woman wearing multi-coloured Doctor Martin boots. A denim jacket hung behind the door and a brightly patterned umbrella rested against the wall. The woman began the conversation.

"Well, thanks for coming over on such a horrid day. My name's Davina, we have chatted briefly on the phone. I am aware that you have dealt with Susie during all the other sessions with Ellie and Harry but we feel that we may now be in a position to finally resolve these horrid events for the children." Tanya interjected almost before Davina had drawn another breath.

"We have had numerous chats with Susie, and conversations with Susie and the children together during our play sessions. We understood that there were no underlying issues to be addressed?"

"And so did we, Tanya, until their last session," Davina continued calmly. "Susie played with the children and read them a story. It was a standard happy ever after book where the children can make up the ending. It is a type of resolution exercise for them where they can choose the ending they would like."

"I can feel an *and* coming," Tanya said, sitting forward on the sofa.

"And……. both the children want to see Karen happy. They became very insistent that she was the hero of the story. Harry referred to her as a 'Power Ranger'."

"A child abducting Power Ranger and that woman didn't even face any charges for what happened. Nobody did really. The bastards were both burnt and sent to hell, while the others were given life sentences for murders and torture. Not one mention of the children anywhere." Stephen took Tanya's hand and gave it a squeeze.

"Maybe that was for the best Tanya and I am not against doing what is best for the kids. What are the suggestions for dealing with this Davina?"

"A supervised meeting for the twins to say goodbye to her. Nobody is suggesting she stays within your family circle, but I do honestly think that the children have unfinished business with Karen. They need to have their say as much as we do. They want to talk to her." Tanya looked at Davina. "We need to discuss this before we give our thoughts, it's a big decision and I want to really believe it is not going to upset the children in any way. We'll go and have some lunch and talk it over. Can we come back this afternoon with our decision?"

"Of course you can, come to the front desk any time after two and I will come down and we can talk again."

Davina's phone rang, it was an internal call. She glanced up at the clock and saw it was almost two thirty.

"Hi Davina, it's the front desk, we have Mr and Mrs Byfield waiting for you down here." She quickly made her way down to the reception area and could see both Stephen and Tanya standing in front of the desk.

"Hi, have you had a chance to think? We can go into a spare office to discuss it if you like?"

"No need," Stephen informed her, "let's do it and get it over with. Phone us when the details have been made."

"Okay, I do need to speak to Karen again so I will contact you during the week." She smiled holding out a hand. "I do think that you have made the best decision. We'll speak soon." They shook hands before she turned and headed back to the office, while the Byfield's headed back home.

Karen was sitting in the Hastings flat. Life had started to move on for her, the Broods were dead and their funerals had taken place. It was a strangely muted affair in comparison to other high profile gangster funerals, almost as though people had taken enough of their crap. She hadn't attended on police advice but in reality, wouldn't have gone anyway. A couple of hundred local faces had turned up, no real friends, just people who wanted to be seen. It had by all accounts been a simple burial in a family plot near the East End before being forgotten by most of those who attended. A lonely police intelligence photographer had sat in a van snapping the faces but even he became bored with the wannabes lining the route and had disappeared early. All in all, it was thought that these two bullies had got what they deserved and it was good riddance.

Her phone rang, it wasn't an unexpected call as she had spoken with Davina the previous day. Karen just hadn't expected Stephen and Tanya to agree. She shook as she discussed the details, partly through excitement in seeing the children but also through the uncertainty of meeting Stephen and Tanya. The following unseasonably sunny Saturday lunchtime, Karen found herself walking towards a large pub garden with a children's play area taking over a quarter of the ground. Large tunnel slides, climbing frames and swings stood out against a tree lined boundary. As she pushed through the waist high swing gate, she instantly heard the laughter of the children and she recognised Stephen and Tanya sitting with Davina at a wooden bench with empty plates and soft drink bottles littering the table top.

Davina was the first to see Karen and walked over the pub lawn to greet her. She hugged Karen and asked her if she was ready for this. Karen nodded unable to take her eyes from Tanya who was now aware of her presence. She whispered something to Stephen who turned straight away to look at her. The walk towards the bench seemed to take forever and her legs felt heavy. Even though she had planned this moment a hundred times the words just didn't come freely. She started to cry, Karen hadn't expected to break down but there was something so overwhelming about the occasion. Tanya jumped up and hugged her and kissed her cheek. "Thank you so much for making sure our children were safe. It was the most devastating few weeks of my life." Stephen nodded in agreement. Karen sat down and explained the story, Stephen and Tanya listened in silence, absorbing every detail. When she had finished, Tanya had a thousand questions for her. Why didn't you tell us? Why didn't you report it? Why did you agree to take them? So many unanswered questions and Karen did her best, but it was Stephen who really answered, by turning to Tanya and explaining that no one would ever understand what it was like to be under the influence of the Broods. Both he and Karen had been there, and were lucky enough to have lived to tell the tale.

At that moment Karen was spotted by the twins, they tore over and smothered her in hugs and kisses and this answered any question Tanya had been having about the impact on what she had done on the twins.

"Karen! Karen! Are you coming back home with us?" Ellie squealed.

"No sweetheart. I can't. I have been given another job. Have you heard of a country called New Zealand?"

"No," Ellie answered, her face dropping with disappointment.

"Well it's a long way away but I can work with doctors making horses better. I am leaving in a while but I will always remember you two tinkers." The twins laughed. "No, doctors don't make horses better silly," Harry informed her, "horses are too big to get into a doctor's surgery." They hugged her again before running back towards the climbing frames. Ellie stopped and turned back. She ran towards Karen stopping only to take off her hair band. "Karen, if you get into trouble again, remember what is in my hair band." She handed it to Karen and turned to run back. "Bye Karen, thank you for our adventure," and she was off back to the irresistible pull of the climbing frame.

Tanya looked at Karen, "You have made a couple of lifelong

friends there. Keep the band safe."

"I will," she promised as she stood and shook their hands before walking back to the car, a tear trickling down her cheek. It was closure for them all.

# CHAPTER FORTY-EIGHT

The Orpington sports bar was empty, the shutters had been down for the past two weeks and the For Sale board standing guard outside was a last reminder to the people of the area that the Brood curse had been lifted. A single light shone deep within the building, the deserted casino area looked like an empty dance floor and the horrors of Green Mile, Paul Parker and the other casualties of greed or revenge were ghosts evaporating into the evening glow, an X-rated Christmas carol fading into obscurity, a world in which Tiny Tim would have been fed to the pigs.

A solitary figure sat in the office tapping away at a laptop. Beverly McCullock, the hard-faced, Irish child stealer. Her phone rang, echoing across the empty room.

"Ernie, thanks for getting back to me. It looks as though we need to meet up, big shoes to fill and all that bollocks. I have a proposition for you and a vacancy needing to be filled. Are you up for it?" There was a short silence before he replied. "Are we back in business?"

"Very much so. I am about to sell the club, I have a friend of a friend who is interested in running a little place in this part of the world. Meet me in the Victoria Pub just outside Victoria station, I should be there around ten tonight. We still have unfinished business. You have something that I have been promised sitting in fucking Umbongo land, and I still want to pick up with the unfinished work from the last occupants of this cold shithole of a club. Be there, we have a lot at stake."

A few hours later the train pulled into a chilly Victoria station. Beverly picked up her bag and stepped out of the first-class carriage. Brought up on the tough Belfast streets, the niece of an active IRA commander, she had a deep distrust of all people, hated the authorities and the idea of working with a former SAS man went deeply against the grain, but business was business. Since her part in the kidnapping of the twins she had watched from the Irish Republic as members of the gang were either imprisoned or killed, and she had kept away from the lime light until it was time to clean up. Then she slipped back into the country as though nothing had ever happened. She didn't appear on the radar, she was just another face coming to town. This was her opportunity to make a mountain of cash and the prestige of becoming a major player within the underworld definitely floated her boat.

Walking across the road she entered the pub, it was not busy and she easily spotted Ernie sitting at the back of the bar. He faced directly down towards where she entered, a door leading to a smoking area standing open to his side. He looked at her but didn't acknowledge her. Old habits. He would wait for her to make her way down towards him, his eyes not leaving the door as anyone following would be easy to spot. If that was the case, he would disappear in front of her eyes with no one willing to witness he was ever there. Nobody followed her in but he remained vigilant.

She knew what he was doing and stood by the bar studying the menu. She was a deeply attractive woman, five ten, slender waist, black shoulder-length hair and dressed to kill.

"A burger and a white wine please, that table over there," she nodded towards Ernie. She paid and again looked over, planning to sit opposite Ernie. He glanced in her direction as she spoke to the bar staff. She had a small overnight bag and he guessed it would be for two nights at the most. He mused, as meetings go this could have been a worse one. She sat down opposite him,

"I have food coming, are you in a rush as I'm starving?"

"No, you tuck on in. Are you expecting anyone to join us?"

"There is no one else Ernie, it's just us." She looked at him. He was unsmiling, wiry and had the presence of total professionalism. She could see that he was not here for a nice time which was a shame as he was a rugged, good looking guy who she wouldn't mind having some fun with. A coke sat in front of him. "Not drinking?"

"Never mix drink and work Bev. And this is work." He took the glass and sipped, the ice clinking against the sides. "What are you proposing?"

"You have a lot of property in North Africa that you can't move and I have the resources to get it into the country. The Broods had a buyer who is anxious to get this deal done. I just need eyes on the ground to ensure that the deal goes through and the equipment gets onto my boat. Do you have contacts over there?"

"Yes, you know I have or you wouldn't be speaking to me. You also know that I am the only person left alive who knows where the stuff is housed. That's why I am drinking watered down coke in a shit hole of a pub." Beverly decided to ignore the jibe and the fact he had decided that they were on such friendly terms that he could shorten her name. She cracked on with the business at hand.

"Okay, this is what I propose Ernie. I get seventy percent of the deal and you will get the rest. I will cover the cost of the shipping which is over a 100K. You can have whatever else is in the stash."

"There's also a bundle of cash Bev. Maybe another half a million and I know that it is all still intact."

"It's yours Ernie, we could both end up very wealthy should this all come off. I can seal this deal, but I wished that I shared your optimism in regard to the cash. Life isn't that easy," she chuckled.

"Maybe you can seal the deal Bev, but do you really think that I would leave my investment sitting in a tribal village in the desert? Save your shipment fees, it's already in the UK, courtesy of the Royal Air Force and before you ask, no I'm not fucking taking you there. You deposit the money into this bank account," he pushed a piece of paper with a number on across the table towards her, "and when that's in the account, I will deliver the goods to wherever you require. And it's fifty-fifty, deal?" She smiled at him, "Tricky little bastard aren't you? Give me a week. For them to give us fifteen million pounds up front could be tricky Ernie. I will get back to you as soon as I've got an agreement."

He nodded and downed the coke. He stood, she could clearly see his toned physique and with not an ounce of fat, he still looked every inch a special forces sort of guy. She filled her nose with his aftershave which smelt expensive, classy and the man certainly had style. In other circumstances she would make a play for him, but this was not other circumstances and she could also see the 9mm inside his jacket. Then he was gone, blending into the London buzz.

She sat alone and pushed the burger to one side as she sipped the wine in deep thought. She drifted into thoughts of her mother, who had recently passed away with a vicious breast cancer. This had shocked Bev as she had considered her mum so strong. Her mum had raised her without a father and until her sixteenth birthday she hadn't given her dad any thought. The TV was playing in the corner while they half watched some hopeless quiz program and Bev remembered the exact moment where her life changed. It was immediately after mum drained the last mouthful of wine from her glass and said, "Bev, I am going to talk to you about your dad. I always promised that when you turned sixteen years old, I would tell you the truth." She could still hear the TV being slowly muted and the clock ticking in the small front room of the terraced house as she waited for her mum to continue.

"When I was your age, I met a young man who had come over from England for a few weeks. His dad was in some trouble with the police and it was thought better that the boy came here. He was the same age as me and his family and ours had been involved in some shenanigans way back. I had to show him Belfast, not an easy job at that time but we got to know each other very well, so well in fact that once he had returned to England, I discovered that I was pregnant. A sixteen-year-old pregnant girl proved to be a very bad situation to be in at the time and my parents kept me hidden during the pregnancy until I had you. Then the story was spread that you were a relative's child who we were bringing up. The boy and his parents kept in touch throughout and provided us with money every month, a lot of money as it turned out. That is why you've had a good school, and this money will keep coming until your eighteenth birthday. Do you want me to continue?" Bev remembered the question sounding ridiculous, did she want to know who her father was. You bet your fucking last dollar she did.

"The boy's name was David Brood. His family have strong links with Ireland and still have the values that we share and they vowed to look after us all. They are involved in a lot of things in the UK that we don't ask about but they also own a big club in the South of England that provides us with the money for rent, food and the little holidays we take, But the biggest thing that the family insists on is when the two Brood brothers have passed away the club will belong to you. I think that they just want to know you will be looked after always."

The day Bev finished her education and the funding from the club had stopped she was sent an invitation to join the family firm in London. By the age of nineteen she had packed her bags and gone off to join the Brood's circus.

And so it came to pass, the Broods had met a sticky end and Bev had inherited half a million pounds because David Brood couldn't keep his dick in his trousers. She had never thought of him as her father, he had forfeited that right when he left her mother to raise her by herself.

Walking out into the Victoria crowds, Bev wandered back towards the taxi rank at the station. She had booked a suite at a hotel in Westminster for the next few days while she sorted out business. Queuing for five minutes the next cab pulled up alongside her. "Crown Plaza, Westminster please driver."

She settled back into the seat and watched the lights of London drift by. She could still smell Ernie and couldn't get him out of her mind. She needed to get a grip she told herself, there was a big deal at stake here and she couldn't afford to be distracted. The cab pulled up outside of the modern building, where a host of doormen were waiting as she swung through the revolving doors and headed to check in.

Once the necessary details were given and her bag taken up to her room, she headed to the bar for a nightcap, her mind firmly on celebrating the sale of the club along with the news that the weapons were already in the country. All in all, a very successful day. She found the bar and saw it was split into two sections, at the front were comfy seats where a host of people sat, either waiting to book in, getting ready to book out, or returning from a night out and like her, having a drink before bed. She slipped into the second half at the rear where it was more private and a little less crowded. She sat and ordered a cocktail noticing a middle-aged business man checking her over. Sure enough, he came and sat opposite her.

"Do you mind if I join you, I am all on my lonesome," he gave her a doleful look hoping for sympathy. She looked at the American balding lard-arse and was about to give him her best Belfast Fuck Off before a familiar scent once again filled her senses.

"Hi Bev, sorry I am late. Can I help you buddy?" Ernie asked as he turned towards the American.

"No, no, sorry, my mistake, have a nice night," stuttered lard-arse as he scuttled off. Bev smiled.

"Ernie, what a nice surprise, and I see you have a whisky."

"Business is over Bev, I was hoping for a little pleasure."

Ernie Stocken and Beverly McCullock looked down onto the hotel bed. Every square inch was covered with money, spilling out of the large traveller's suitcase that squashed the luxurious pillows at the top of the king-sized mattress. A hefty down payment for services provided. The expansive windows overlooked the River Thames as it crept under Westminster Bridge and past the Houses of Parliament, made an impressive backdrop to the London skyline.

Chinking together two expensive crystal champagne flutes

they kissed and laughed for the umpteenth time.

"See Ernie, you may be a former Special Forces kind of guy, and I may have been a crazy IRA type of girl, but who says that we can't do business?"

"Good point Bev, I can think of fifteen million other reasons why we are a good team. Now we just need to plan how we are going to take over this town."

They held up the glasses and in unison said. "To the Broods."

# AFTERWORD

Follow Stephen Byfield in his quest to uncover corruption within the prison service and the Government, in the last of the Byfield trilogy, BETWEEN THE SHADOWS, out now, (Link to Amazon on following page).

# BOOKS BY THIS AUTHOR

## High Risk

The first in the Byfield trilogy.

Can prison stop this serial killer?

When Stephen Byfield takes on the challenge of becoming the youngest governor of a high secrity prison, he fails to realise the depth of devious behaviour plotted amongst his own staff and the murderous intent from the psychopathic serial killer, Martin Heard.
This convicted murderer of a previous prison governor holds a deep rooted hatred for the Byfield family stretching back to his drug addled past. He will stop at nothing to kill every last person who stands in the way of vengeance being served.
Stephen Byfield's loyal Deputy Governor, Terry Davies, a battle hardened former Royal Marine, once again stands in the cross hairs of the enemies sights, without realising the consequences faced by his own family. The true cost for adopting a cold blooded killer's baby son years before will be paid in full as Heard's murderous rage will remain unsoothed until he can take back what is his.
Can Stephen Byfield keep this figure from all our worst nightmares locked inside his cell, or can Martin Heard's calculated mind plot a way out?

## Resolutiom

How far would you go to save your children?

As a hardened Prison Governor, Stephen Byfield thought that he had seen everything that life could throw his way. The moment he dismantled the Brood family's drug trafficking business into Her Majesty's Prisons, he saw a level of vengeance waged against him that he could never have foretold. Not in his worst nightmares, could he envisage what his children would face in the name of revenge. No horrors are out of bounds for The Broods as the gang attack anything and everything that stands in their way. Can the Byfields ride the storm, or will this hurricane of violence destroy them for good? One thing is for sure, Stephen Byfield will die trying.

## Between The Shadows

Does Your family always come first?

Beaten and bloody in the depths of a cargo ship in a Tunisian port, Stephen Byfield wracked his brain to answer the questions fired at him from a murderous, mysterious English interrogator.
"Where is the parcel?"
If Stephen had known, he would have spat the words out along with his broken teeth. If British Security forces knew its whereabouts they would have let his murder happen. If an early morning phone call from Whitehall to a waiting vehicle hidden in the dock yard hadn't ordered an intervention, you would be reading an obituary.
With breathtaking action swinging from the dusty, lawless roads and alleyways of a Cape Town township in South Africa, to the oak lined offices in government in London, England, revenge and menace are relentless and indiscriminate. Byfield is on the cusp of understanding this.
Selected by Whitehall to investigate corruption amongst high ranking officials takes Stephen into a world of murder and betrayal. A world where the most senior Government officials are

legitimate targets and collateral damage is nothing but dust on the polished wooden office floor.

What is contained within that envelope that is so good people would die to own it? Stephen is about to find the answer, and with that secret comes misery as MI6 systematically try to destroy him for the contents. Framed and falsely imprisoned within a bleak Scottish prison, can Stephen save his family from the stalking assassin sent to kill them all, and blow the lid off the corruption happening at the highest levels?

# ACKNOWLEDGEMENT

Working in the prison service for so many years had its ups and downs, but what it did do was provide me with the experiences which allow my imagination to create these stories. Some readers ask me why some of the storylines must be so barbaric, and my reply to them is that people who use such violence really do exist. I would not be representing the full horrors of gangs such as the Broods if I did not portray what they are really capable of. The same is true of my descriptions of the riots within the prison, these really do take place and the lives of prison staff are put in danger daily.

As usual, my foremost thanks must go to my wife Jo who patiently edits my work from start to finish. I would also like to thank Melissa Jagger who painstakingly read Resolution page by page, giving helpful suggestions in order to improve the reader's experience.

# ABOUT THE AUTHOR

## Adrian O'donnell

Adrian left home at 16 years old to join the Army in the late 1970's serving in the Queen's Regiment in various countries around the world. A further challenge called when he was 24 years old and he joined Her Majesty's Prison Service, serving in some of the most difficult prosons in the UK.
Retiring in 2016 after 32 years service, he took the opportunity to work in the Middle East advising overseas governments in security procedures. He is married to Jo and presently living in a small village in the South West of France. They have a large family of five sons and four grandchildren.
Resolution is the second novel in the Byfield trilogy.

# PRAISE FOR AUTHOR

*"It's easy to tell the author worked in the prison system and he found that delicate balance between realism and excitement without over-stepping the boundaries."*

*"The perspective given is fascinating and a welcome break from all the 'behind bars' prisoner type journals."*

*"Adrian's writing style is not dissimilar to David Baldacci, another great author. Waiting with great anticipation for the next in the series from this new author."*

*"What intrigued me about this book was the author based it on his real life experience and this experience of working in the prison service is clear because the detail in this book is both fascinating and interesting."*

*"The author's ability to communicate with the reader on behalf of each character is brilliant, detailed and convincing."*

*"I do believe James Patterson better watch out!"*

*"For a writers first book absolutely brilliant" (High Risk)*

Printed in Great Britain
by Amazon

28287456R00164